First Woman on Mars

John Minichillo

Denver, Colorado

Published in the United States by:
Spaceboy Books LLC
1627 Vine Street
Denver, CO 80206
www.readspaceboy.com

First printed September 2019

ISBN: 978-1-951393-99-1

For Katrina

Part 1

1

From space, the Findability campus resembled the Pentagon, with sixteen curved parentheses-shaped office buildings in concentric rings around Donut One—the building where Maxim Brez worked, the founder, always within walking distance of the rest of the Findability family. In her cubicle, at her computer with two large flat screens, Peg Myers hovered the Findability Maps satellite view over Donut One, she tilted to Street View, and she zoomed in on a line of windows where she suspected Maxim Brez's office was. Lots of people had met Maxim Brez. He was a frequent topic of conversation. He was the face of the company and a genius. He lived with a supermodel, who was also somewhere inside Donut One that Findability Maps wouldn't reveal.

Peg Myers was envious of anyone who had ever caught a glimpse of the supermodel. She hoped one day to see the supermodel with her own eyes, supermodel otherworldly, with parchment-white skin, long limbs, long fingers, a long face. Her jet-black hair seemed to luminesce violet, and Peg had never seen a photograph of her without her trademark candy-red lipstick. The supermodel was a woman possessed of obvious great luck.

They were American royalty, they were angels, Brez and his supermodel, and Brez had been to space. He was rich enough that he'd bought a round-trip ticket to the International Space Station, and NASA had let him go. Findability owned a private space venture, Launchability and NASA saw Brez as more of a business partner than a space tourist. Other billionaires would have paid to go, but Brez propositioned NASA and they took his offer.

He blasted off in a Russian Soyuz rocket and it was a live news event- everyone at Findability watching instead of working, on the big screens in meeting rooms and in the auditorium, on the flat screens along the moving walkways, and on all the desktop screens. Everyone everywhere at Findability watched. None of the family worked the day of his spacewalk, not during any of Brez's live appearances, and no one worked the day Brez touched down in a field in Kazakhstan. TV cameras cut to the supermodel in the crowd, who was captioned: "Girlfriend of Maxim Brez." Peg Myers repeated the phrase, "Girlfriend of Maxim Brez" as she scrolled around the Findability Maps image of Donut One and looked for signs of the feminine.

She zoomed out and scrolled over to Building Eleven, where Peg worked. She found the window nearest her own workspace, a cubicle surrounded by the cubicles of nerdy men, most of them with large dual flat screens like her own. Peg kept her second flat screen on her so-called "work," a readout of numbers and abbreviations in columns that Peg may or may not interpret later. From the satellite view of the second flat screen she zoomed in on her own spot on the parenthesis, all the parentheses-shaped buildings alike. She copied the location from the address bar and plugged it into an animated Findability Maps GIF that zoomed out to a view of her from above the stratosphere, rolled once around the Earth, and dropped back down to the window nearest her workspace, the animation repeated in a loop. One of her office mates had once told her, "If you attach that GIF to emails it will be a map for the UFOs to find you."

As with most of the men Peg worked with, she was unable to tell if the guy was joking.

"You think aliens monitor the Internet?" she asked.

"*Of course* they're on the Internet," he said.

"If the UFOs find me," Peg said, "They'll find you too."

"I'm not scared of UFOs," he said.

"Who said anything about being scared?" Peg said.

"You're not scared?"

"You just said *you* weren't scared."

"I might be scared," he said. "I mean, what do they eat?"

Peg considered these kinds of conversations to be work. Her title was Findability Expert and her job was mostly to answer the Findability prompt, "What are you looking for?" Her activities were logged, and Peg Myers was paid to explore the far reaches of the Web. Like anyone she had interests, which also seemed to be where she most often went: to the same astrology sites, the fake news sites, sites like Cakewrecks, and Fail-Fail-Double-Fail. She wasn't a political expert, a sports expert, a books expert, a general knowledge or regional knowledge expert. Peg Myers mostly tracked the megatrends. She chased anything with megahits, and anything with megahit-itis, a term she herself had coined. Some days she looked at pictures of corgis, some days pictures of pugs. Some days Justin Beiber, or corgi puppies, or pug puppies; she was easily drawn to pretty much any species of baby animal. She spent weeks on Star Wars, months on Kardashians, panicky whole days in the shadow of each near-miss asteroid. She kept returning to Tsunami footage, honey badger footage, Honey Boo Boo footage, miles of bloopers (though no one called them bloopers anymore). She followed the hit spikes around the recently dead, each chessboard move in each new geopolitical crisis, and of course, the memes. Peg Myers's favorite Internet phenomena, by far, were the memes—so many they were overwhelming to keep track of, and she went about it casually, setting off each morning in search of megahit-itis and the inevitable aftermath of related memes.

Peg stopped the Findability Maps GIF animation and scrolled back over to Donut One in Street View. Brez was giving a speech in the auditorium later, so Peg, like most of the Findability family, stalled in her unquantifiable and immeasurable work. Brez had an announcement to make.

Eventually, she closed Findability Maps and opened the live stream of her daughter's Montessori classroom. Her daughter, Erin, was in fifth grade, at the outer periphery of the Montessori experience-all paid for by Brez, with most of the Findability kids enrolled in one of seven on-campus daycares and schools. Peg habitually dropped in on the camera feed, Erin always at a touch screen turning pages of text. The layout of the class was open, the kids from various grades encouraged to wander, which was the Montessori Method, with wooden blocks and stacking puzzles scattered about, though the kids tended to gravitate to the touch screens, because this was a Findability classroom and worlds would collide.

Peg typed, "What are you reading?" in the instant messenger in the sidebar but she didn't send it. Erin would surely scold her with *"Why are you watching me? What do you do all day? Why aren't you working?"* The kid was severe.

Like the children in the Montessori classroom, Peg mostly wandered around until she was eventually pulled back to the Findability prompt, "What are you looking for?" Today Peg Myers was fearless in her avoidance of even that work. As far as Peg knew, no one had ever been fired. People left, but only for higher paying positions at less successful tech companies looking to acquire a touch of the Findability magic. A whole round of the family retired early, after the stock splits, well before Peg's time, with too many workers now to offer the same kinds of bonuses. There were perks, no doubt, mostly on campus, with the calculated effect to entice the family to never want to leave. They had everything: they ate well, snacked well, jogged, biked, swam, sauna-ed, got massages, took naps, caffeinated, anti-oxidated, played ping pong and air hockey. Peg was already thinking of leaving her cubicle to watch The Findability Channel on the flat screens that rolled by on the moving walkway when her computer chirped with an instant message that pulled her out of her reverie.

The instant message appeared in the sidebar, next to a thumbnail of Brian Clark. Peg imagined herself sitting in the audience at one of Maxim Brez's press events with the camera panning to her, and with the caption, "Girlfriend of Brian Clark." She repeated the phrase but didn't like the feeling of being connected to him. He was nice enough and was well paid, but everyone at Findability was. Peg could almost see it happening, and for that reason she never blew off Brian Clark, or let her true feelings be known, because Brian Clark was just a friend. He wanted to be more, she was sure, so she remained his buddy and always kept an eye out for someone else.

Brian Clark's message said, "Brez is announcing a contest. It's got to do with Launchability."

A contest didn't sound to Peg like the version of Brez she had dreamed up. Everything at Findability was free to employees, with no competitive incentives, no raffles, no inequitable distributions. Competitive incentives weren't Brez's way.

"What kind of contest?" Peg typed.

"Someone from the family is going to space."

"Didn't Vulture Twelve fail on the pad?"

"That was months ago. They worked it out. All systems go."

Peg stared at Brian Clark's thumbnail. He was balding, smiling, and with wire-rimmed glasses. He resembled exactly who he was.

"How will they decide?" she typed.

"Last man standing," he said. "Maybe like one of those shows.

"Last *person*," he corrected himself. "I meant to say *person*."

"I knew what you meant," Peg typed, exactly the kind of conversation she didn't want to get into.

"They don't need a mathematician," Brian Clark replied. "Although I would thrive in an atmosphere devoid of allergens." He paused, then Peg's computer chirped again with his follow-up message, "Achoo!"

Of course there would be allergens: latex and whatever other plastics they used in the spacesuits. The spacesuits were airtight. He'd be trapped in there with plastic fumes. It couldn't be healthy. It couldn't be enjoyable. But she didn't mention that. Instead, she hit the caps lock, and typed, "LOL."

"Sit with you at the speech?"

She could sense his heart in his throat as he typed that, so she waited for an uncomfortably long moment before she replied, "I'll look for you."

*

The moving walkway was abuzz with members of the family on their way to meetings or away from their desks to grab a bite. Many of them kept to the left and walked, so that the combined velocity of their walking and the conveyor occasionally blew back their hair. Peg kept to the right where she gripped the moving handrail and rode twice around the circuit of buildings before settling on a food court where she stepped off. She was torn between the build-your-own omelet kiosk and the build-your-own fajita kiosk, the stands and add-ons identical except for the choice of cage-free organic eggs or multi-grain organic soft tortillas. Peg stood between the two lines, tried her best to keep her place in each, and she eavesdropped on the conversations around her. Everyone talked about Brez, about the contest, and about going up into space.

"I heard he wants to build a space hotel."

"An orbiting hotel?"

"A hotel on Mars!"

As Peg moved forward the two lines further diverged, and she would have to make a choice. She loved eggs late in the day and fajitas early, so brunch was a toss-up. What she really wanted, she decided, was mini-omelets with fajita fillings wrapped in little tortillas, something to gobble up as she rode the walkway. She held her arms out in a Jesus pose, an attempt to approach the two stands at once. Everyone behind her seemed to understand her gesture, and they allowed her this indulgence. When it was her turn, she got the attention of each of the kiosk cooks, who looked at each other and nodded, and they gave her exactly what she wanted. Peg walked away, paper sack full of steaming rolls of food wrapped in foil, and the two lines became one as they all clapped and the cooks coordinated the orders of breakfast omelet fajitas for everyone behind her. This was why she was hired, she thought. This was what she brought to the company. Everyone talked about thinking outside the box, but Peg *lived* outside the box. When she'd ridden the entire moving walkway around the corporate campus twice more, with her brunch eaten, it was time to head back to her cubicle and try to do some work.

Peg's cubicle had a miniature battery-powered waterfall and rock garden, a pair of motion-sensor-activated animatronic love birds, a rusty vintage tin Coca-Cola sign, a print of Van Gogh's bedroom, and a blown-up and framed Hanged Man card from the Russell Crow Tarot Deck. Peg's computer had two nineteen inch monitors, one of which was used almost exclusively for a slide show of her all-time favorite memes: Picard telling Number One to "Make it [something that rhymes with 'so']," Gene Wilder as unimpressed Willy Wonka, Michael Cera photo-bombing, intense Nicholas Cage, unemotional Christopher Walken, Pepper Spraying Cop, Overly Attached Girlfriend, White People Problems, Grumpy Cat, Ridiculously Photogenic Guy, and her absolute favorite, Ermahgerd! Instead of working she watched her monitor cycle through the memes. She'd seen them here every day at work, but eventually Peg would bubble up to a chuckle, and that was the measure of a good meme, funny on the worst day, funny no matter what.

Peg had emails in her inbox from the people she worked with: invoices to cut and paste into spreadsheets, chat box conversations to log, and attached to the signature lines of many of the emails was an ascii art doodle of the Findability Campus made from a capital O swarmed with parentheses. This particular ascii doodle art had always looked to Peg Myers more like ascii doodle art of a vagina. When she saw it she sometimes said to herself, "Girlfriend of Maxim Brez." There *was* work to do, work she was being paid to do, but all of that could wait. Because the amount of time left before Brez's presentation had dwindled, and she wanted a smoothie, which had a slow-moving line at the kiosk. So this was it. Her day was done. She had time to throw the I Ching and then she needed to get going to be able to slowly sip her smoothie before Brez's talk. She really loved working at Findability, but any day that centered around Brez was special. Peg Myers was his flag bearer, his most devoted disciple, and his number one fan.

2

Maxim Brez stepped out onto the stage in black jeans, Doc Martens, and a Findability trademark blue fleece pull-over with the NASA logo stitched above his heart. Peg had gotten a seat up front, possibly as close as she'd ever been to him. Brez was shorter than she'd thought, maybe even shorter than she was. Like everyone around her—and the Findability family was nearly all men—she whiled away the minutes by giving her full attention to her Findability touchscreen phone. Brian Clark had messaged her, "Where are you?" but she'd gotten there early, hadn't thought to save him a seat, and so she waited until Brez took the podium before she typed, "Oh shoot, it's starting. Powering down."

Behind Brez was the forty-foot screen he used for presentations and it made him somehow larger. Brez took the remote, the Findability logo appeared on the screen, and with a trick of animation it morphed into the Launchability logo. He leaned into the mic and said, "Are we ready to launch into a new era?" and the place went wild. Whenever the Findability family was assembled, it was like a Star Trek convention minus the costumes. They were self-proclaimed nerds, though Peg preferred the term "introvert." A walk through any office floor revealed cubicles crammed with graphic novels, Star Wars figures, and Anime posters. All these balding pot-bellied men were still twelve on the inside, and they always would be, eventually hauling their comics, sci-fi toys, and DVDs with them to the old folks' home. When Peg first started working at Findability—after the initial shock of actually having landed such a coveted job, and after she realized that she was most likely an affirmative action hire—the men were nervous around her. She was younger and people told her she looked like Jodi Foster, and she did on a good day. The men would stammer, they wouldn't know what to do with their hands, they would sweat. She supposed they all thought Brian Clark was her boyfriend, and so it was necessary to lose him in the crowd like this from time to time.

"Ladies and gentlemen," Brez said as the familiar satellite image of the Findability campus became smaller and smaller on the screen until they were looking down on the coast of California, then the whole continent, until the blue ball of the Earth shrank away to a dawdle, "seeing the Earth from space was a feeling I will never forget. Our inventions and our accomplishments appear small compared to the greater web of being. We've helped to create a parallel virtual universe of human connections where we meet each other across vast distances with networked computers. But our next challenge is perhaps our greatest."

Brez thumbed the remote, the small Earth rotated away until a pink star was centered on the screen, the Maps view accelerated, and someone shouted, "We've mapped Mars!"

It was true, this new Maps feature had been under wraps and in development. But Brez shook his head and smiled. "Ladies and Gentlemen," he said, "may I present the Vulcan Fourteen," and the view rotated back to trail an enormous staged rocket as it blasted toward the red planet that slowly enlarged into a basketball.

They'd skipped the number thirteen. The last Vulcan was XII and that meant this was really the Vulcan XIII. Most of the family seemed to think Brez selected the name Vulcan as a nod to his Russian ancestry, but everyone Peg knew called them Vulture, since they hadn't been reliable and were seen as a bit of a joke. One of the stages of the Vulcan XIV exploded off and drifted away, and the shorter rocket continued ahead toward the red planet. The Vulcan XIV had the same recognizable lines as its predecessors, with a six-pack of thrusters at the bottom and a wide cylinder that slimmed all the way up the rocket to the last stage, which was straight, with the cone-shaped capsule on top. This rocket was three or four times longer and wider in scale than the previous Vulcan, so they'd really upped the ante, and had also managed to keep quiet about it.

"We're going to Mars," he said, and the rows of reporters in front of Peg left their seats to kneel in front of Brez, camera flashes bursting all around.

"*I'm* going to Mars," he qualified.

And then, after he paused long enough for the crowd murmur and photographic activity to finally die down, he said, "And one of *you* will be going with me."

So Brian Clark was right, and if Brian knew, most everyone knew, this staged event more for the world than any of the family, Brez's big announcement surely leaked ahead of the speech for maximum effect.

"I know this dream of mine is a shared dream," he said. "With our private venture, in cooperation with NASA, but funded with our own resources and brain power, we're going to select *one of you* to journey with me: to be among the first men to walk and eat and sleep on another planet."

Brez had announced the Findability Phone with the same kind of overreaching flourish, so the tenor of his talk was familiar. However, if what he was claiming to want to do could be accomplished, it was a truly remarkable endeavor and they'd all been a part of history today. Without having any control over her body, Peg stood and cheered with everyone else, and Brez raised his hands over his head in acknowledgment. Brez stepped away from the podium, followed by a cloud of reporters as he walked over to the supermodel, who Peg only then noticed had been seated at the edge of the stage not very far from her all along. They were a beautiful couple, his daring brains and her perfect breasts, which hung in her loose silk top without a bra, the dark points of her nipples speaking to everyone in the crowd and only overshadowed by the enormity of what Brez had just said.

Everyone waited around, embraced each other and shook hands, with signs of excitement in every interaction. As it became apparent there would be long lines at the food courts, the family filed out and excused themselves to "get back to the office," but there wouldn't be any work at all today, and as the crowd thinned, Brian Clark spotted Peg and came over to her.

"Was I right?" he said.

"You must have good sources," Peg said.

The breakfast fajitas rolled around in Peg's stomach. She'd long been uncomfortable with her body and she felt bad about what she'd done to herself, yet again, by eating too much. There was no way her physical specimen could be considered a serious candidate in contention to go to Mars, but she knew Brian Clark was going to ask, and when he did, the idea of dropping pounds appealed to her so much she decided to say she had to at least try, and maybe today was the day to finally start a diet and exercise regimen. She wanted to look better and she wanted new clothes. Maybe then she could attract the best among the men that the company could offer.

"Are you in?" Brian Clark said, and Peg's Findability Phone vibrated.

She saw it was her daughter, Erin, and nearly everyone was gone from the auditorium, so she held up a finger to Brian Clark, and she answered her phone.

"I know, I know," she said to Erin. "Yes, I was there. I'm still here. Was I on TV?"

Erin said she'd been reading about Mars, and so it was an amazing coincidence. Then Erin asked the same question Brian Clark had just asked. And while she was prepared to tell Brian Clark "yes," as an excuse to get away from the desk more, to maybe jog around the track or go swim laps, she knew, that even though the company might select a woman astronaut for the P.R., there was no way they'd ever pick a single mother.

"Do it!" Brian Clark mouthed to Peg who listened to her daughter tell her about Mars.

"I hadn't even thought about it," Peg said. She rolled her eyes and waved him away, and so he left her there in a conversation with her daughter about our neighboring planet, and Brian Clark, like all the other introverts, wandered back to his cubicle to see what everyone was saying on internet forums.

Peg dreaded going home, because some time that night, because of Brez's press conference, she could expect a call from her ex-husband. She liked Ronny, he was a nice enough guy, and easy to talk to. When they were married she put him through grad school, and he had the habit of staying late at the library to study, only she later learned he hadn't studied at all. She had yet to forgive him for his affair with the new woman—or *girl*, she was a girl then—Cecilia, who reminded Peg how much she'd let herself go and how there was also no new Ronny on the horizon. Her job as a Findability Expert had given Peg the resources to pay for Ronny to go to college, and it also made it so he didn't fight her when she asked for full custody of Erin. She knew she was better off without Ronny around, but from time to time, because of Erin, she still had to talk to him or see him.

Ronny finished his MBA with student loans and he became a traveling sales manager. He sometimes scheduled sales trips to visit Erin, which Peg was grateful for. She would honestly be fine never seeing him again, but his efforts with Erin made a difference. Erin didn't feel abandoned by Ronny and she grew up knowing her dad well enough to also know her staying with her mother was the best for everyone. Peg would eventually be glad that Ronny was gone, and she would feel sorry for Cecilia, who appeared to be stuck with him now, to the point that Peg became anxious when she imagined being in Cecilia's shoes, knowing that Ronny would always be off on a trip, and what he might do again if he met a young girl.

Before they pulled the Corolla in the drive, the call came. Peg put Ronny on speakerphone so he could run through his usual shtick with Erin, "How's my girl? How's school? Any boys I should know about?" and while he often left it at that, this time Peg knew he'd end with, "Let me talk to your mother."

"I'm here."

"We read about your boss. How he wants to be an astronaut."

"He *is* an astronaut."

"He wants to go to Mars."

"Someone from the company is going too."

"Cecilia and I were joking about it," Ronny said. "Like what if they picked you."

"Do you think it's funny?" Peg said. "Am I a joke to you two?"

"We didn't mean it like that," he said, backpedaling. "It's just. I mean being an astronaut is physical. It's really hard."

"I could do it," Peg heard herself say and she almost believed it.

"I don't know," Ronny said. "Remember The Six-Million Dollar Man? They put him in a centrifuge."

Peg was increasingly unsettled. First, Ronny had called her to make small talk that belittled Maxim Brez, one of the century's most successful programmers and business leaders. Ronny had suggested in no uncertain terms that she couldn't get in shape. And to hear him say "centrifuge" was infuriating. She wouldn't have guessed he'd have even known that word. She tried to place the reference and she imagined The Six Million Dollar Man theme music pumping along to sped-up footage of the astronaut Steve Austin spun around in some kind of fortified high-tech carnival ride, and she decided that if she found a still of that, it might make a really good meme.

"I don't remember that episode," she said. It wasn't a show they ever watched together, just one they grew up with, a show from their separate childhoods. Ronny had had The Six Million Dollar Man doll and had wanted to be like him, an ex-astronaut with bionic strength. She remembered him telling her that.

"Your boss is going to get himself killed," he said.

At that, Peg snapped. She had put up with a lot from Ronny over the years, and there was so much she had wanted to say. Even after divorcing him, there was still more to say.

Instead she said, "I *am* entering the contest and it doesn't even matter if I win because *I'll* know I'm good enough to go to Mars and I don't need you or anyone else telling me I can't. Fuck you, Ronny! And fuck Cecilia too!"

She hung up before he could say anything and Erin pumped

her fists over her head and shouted, "Hell yeah, Mom!"

Peg's victory was short-lived. The next morning she remembered putting Ronny in his place, but it wasn't until she was in the Corolla with Erin that her bold promise descended on her in the form of unreasonable cheer on the part of her normally solemn daughter.

"Did you know NASA doesn't even have a spacewalk suit for women? You should bring that up. The spacewalk suits are hard shell and designed to fit men's bodies."

Peg imagined being crammed inside an oversized tin man suit and trying to make her limbs move when her joints were misaligned with the moveable points of the suit.

"The first woman in space was a Cosmonaut," Erin said. "We think we're so progressive, but we didn't put a woman into space until 1984."

The thought of communist Russians and that ominous year made Peg think of Big Brother and his round omnipotent face staring down from a billboard.

"1984!" Erin shouted and Peg was spooked.

Even if she could get herself in shape and somehow get selected, there was no way she'd be able to deal with the cameras. Brez seemed to woo them. She shuddered at the thought of reporters shouting questions at her. She decided to undo the damage and go ahead and tell Erin she was put off by Ronny, but that she didn't intend to enter any contest.

"Even if you died I think I'd be okay because I'd be so proud," Erin said. "I mean can you imagine it, standing on Mars? It would be amazing!"

It really would be amazing, and Peg hadn't thought enough about that part: *her* footprints on another planet, *her* name forever associated with Neil Armstrong's. And then the speaking tours. She would go to middle schools for the rest of her life and be a professional role model for girls. She could sell autographed photos.

They'd put her on a Wheaties box. The more she thought about the contest the more appealing it all was, except that that life would be a lot more work than her average day at Findability. She'd still get a check from Findability, she supposed, though her title would have to change, getting paid to be some kind of media representative. She'd make PSAs or judge science fairs. And then it dawned on her that maybe that's what Brez was really after all along. Getting to Mars was going to cost him but would pay back several-fold in image marketing. Every news organization would cover the Mars story for years, and Findability would remain in the spotlight.

"I mean I'd be really sad if you died," Erin continued. "I would miss you. But it would be so worth it. You'd be a hero."

"There are going to be a lot of people in this contest," Peg said.

"Visualize winning," Erin said. "That's what Olympic athletes do. They imagine themselves wearing the gold medal and it works."

"I've never won anything," Peg said, and she wondered what would happen if the reporters took the time to interview the losers, if they'd say they'd visualized winning too.

"That's a horrible attitude," Erin said. "We've got a lot of work to do."

In the Findability parking lot Peg was reminded of how many other employees there were and how most of them had a better shot at going to Mars than she did. They were smarter, they were in better physical condition, and they were motivated. She'd been using the job as a placeholder in her life and she'd been lucky. She'd gotten away with doing next to nothing for a long time. The change wouldn't be easy, but it was necessary.

She walked Erin to her classroom in Building Four and rode the moving walkway over to Building Eleven. But then she kept going, over to Building Sixteen, the one with the gym and the pool.

3

She hadn't brought workout clothes with her, but they were available at the desk, Findability T-shirts and sweats that were deducted from her pay. They even had white Nikes with the swoop in the trademark Findability blue. She was in and out of the locker room in no time and running around the track that encircled the upper level of the gym. There was a lot of the family doing just what she was, though most had thought to wear their own t-shirts: Spiderman, X-Men, Atari, Star Wars, Mountain Dew, Scrabble. There were all kinds of t-shirts and logos with not a single professional sports team represented, with nearly everyone an awkward jogger: trying too hard, or with a jerky gait. Peg would never wind up on a real Survivor-type reality show, but with this motley group of computer geeks she felt she actually stood a chance. After her fourth or fifth time around the track her stomach tightened and she slowed to a walk. She needed water. She needed to sit down.

A blur flew past her and she recognized the form and efficiency of an actual athlete. She knew right away this was Claudia Burkhardt, who was a Facebook friend, and Peg couldn't stand her. She was thirty-one or thirty-two and she ran marathons. She posted pictures of herself at the after-parties drinking with a different man each time and she didn't just run marathons she ran *extreme* marathons. She ran a fifty-mile race, a race up a mountain face, and a triathlon that was stretched out over three days. Claudia Burkhardt didn't mess around in life and she was here to let everyone know she was going up in the Vulture XIV.

Peg found a second wind when Claudia zoomed by, and Claudia shouted, "Keep your toes forward. And move your arms."

Peg looked up as Claudia ran backwards to offer this advice, and she was faster than Peg was running forwards. Claudia could go for miles without effort. Peg waited until Claudia turned back around, and she muttered, "I hate you." But then she did concentrate on keeping her toes pointed forward and it made a difference.

A crowd of boyish men gathered at the water cooler to watch Claudia. Peg stopped because she was genuinely thirsty.

"Has there been an email or anything?" Peg said. "How do we sign up?"

"There's supposed to be an announcement later today," one of the men said. His arms were too long for his short trunk. He talked to Peg but didn't take his eyes off Claudia. When she ran past, their heads turned in unison. Peg wanted to give up and go back to her cubicle. Instead, she downed a paper cone full of water, then another, and she went back to running in circles. She felt better about Claudia as she did. They were the only two women at the track, they were Facebook friends, and so she saw Claudia as an ally and someone who apparently knew a lot about staying in shape. The next time Claudia came up from behind, Peg gave a little wave, and Claudia smiled. She'd *smiled*. Peg couldn't remember the last time she'd gotten a genuine smile from anyone other than her daughter or Brian Clark, and it felt really good. Peg's body, however, felt awful.

For her last lap, she tried to run while holding her breath. She decided lung capacity might be an important measure of her compatibility with space travel, and she would try to make it around the track in as few breaths as possible. She got in eight or ten paces before she became light in the head but kept pumping. She'd told herself she didn't need air. Except she did need air. She quickly took a deep gasp, and the sound magnified in the gym and shocked all of the men around her. She'd wheezed air like she'd returned from the bottom of a lake, and she bent over and paused for a minute to breathe, hands on knees, like she might vomit, like she'd given in. Then she held her breath again and took off running, this time halfway around the track before she took her next breath, a single drawn-out deep inhale, without gasping, and without stopping. She made it all the way around the track in two breaths, and she felt stronger. She went once more around to prove it wasn't a fluke, and then she quit running and went to the locker room to put on her navy blue suit and sensible flats. She rode the moving walkway back to her cubicle where she studied the Mayan Apocalypse, unsatisfied with any of the theories of why their magnificent cities were abandoned. It was clear to Peg that if the reward for the *best* athletes was human sacrifice, then all of the smart and able-bodied people had left. Then Peg was diverted away from this research by Mayan Apocalypse memes where Peg spent the rest of the afternoon.

After returning to her cubicle, Peg was tired and hungry, and she left again to browse the food courts. Because her legs were sore, on this trip she let the moving walkway do the work, and she wasn't the only one. She recognized fatigue in the postures of all of the introverts around her, who had also gotten it into their heads they'd give the competition a shot, just as she had, and they'd all come on too strong on this, their first day.

She was torn between a chicken teriyaki kiosk and one that served veggie burgers with sweet potato fries. The line for the veggie burger was shorter, so her legs made the choice. When she got to the head of the line, however, she asked the cook to give her chicken teriyaki on the burger bun with melted American cheese and lettuce and tomato, a chicken teriyaki sandwich. The cook stepped away from the stand with a bun and came back with the chicken, which he assembled into just what she'd wanted, with no indication of surprise, as if it were something people often ordered.

She didn't eat on the walkway but went back to her cubicle, where she sat down and watched her daughter on the video feed. Nearly everyone she passed was in some kind of workout attire, a lot of the family in Findability blue sweats and Nikes like she was, and it made her want to disappear back into her cube as soon as possible.

She took a few bites of the teriyaki sandwich, which she felt she'd earned, because her body *needed* calories for a change.

"What are you reading?" she typed into the instant messenger.

"There's a face on Mars," came the reply. Erin turned around in her seat to look over at the web cam and she waved. "Viking spotted it. With this Egyptian pyramid nearby, except the pyramid is a pentahedron. The face is like a Martian sphinx or something. Martians might still be there!"

As a Findability Expert, Peg had heard of the face on Mars. NASA had debunked it, but no one believed them. Peg was unconvinced of the authenticity of the moon landings, all of the moon shots occurring while Nixon was president, and a distraction from Vietnam. Nixon was a bully and the natural enemy of nerds, who hated him and thought him capable of juggling multiple deceptions. America wanted to believe, but a significant faction of the Findability family was convinced Nixon hired Stanley Kubrick to fake the footage. Among the Findability family was an unrepresentative number of web junkies who were also conspiracy junkies, and well-versed in, if not wholly religious about: aliens, illuminati, chupacabra, Mothman, Bigfoot, ghost hunters, chemtrails, Nikola Tesla, MK Ultra, Reptilians, Skull and Bones, the HAARP weather weapon, Loose Change, CIA crack cocaine and DoD AIDS, all of which cumulatively substituted for God and mythology. Most of the supernatural phenomena worth believing in, for programmers and introverts, had a nefarious edge. Presidents and governments were out to get us. They were in cahoots with the Grays, and in the constant pursuit of absolute power. Every now and then the wallpaper of reality peeled back and we were given a glimpse: a UFO over San Francisco or a famous astronaut admitting at a MUFON conference that he'd seen something inexplicably strange. Peg knew how to navigate this sea of alternative belief systems without necessarily believing in them, so that when they came up she mostly let her coworkers, who were men, interrupt each other and talk and talk.

Meanwhile Brez had bought into the science side, that we *had* landed on the moon, and that *he* would outdo those heroes, the real heroes being the engineers. One could believe in both science and conspiracy, Peg supposed. Because a little skepticism was healthy and there had been times when those at the top had certainly lied. Nixon was proof of that. The main thing for Peg was that a computer in 1968 didn't really amount to much. She couldn't imagine them calculating orbits with their slide rules. There was too much uncertainty and too much radiation. The more she looked at the footage the more it seemed faked to her. She kind of hoped she'd win a seat in the Vulture XIV just to prove herself wrong. Because she didn't want to be like that: disbelieving all the grand stories, or always believing the worst. Though it was true, that *simulating* reality was without a doubt what we'd gotten best at.

"Do you think I've got a shot?" she typed to Erin.

"As good as anyone," came the reply.

She didn't know why her daughter would feel that way. What had Peg ever done to instill that kind of confidence? She'd raised her, yes. She'd made a good enough living and they had a nice life. Compared to Ronny and Cecelia Peg was a genius. But an over-achiever? A go-getter? She'd never thought of herself that way and didn't understand why Erin would either.

"I've gotten fat."

"You can lose weight."

"I don't do well under pressure."

"You haven't really been tested."

"I'm indecisive."

"So?"

"I get sick easily."

"You know all kinds of stuff."

"On Earth. I know pop culture."

"That's important."

"For what?"

"For having a conversation. You're going to be cooped up in a space capsule for *two years*."

"You really think I'm interesting?"

"Now you're fishing for compliments."

Peg realized then what winning the contest would mean. She'd be in the Vulture XIV with Maxim Brez, *for two years*. She'd really get to know him. She'd be his friend. She imagined herself living in a space capsule as something that could actually happen.

And then someone on her floor shouted from his cubicle, "Check your email everybody!" The official contest rules had been sent and when Peg clicked on her email inbox there it was, a message from Brez with the subject line, "Come with me to Mars."

Peg didn't open the email right away. She couldn't. She was hungry again, extremely nervous, and out of sorts from her jog earlier. She thought about running, how it wasn't so bad, and she would run every day if that's what was needed. But she supposed she'd have to lift weights too. And take supplements. Which ones were best for going into space? Calcium and vitamin D, she assumed. But what else? And who would know? She wanted to go back out on the walkways but she knew everyone would be talking and she wasn't ready to hear about the rules yet.

She got online and went looking for memes. For sure there were already Maxim Brez / Launchability memes. She used the Findability image search to find them: one was a shot of Brez at the podium with the Maps image of Mars on the screen behind him, and the caption, "Because we've catalogued every known fact on Earth," with the British spelling of "catalogue," though she suspected that whoever made the meme wasn't a Brit. She imagined a Brit would be nicer. As a meme it seemed lacking. It might get circulated on Facebook, but that wasn't saying much. "Cataloguing" wasn't quite what Findability did. It wasn't quite funny enough and you had to know for sure who Brez was and this particular speech. It was odd to Peg that there were people out there on the web who might not recognize Brez, but of course there were. As a member of the Findability family, her point of view was skewed.

Brian Clark stood at the threshold of Peg's cube, also wearing Findability sweats and Nikes. He was beaming. Peg knew this had something to do with the rules of the contest and that she wouldn't be able to put off hearing about the contest any longer.

"So..." Brian Clark said, and he nodded.

"I haven't looked."

"There's no physical fitness requirement!" Brian Clark shouted, and someone from a nearby cube responded with a "Woohoo!"

Peg didn't know if she should be relieved or insulted.

"We sit at our desks all day," he said. "And the winner will sit in a capsule for two solid years. Our lifestyle is already compatible. Physical fitness is not discouraged *but*: it, is, not, a, requirement."

She was sure now. She was insulted.

"You were working out too?" she said.

"And *you!*"

"Erin talked me into it. All this role model stuff."

"You would be a *great* role model."

"You don't think I already am?"

"'Female astronaut' is inspiring."

"I'm going to keep jogging," Peg said.

"I was thinking the same thing," Brian Clark said.

She saw how he was trying to turn this into another way of spending time with her and she didn't want that.

"I need to do this on my own," she said.

"I didn't say," he began. Then he corrected himself, "We could motivate each other."

"I am motivated."

"It would motivate me," he said.

"Seeing me sweat?"

"Yes."

"I guess I can't keep you from using Building Sixteen," she said.

"But you don't want me to?"

"I don't want to run into you there," she said. "I think I've met someone."

"Oh."

"Not a man but someone who can help me."

"A trainer?"

"Kind of."

"Good," he said. And he nodded. "I'm okay. This is good."

4

Over the next few days there were fewer and fewer members of the Findability family wearing workout clothes or crowding Building Sixteen. Peg still hadn't gotten up the nerve to read the contest rules, but she knew, from what people were saying, that she had some time before she had to sign up. There was an application with a few basic questions that also asked for a headshot, and for the first round that was all they wanted.

She turned off the slideshow of memes on one of her monitors and brought up the web cam at Erin's Montessori. There she was at the computer terminal researching Mars, and Peg was going to hear about Mars a lot. On the second monitor she opened up the photo booth and leaned in, so that her face filled the large screen. She tried to smile naturally as she looked into the camera eye at the top of the monitor, and she clicked on the camera icon with the mouse, which took her photo with a slight delay, so that her smile had already faded. She wasn't photogenic and she wasn't coordinated, and getting a good headshot might take her all morning. An instant message popped up on the monitor trained on Erin's Montessori classroom and Peg was happy for the interruption. It was Erin's teacher and she was asking about sign-ups for parent-teacher conferences. When could she come in? Peg could stop in any time. She could go over right now if she wanted.

"It's been so busy," she typed. "But I've been meaning to talk to you."

"We're always here," the teacher typed, and then Peg recognized her sitting at the terminal next to Erin.

"I haven't told Erin yet," Peg typed. "But she's going back to stay with her Dad. Maybe for good."

There was a pause, and the teacher replied, "I'm very sorry to hear this. Are you sure this is what's best for your child?"

"It can't be helped."

"She's thriving here. I'd hate to see her development stunted."

Peg could hardly believe this. As far as she could tell, and she dropped in on Erin's classroom *a lot*, the Findability teachers had it easier than she did.

Peg closed the photobooth and she opened her email to download the Launchability Mars contest application. She scanned it quickly to see several lines for spouses and dependents: are you married, divorced, any children living with you? It was to be emailed back to Findability human resources, and the deadline was sooner than she'd thought. Dependents? Yes, she clicked, and she typed in Erin's name in the box.

Another instant message popped up from Erin's teacher, "Maybe you and Erin's father could both come in and we could work something out. What is most convenient isn't always what's best for the child."

Peg backspaced over Erin's name until it was gone, and she unclicked the box marked "dependents."

"If you haven't told Erin yet," the teacher continued, "we should maybe all talk this over before you make any rash decisions. Before you upset her."

She typed Erin's name on the line again but clicked a different box, "dependents, not living with you."

It seemed like a betrayal, but she had to get this thing in.

She opened a separate instant messenger and asked her

daughter directly, "You want to stay home tomorrow? You could play on the laptop. As far as I can tell your day would be pretty much the same."

"I can make my own lunch?"

"Just don't use the stove."

"I can sleep late?"

"When have you ever slept late?"

"I'm old enough to use the stove."

"Don't say anything to your teacher. I'll talk to her."

The instant messages kept coming in from the teacher. It gave Peg the feeling the woman earned a bonus per child. She seemed to want Erin there very badly.

"I'll talk to you tomorrow," Peg finally typed to the teacher, and the flurry of messages stopped.

As she rode the circuit of campus on the moving walkway, she held fried rice wrapped in a large spinach tortilla, not a very good combination, a starch wrapped in a starch, and no one in the lines behind her had copied her order. She'd had her fill of rolled-up rice and she was looking to step off the conveyor to toss it into the garbage when a tall powerful woman zoomed by. Peg recognized Claudia and was immediately inspired. She stepped over to the left side of the walkway and she walked as quickly as she could while holding her food out in front of her. She felt the exhilaration of stepping briskly and she was nearly as fast as if she were running, her walking combined with the motion of the walkway. She exited at the first opportunity and nearly fell from momentum as her legs adjusted to the unmoving carpet of the long hall. She slam-dunked the Chinese burrito into a slender aluminum waste receptacle and instead of stepping back onto the walkway she started to run. There were members of the family who chose not to use the walkways but they were scarce, and Peg jogged past them uncomfortably in one of her sensible navy blue business suits and flats. As she approached the fast-walking Claudia, Peg puffed and panted and drew a lot of attention to herself. Claudia sensed Peg closing in and she looked over her shoulder just as Peg burst forward into a sprint and put distance between them.

"You go!" Claudia shouted, and Peg felt good inside because of this younger, better-looking, more athletic, more-put-together woman, who was clearly on her side. And Peg continued on, unselfconsciously chugging ahead of everyone down the long hall, until she came to a crowded food court and she had to slow down, which was her undoing, and she stopped. She was leaned over with her hands on her knees trying to catch her breath when Claudia came up to her.

She placed a hand on Peg's back and said, "We're going up in the Vulcan together, me and you. Ain't none of these boys going to stop us!"

Peg couldn't speak but she managed to give Claudia a thumbs-up.

The specs for the capsule hadn't yet been revealed but it was a long flight and a very large rocket. If Apollo carried three, the Vulture might take six or seven. If one was Brez, two or three were pilots, a couple of scientists, and so maybe, if it came down to two, if there was a dead-even Findability family tie, there could be two who would win. Peg loved the idea of winning but of also sharing that with Claudia. Over the years, at least not since landing this job, she had gotten used to not dreaming of things, but she was there now. As she stood up to look Claudia in the eye and to smile at her, she felt dizzy and the backdrop of the food court dissolved as she imagined the rust sands and yellow sky of Mars stretched out all around them. They would be wearing space helmets, she had to tell herself, and so she quickly revised her daydream with Claudia facing her in a sexy Martian spacesuit. *"Was that even possible?"* she wondered, the suit bulky, reflective and completely covering all of Claudia's athletic body. And then Peg looked her new friend up and down. She really saw her for the first time. She was beautiful, yes, she had a beautiful face, with flowing auburn hair, and a beautiful body, in a gray business suit and violet silk blouse that fit her well but also didn't really represent her. Claudia was more herself in her jogging suits, with the freedom to move.

Peg basked in the rays of Claudia's sex appeal, and while the magnitude of her attractiveness wasn't as immediately apparent as it was with the supermodel, Peg thought maybe Claudia, once you stood next to her, was actually more beautiful. And Peg got the feeling that being with her like this and getting Claudia's approval made Peg more beautiful too. It was exactly the kind of moment that would normally be spoiled by Brian Clark coming up to her, but he was nowhere to be seen, and now that Peg thought about it she hadn't gotten a phone call, text, email, or instant message from Brian Clark all day, with a touch of sadness that maybe the last conversation had gotten through to him, coupled with the levity of the possibility of being free of him.

What seemed so remarkable to Peg—a good girl friend—maybe a lot of women had. She had watched her daughter often enough to know Erin didn't have girl friends, but she decided to ask first, before she pulled her out of class. She would hate to stand between her daughter and that kind of feeling. Peg had assumed they were both loners, a Myers trait they were cursed and blessed with. When Erin's class let out, Peg stayed in her cube and acted busy, so she wouldn't have to interact with Erin's teacher. After school, Erin took her time on her way from Building Four to Building Eleven. She took the long route so that she got to walk through Building Fourteen, the Launchability headquarters, where there were video loops of animated renderings of the future of space tourism, with Brez narrating the voiceovers.

Most of the work of Launchability was done in Huntsville, where Brez was courted by the state of Alabama to build a twin site to the NASA Center, where the rockets were built and tested. Here at the Findability campus were some of the architects and engineers who refined blueprints or analyzed data. They stood in line for cappuccinos and smoothies, just as Erin would, and none of them talked much, but when they did she got a glimpse of the work, physics and math like Chinese to her—and what she wouldn't give to know what they knew.

By the time she'd arrived at her mother's cube she'd bought a solar-powered paper airplane and two freeze-dried ice creams. As she crossed the threshold of her mother's space, Erin slurped at the remains of her smoothie and tossed one of the Mylar-wrapped ice creams onto her mother's desk.

"It's what astronauts get for dessert," she said.

"Have you been charging to my account?"

"A little."

"What else did you get?"

"Check it!" Erin said and she gave Peg the airplane. There was a plastic propeller and a solar cell as well as a large sheet of heavyweight paper that was printed with dotted fold-lines and colored lines that represented the windows and jet engines of a space shuttle.

Peg paged through the instructions. "This looks complicated."

"Get your boyfriend over here."

"He's *not* my boyfriend. Besides, he's working."

"Are you kidding? He'd be here in a flash."

"He *would* be good at this," Peg said.

"So?"

"I'm trying to give him distance."

"What did he do?"

"It's not him, it's me."

"I'll call him," and before Peg could stop her, Erin had called Brian Clark on Peg's phone. "This is Erin," she said. "Can you get over here? We need your brains."

While Peg had always felt more than comfortable around Brian Clark, because she had let him know she wanted some space, she was anxious. She opened the package of freeze-dried ice cream. It was a small rectangle of Neapolitan that was like a brick of chalk.

"I got it at the Launchability Store."

Peg took a bite from the stripe of chocolate. The freeze-dried ice cream became a milky liquid in her mouth and was quite good. Not at all like the real thing, but she would give up ice cream to sit next to Brez for two years. She took a bite of strawberry and vanilla and let them mix in her mouth, then she alternated, chocolate, vanilla, strawberry, until it was nearly gone and Erin hadn't even opened hers. She was always saving things: her allowance piled up in a bank account and she sometimes left her lunch untouched until just before bed. "Eat it!" Peg wanted to tell her, except she knew where that conversation would lead. Erin didn't need to give a reason for wanting to save her freeze-dried ice cream, and the only reason Peg wanted Erin to go ahead and eat the stuff was so she wouldn't be drawn to it herself.

Brian Clark appeared and went right over to the solar-powered paper airplane. He took out the instruction book, and he went about folding the paper.

"I love these things!" he said.

When he had it looking like a space shuttle, he affixed the propeller and solar panel, which he held close to Peg's desk lamp.

"Does that really fly?" Erin said.

"Just you watch."

Brian Clark adjusted the ailerons and the vertical stabilizer, he lifted the airplane up over his head, above the height of the cubicles, and he gave it a toss.

Erin giggled, but Peg said, "You can't throw that in here!"

Brian Clark shrugged his shoulders, and said, "It's harmless."

"People are working!"

Erin stood on Peg's office chair to watch the airplane as it flew a slowly descending circle over the cubicles and eventually disappeared into one.

"Hey!" someone shouted.

Peg made a face of concentrated irritation and her arm shot out to point at the entrance of her cubicle, where Brian Clark should go to retrieve Erin's airplane.

Erin ran over to where the plane landed and there was a fat man with glasses and a gray beard who sat at a Bowflex workout machine that had been crammed in next to his desk and computer. He wore an orange and magenta outfit of jogging shorts, tights, and a sweatshirt, with a white towel draped over his shoulders. His sweatshirt had, spelled out in iron-on letters: "Nerd Squad." He held down a bar in front of him and he strained against the resistance. There were two large monitors on his desk, with one monitor displaying some kind of Findability-related spreadsheet, the other playing a workout video from YouTube. The man had been trying to keep up, but the airplane had apparently disrupted his concentration, displeasure evident on his face, and he released the bar out of rhythm.

Erin waved and picked up the airplane.

"Sorry!" she said, which disarmed the man, because he'd expected the transgressor to be a coworker.

Brian Clark quickly followed and offered up his own apology, "I did it. I'm at fault."

The frown returned to the man's face, which caused the long gray beard to curl toward his chest. He let go of the bar and pointed at himself, "You hit me on the nose!"

Brian Clark apologized a second time, though with less sincerity, because the man was protected by his wide thick glasses, and the plane was light. "I just can't help myself," Brian Clark said, "when it comes to kites and things."

"There's a courtyard."

"I know, I know."

"Love the setup," Erin said of his cubicle. "You going to win that contest?"

The absurdity of it all embarrassed the man and he blushed. The workout instructor on the YouTube video kept barking out motivational quips. Brian Clark took the liberty of sitting in the man's office chair.

On a shelf above his workstation was a diorama of The Battle of Hoth, with two imperial walkers advancing on a line of rebel infantry in a snow trench and firing a laser cannon and a snow speeder with a miniature cable trailing, in the act of tangling up one of the walkers. The models were painstakingly painted with carbon scoring for battle-realism and the snow speeder hung from a fishing line with a stream of gray cotton puffing out of the engines for contrails. Brian Clark reached up and touched a wing of the snow speeder, which made it spin. The shape of the snow speeder was close enough to the paper airplane that it gave Brian Clark an idea.

"Can you help me with this?" Brian Clark said and he rifled through the desk looking for a scissors and a straight edge, which he found. He unfolded the airplane and redrew the lines for a closer match to the snow speeder, until the fat man got down on a knee to be next to Brian Clark, and he took over. He refolded the airplane, which wasn't close enough to the shape of the snow speeder to satisfy them, so they unfolded it and tried again. Erin sat down on the Bowflex bench, pumped the bar a few times, which made it clear how strong she was, as well as how weak the man was, but she quickly became bored, so she got up and wandered back over to her mom's office.

"Where's Brian?" Peg said.

"Made a friend."

"He's good at that."

"Can we go home now?"

"Just let me finish this," Peg said, and she paged through a website of low-carb recipes.

"You're really serious about this?" Erin said.

"I didn't want to be," Peg said. "But now I think I am."

"That one looks good."

"We don't have any of this stuff."

"Go to the store."

"Not up for it," Peg said. "Would be nine before we sat down to eat."

"Get it delivered."

"They do that?"

"*You're* the one who works for a tech company."

"I guess I knew," Peg said. "We've just never tried it."

Erin waved her mom out of her office chair and she sat down. She clicked on an icon that opened a printable copy of the recipe, which she highlighted and copied. She went to the website for Organic Grocery Delivery, set up an account, and she emailed them the list after adding a few items of her own. She hit "send" and said, "Groceries will be there when we get home."

Erin got up to leave, and Peg sat back at her computer. "I was thinking maybe I should try a raw diet, and she typed her search into the Findability window."

"I don't know," Erin said. "If you win this thing you won't be able to eat raw. You'll be eating processed goo out of tubes for two years."

"*You're right!*" Peg said and she typed in a new search and clicked on the image icon to fill her monitor with an array of military MREs and even some space food for purchase. One website was in

Russian, but it looked like a lot of the same products were available from Amazon.

"You've got to be kidding me," Erin said as Peg filled her cart with hundreds of overpriced foil packages of what appeared to be food in name only. The reviews were rarely above one star, and when they were, there was always the disclaimer that self-contained ready-to-eat vacuum-packed individual meals should never be compared to real food, not even to heavily processed, canned, or preservative-infused edibles. The sole purpose of the units was to deliver calories under extreme circumstances while taking up as little space and with as little weight as possible. Peg spent enough on all the food-packs to qualify for Amazon Prime for a year and to get free overnight shipping on her order. And then as an afterthought, she went back and added six tubs of Tang to her order.

"You are not serving me that stuff," Erin said.

"Have you tried it?" Peg said.

"I've had Kool-Aid."

"Not at all the same," Peg said.

"You really are an astronaut."

Just as she stood up to go, Peg had to duck to avoid being hit by Erin's paper airplane that had been transformed into a snow speeder, and it flew faster and in a tighter arc. Brian Clark and his new friend were heard cheering, and Peg said, "I already live on Mars."

5

When Peg left in the morning, Erin was still asleep, and driving to work felt strange without her. Peg missed not having Erin's iPod with Erin's singer-songwriters, and her unending insistence that the speed limit was, for all practical purposes, five miles above the posted speed limit. At work she still parked over by Building Four, which felt like a mistake when Peg remembered Erin wasn't with her, except that she'd promised to talk to Erin's teacher, something she didn't look forward to.

This was the first day of work since she'd officially entered the contest, and she felt envy and resentment for everyone around her on the moving walkway, because she was sure one of them would be the one to go. Of course they weren't calling it a contest, but a job search. Technically, she had applied for an internal hire, for the job of Launchability Astronaut, the list of qualifications set off with bullet points. While it was well known that pilots were required to have 20/20 vision, it was assumed that no one at Findability did, and so this was not a requirement. There was a question about citizenship, apparently for tax purposes, because foreign-born members of the Findability family were encouraged to apply. There was no indication yet as to what might be used as the criteria for selection. Human Resources already had her resume on file, as well as her letters of recommendation, none of which would have in any way addressed her astronaut potential. But she supposed that was true of everyone else, and Peg realized she'd been standing on the moving walkway instead of walking or running as she'd gotten into the habit of doing. Here she was wasting time that could be spent exercising. But she also didn't feel like running and she decided that was okay.

There were two men in front of her in white lab coats with goggles on top of their heads that caused their hair to shoot out at odd angles. She knew from their attire that they were chip architects. They strove for smaller, faster, more powerful circuits and that was their life's goal. It was that simple, and also that complicated. They were engaged in a spirited conversation with no awareness that someone behind them might want to pass, and when Peg listened, what at first sounded like a description of a rape, or of some kind of fetishistic pornographic movie, Peg eventually recognized as a Nerd debate when she heard them say "Superman" and the whole conversation was illuminated. The chip architects were arguing whether or not sex with Superman would kill Lois Lane, one sure it would and evidence of Superman's homoeroticism, the other more of a romantic and seeming to want Superman's love consummated no matter what, which he morphed into an argument that not only could Lois take it, but she would very much *like* it. The back-and-forth was one the two men had probably first had when they were fourteen or fifteen, with their middle-school friends, and they rehearsed the same points of argument except that they'd thought the problem through for years and years. One suggested a small piece of Kryptonite as a marital aid.

"A Kryptonite ass plug?" the other said, mocking.

"She wouldn't have to put Kryptonite in his anus. The comic book record makes it clear beyond a doubt that Superman is affected by simply having Kryptonite in the room."

"Wouldn't that be dangerous? What if he fell asleep? He could die!"

"He would trust her. It would make him vulnerable. The Kryptonite a perfect metaphor for love."

"I don't think there's a bedroom in the fortress of solitude."

"He has a bedroom in his apartment in Metropolis. Or he could go to her place."

"I don't like it. He has to try to win her over as Clark Kent and it'll never happen because she's a beautiful woman and Clark Kent is a nerd."

"*You're* a nerd."

"I'm half the nerd you are."

"Clark Kent is only pretending to be a nerd. He has Superman's penis and she knows this instinctively and he'll reveal himself to her at the right moment because he's a man and his happiness depends on it."

"His entire race died in a planetary explosion. Who says he ever gets to be happy?"

"I'm going to be happy when I'm standing on Mars and you have to look at me through a telescope."

"When *I'm* standing on Mars and you're watching me on CNN."

"When your kids read about me in history class."

"Well, even if Clark and Lois could have sex, if she got pregnant a Superbaby would kill her for sure."

"I'll give you that."

"Ha!" the slightly more misogynist chip architect shouted and he leapt into the air in excitement, which made the moving walkway jerk when he landed, and the two men were suddenly aware of their surroundings, and that Peg, a woman, was right behind them.

She tried to imagine what it was like in their office, with the two of them putting each other down and disagreeing all day. They blushed when they saw her and Peg said, "Lois could handle him. They're all boys inside, all of them," which included Brez too. The chip architects argued their candidacy for the space mission by how much of a nerd they believed themselves to be, which was seen as having great merit around Findability. And maybe that was it. Maybe that was the key to the contest. Brez was offering them something they never should have had access to. They were the introverts, not the explorers. They were the men in the control rooms at the monitors with their equations, not the guys who splashed down and got the girls. Brez was subverting the natural order. He'd built a geek family and now he'd proposed crowning a geek king. They'd all grown up on sci-fi but imagined themselves as the Spock, or the Data, or the C3PO, while the jocks were the Kirks and the Han Solos. They hated the jocks but were tricked into rooting for them when the jocks were out in space. Space should have been nerd territory. They knew best how to survive in it. They knew the truth about black holes and gamma rays. That it was zero degrees Kelvin, there was no north, south or west, no friction, no end to momentum, and no one heard you scream.

"She likes Clark," Peg said. "She's just waiting for him to come out and say what he really feels. Superman is her fantasy but she knows it would never work out. He'd eventually fly off and pick up some other girl. Clark's got a good job. He's kind. He's smart. He just needs a little self-confidence."

The men clammed up, and one of them stepped aside to let her pass. But Peg didn't walk by, nor did anyone else behind them. And then, as if she hadn't said anything, one of them said, "She could have a little Kryptonite in a bedside nightstand."

In her cubicle, her second monitor was still trained on Erin's Montessori classroom and Erin's absence depressed her. She called her on the phone and told her to get on Skype. There was Erin in her monitor again and Peg felt better, until she realized Erin was sitting on the couch with the laptop, and watching TV.

"You're supposed to be doing schoolwork," Peg said. "Or whatever it is you do at school."

"I'm cleaning out the Netflix Queue. You realize you've got like 800 movies on here? Just the streaming?"

"I want to watch those."

"When are you ever going to watch them?"

"I want to watch them."

"When was the last time you watched a movie?"

"We watched that Wes Anderson movie."

"That was pay-per-view."

"We watched Traveling Pants Two."

"That was *my* pick. It wasn't from your queue."

"I don't know. I like knowing they're there."

"I'm deleting them."

"You can't *delete* them."

"Not all of them."

"Tell me which ones you're deleting."

"Garfield, Uncommon Truth, Star Trek Voyager..."

"No..."

"Voyager?"

"I want it in there."

"Okay, okay. Nova. Transformers: Dark of the Moon. The Hulk."

"Which one?"

"Ed Norton."

"Not Lou Ferrigno?"

"I left those."

"All right."

"Richard Dawkins. Fleetwood Mac Rumors. Ancient Alien Encounters."

"Leave that one."

"You've seen it."

"I have not."

"It's from the nineties. We watched it together."

"I don't remember it."

"Some stupid Egyptian hieroglyphs. Same old stuff."

"Well how did they build them then?"

"I don't know," Erin said. "With slaves."

"The great pyramids are a technical feat beyond what we can do even today and a message to the heavens. There really were E.T. visitors, and they've been here with us for a long time."

"Whatever," Erin said. "It's just not a very good show. You won't watch it."

"I'll watch it."

"I'm deleting it," Erin said. "Tell them 'hi' when you get there.

You're down to 750. I'm about to get ruthless."

"Leave them. *I'll* do it."

"Your astronaut food came."

"*Why didn't you tell me?*"

"I'm telling you now."

"Open it! Open it!" Peg said. "I want to see it."

Erin carried the laptop into the kitchen and set it on the table so the webcam was pointed at the stacks of boxes she'd placed on the counter. One at a time, Erin took out the tubes of the identical-looking meals and read the labels to Peg: "Peas, black beans, carrots, brown rice cereal, *wait a minute!*"

"What?"

"Yogurt. This one is yogurt."

"So?"

"It's basically go-gurt. You paid seventeen dollars for a tube of go-gurt."

"It's packaged for space. You can't take go-gurt up into space. It might pop or something. Could get on the equipment."

"You're *not* in space. You're practicing. How many of these did you buy?"

"I like yogurt."

"I can tell."

"Try one."

"I don't want any of this stuff."

"Just try one. Tell me if it's good."

Erin opened another box and rifled around in it. She held up a tube and said, "Boston cream pie."

"Go for it."

Erin pierced the package with a built-in straw and sucked as she squeezed. She let it set in her mouth, and she swallowed. She took another long drag.

"How is it?"

"Like confused pudding. Not sure if it wants to be chocolate or vanilla."

"Cool."

"Try the apple pie."

Erin set the tube on the table unfinished. "I'm not filling up on this stuff. I'm heating up a pizza."

"And then you're doing homework."

"I never had homework before."

"I'm talking to your teacher today. If she emails you after this, tell her you live with your dad now."

"Won't she know I don't?"

"How would she know?"

"Don't schools contact each other when someone transfers? Wouldn't Dad have to sign papers or something?"

"I don't know. Your teacher doesn't strike me as all that bright."

"What gives?"

"I really want to win this," Peg said.

"You think I'm holding you back?"

"*I* don't, but they might."

"Did you Findable that? First single mom in space?"

"I don't need to. I just know it."

"Okay, you're right," Erin said. "All I'm getting is porn."

"Please use the safe search."

"Safe search is boring."

"You're only *eleven*. Turn the safe search on."

"I'm putting it on 'moderate'. Still no single-mom astronauts. You could break the mold."

"Only if they don't know."

6

Peg sat with Erin's teacher at one of the classroom tables, both of them in the kid-sized chairs. Erin's teacher had Erin's portfolio spread out in front of her, a battery of documents Peg had never seen. Painted Styrofoam balls that represented the solar system hung from the ceiling tiles at intervals. Peg tried to maintain eye contact with Erin's teacher but her gaze was pulled to Mars that hovered in the classroom sky beyond the teacher's shoulder. The planet had been spray-painted in streaks of red and gray, the red much too bright, making the red planet look magenta.

"Are you doing this because of the contest?" the teacher said.

"It's not a contest. It's an application for an internal hire. And no."

"Your timing seems suspicious," the teacher said.

"Have other parents…"

"Yes," the teacher said. "Claudia Burkhardt pulled her son out yesterday. I've seen you two together. Seems fishy, you must admit."

"Claudia? I didn't even know she had a kid."

"Don't be coy, Ms. Myers. We're talking about Erin's education. Don't you think that's more important?"

Peg leaned forward, and said, "You're like one of those Disney villains."

Erin's teacher sat straight, then she collected up Erin's portfolio and slid it across the table to Peg. "You figure all this out," she said. "Just remember I don't have to take her back."

"I think you do," Peg said, and she got up and left without taking Erin's folder.

The next day a coworker with a long gray beard stood at the threshold of Peg's cubicle. He was dressed in purple jogging shorts with yellow tights under them and he held Erin's solar-powered paper airplane. His t-shirt spelled out, in iron-on letters: "Jedi in training."

"Brian said this was yours," he said. "I would have given it to you sooner, but I'd thought it was his."

"It's my daughter's," Peg said. "But thank you."

"My name's Kevin," the man said, they shook hands, and both Peg and Kevin extended the handshake, tempted to break out secret nerd-society handshake maneuvers.

"Erin doesn't care about the airplane," Peg said. "You can have it."

"Thanks," Kevin said. Peg noticed he had a drafting pencil sticking out of his beard. "Turned out pretty cool." He held up the paper snow speeder and moved his hand slowly, like it was flying over a long barren expanse. "Normally, aesthetics and functionality are at cross purposes."

Peg nodded. Kevin had certainly improved the airplane.

"Which is why I think I can help *you*," he continued.

Peg waited for him to clarify.

"I can coach you," he said.

She pointed at his outfit and said, "Aren't you in it?"

"I'm kidding myself," Kevin said. "I'm really just a big chicken. I'd have a two-year-long panic attack. It would be horrible."

"You think you can help me?"

"I don't know if I can explain this," he said. "I spend a lot of time on Reddit and the sexism is really off-putting. There's this change that has occurred, that some of us haven't caught up with, and I feel like we need to revise the stories. In fantasy: no more saving the princess. In sci-fi: Leia gets a light saber. Seeing you on Mars would be so cool. It would be the right thing, the better thing."

"You want to help me because of Reddit?"

"Basically, yes."

"And *how* can you help?"

"I'm the Findability sci-fi expert."

"Okay," Peg said. "What can we do?"

"Whatever you research here," he said, "put it on hold."

Peg looked uneasy. "Memes," she said.

"Definitely no more memes," Kevin said. "There's so little time. We'll start with *Dune*, then move on to the Star Trek series. I'm going to assume you know Star Wars, so we won't bother unless you're really that oblivious. And Arthur, you'll need some Arthur."

"As in King Arthur?"

"You're a Knights Templar on the quest for the grail and we are going to subvert the structure. The damsel is leaving the tower to go on the quest herself."

"Damsel?"

"Hear me out on this. If the table is truly round they are going to have to give you a place at it. Brez understands this. If you ever get in the room with him, you'll be speaking his language."

"You want me to read *Dune* so I can be an astronaut?"

"Okay, maybe not *Dune*. How about Ray Bradbury?"

"I read *Fahrenheit*."

"No, you want *Martian Chronicles*."

"Is it on audio?"

"Good thinking," Kevin said. "You can listen while you jog."

"You really think it will make a difference?"

"*All* the difference. That and t-shirts."

"You want me to wear t-shirts to work?"

The idea was not all that unusual. Plenty of folks in the Findability family wore nothing but t-shirts to the office. Kevin was one of them. And the t-shirts tended to be valuable, even costing more than dress shirts, coveted t-shirts like vintage Pink Floyd, or tees of long gone uncool 80s bands probably worn ironically (though no one was ever sure), $80 hand-screened tees with detailed renderings of favorite superhero panels, jokey t-shirts, as well as the occasional solid color Gap tees with no writing or graphics and surely no more than eight dollars a piece.

"Vote for Pedro," Kevin said. "That kind of thing."

"I don't know," Peg said. Though she'd never felt good in her sensible navy blue business suits and flats, so she had nothing to lose. No one had ever been fired, she reminded herself.

"Let them know you're here," he said.

"Do we go shopping?"

"I'll take care of it," Kevin said. "Meanwhile get Brian to tell you everything he knows."

"About math?"

"About anything."

"I've just told him I want distance."

"*Un*-distance him."

"Won't that be confusing?"

"Let me tell you about every man who works here," Kevin said, "with the exception of Brez. Women are mysterious. He *expects* you to contradict yourself."

"I don't want to lead him on."

"It's not you," Kevin said. "He's going to be lead on whether you do the leading or not. Quit feeling bad about it. He'll meet someone eventually. For now, be his friend. And let him help you."

"But he wants to go," Peg said. "Since he was a little boy, probably, he has really really wanted to be the one to go."

"He's used to coming in second," Kevin said. "Or fourth. We'll get him a t-shirt. He'll wear the t-shirt. He'll be happy for you. He really will."

"Vote for Pedro?"

"*First woman on Mars!*"

"Holy shit," Peg said. That was putting it out there. Brez could be the one to step on Mars first and her shirt would still be true. There would be a first man and a first woman on Mars, which was a win / win for Findability. She knew now that she needed Kevin in charge of her campaign, and that it was a campaign.

"I've got a place," Kevin said, and he pointed at the saying on his shirt. "We can have you something by tomorrow."

"Will people know it's me?"

"They know you're a woman."

"You like pie?" Peg said.

Kevin shrugged his shoulders, but he was curious. Peg dug around in the desk drawer that she'd filled with astronaut MREs until she found the tube she was looking for.

"The cherry pie is really good."

First woman on Mars, Peg was thinking and her new friend squeezed the tube of red cherry gel into his mouth, with a smidge dribbling onto his beard. She made the gesture that he should dab at it, but he didn't get her, so she took a Kleenex and dabbed at his beard herself. It was like babying him, and she could tell he liked it, but he also instinctively shrank away.

"I do like pie," he said, and as soon as she was done with him, he turned and left. He moved down the hall stealthily, a ninja in his own mind, and she saw he was short, rotund, and could never possibly sneak up on anyone, though he really seemed to live inside that possibility.

At home, Peg stared into the refrigerator. She had to cook something for Erin, but was hindered by the portion. Cooking for two made more sense but she wasn't hungry in the least. At least not yet. With the astronaut tubes she swallowed small portions all day long, which kept her satisfied, if only momentarily. In the eight hours she was at work, she'd tried all the tubes of pie: lemon meringue, key lime, strawberry, cherry, blueberry, pumpkin, apple, peanut butter cup, New York cheesecake, French mousse, banana cream, coconut cream, grasshopper, pecan, custard, Oreo, and tiramisu. Living like an astronaut was a lot easier than she'd thought. In the future, she decided everyone would eat this way. After two years of eating tubes of pie in zero gravity with Brez, it was going to be hard to switch back.

"Pot pie?" she said to Erin who sat on the couch with the laptop.

There was no reply.

"Don't you ever watch TV?" Peg said. "Kids your age are supposed to watch a lot of TV."

"I want a laptop."

"You know you can use mine whenever you want."

"Your desktop is a mess."

"Just put everything in a folder."

"*You* put it in a folder."

"Okay," Peg said. She worked in tech. Everyone she worked with had bought their kids computers. Good computers. Expensive computers. She had the money, she was keeping Erin home from school, and she couldn't think of a good reason to say "no." Why did she always start with "no," and work uphill toward "yes"? There were people out there who started at "yes" and didn't question themselves.

"Okay, you'll put it in a folder, or okay, I can get a computer?"

"Both."

Erin carried the laptop into the kitchen and she held it up for Peg. Erin had a computer picked out and all of Peg's information was filled in so that all Peg had to do was click on "accept" to finalize the transaction.

"This is the one you want?"

Erin nodded.

"You had my credit card number?"

Erin shrugged her shoulders. Peg bought the computer.

"What do you want for dinner?"

Erin took the laptop and opened another window. There was another merchants page, this one familiar to Peg, their favorite Chinese restaurant, The Happy Palace. Erin had ordered stir-fried noodles and crab rangoons, and dinner was taken care of.

"Find me a good treadmill," Peg said.

"Any specs?"

"Some kind of human hamster wheel."

"I'm on it," Erin said, happy to have a task on the laptop.

Peg sat next to her on the couch and soon realized Erin was right not to watch TV. There was nothing on that was worth their time.

7

When she got to her cubicle the next day, Kevin and Brian were there to greet her, both of them in red t-shirts with white all-caps, block-lettering, that spelled, "First woman on Mars." Kevin held a box of them in various sizes, like he was their softball coach, and he set them down in her space for her to rummage through. Kevin held one up to her to assess the size, and he had to put it back and go up a size. He'd gotten half of them in a slim feminine cut with dropped neckline, and he set several on Peg's work area for her to keep. The rest he would pass around to the other members of the family. Peg was going to be the first woman on Mars, and these t-shirts would be collector's items. If they worked anywhere else he could sell them, but since everyone at Findability was used to getting things for free, handing them out went much better with the workday flow. No nerd in their right mind would turn down a free tee, especially one that was gender-busting and Mars-related. The only thing missing, from a nerd's perspective, was a female Silver Surfer, or female Green Lantern, which just wasn't Kevin's style. For him, the message was all that mattered, and the words would be remembered to take on a life of their own.

Peg took off her jacket and blouse in front of them and Brian Clark was immediately blushing. They'd always kept their friendship genial, and here was acknowledgment of Brian Clark's physical desire. She was annoyed by his reaction and felt she should be able to take off her shirt in front of him without worrying about his feelings. But here he was, dumbfounded and meek and in the throes of a fantasy her disrobing flung him into. Soon enough she was wearing a red t-shirt, and Brian Clark continued to stare at her with awe.

"Perfect!" Kevin said, and Peg walked over and gave him a hug.

"I love it!" Peg said. She slipped on her jacket over the t-shirt, but it covered up the iron-on letters, so she took the jacket back off, and just like that she was done with wearing business suits to work.

Kevin left with the box of tees to hand them out. And Brian Clark lingered a little longer, the two of them facing each other in matching shirts.

"I really hope it comes true," Brian Clark said, which would mean he wouldn't be the one to go, he wouldn't see her like this for two years, and he'd also have to share her with the rest of the world.

On the moving walkway Peg attracted even more attention than when she was the new girl at Findability. Each of the men she passed read the t-shirt, and sometimes she got smiles. It meant they could look right at her boobs, and that she was encouraging them to do so. However else Peg felt about her body on any given day, she had a pretty good set. Halfway around the campus she saw a man wearing the identical t-shirt, who waved. And she saw Erin's Montessori teacher, who didn't smile back, and Peg pretended not to see her. She'd brought tubes of pie with her and eventually she would get off the walkway and jog, but so far this morning the idea was to be seen. These folks were the curious type, and when they saw a t-shirt they would always, all of them, get the urge to read it. She was becoming the first woman on Mars already. Whatever the selection process entailed, they'd have to give her serious consideration now. She had let herself be known. She had felt their eyes on her and her life was different. And then it happened. She couldn't have planned things any better.

She didn't even realize it was happening until she made eye-contact with him: Brez was out on the moving walkway, surrounded by his entourage. Peg was jogging down the long carpeted hall between the walkways when she saw them coming, a huddle of well-dressed younger men in much better shape and better groomed than the rest of the Findability family, and one of them looked at her, then another, and they parted and there was Brez reading her t-shirt, and he smiled.

As soon as he appeared he was gone, but his look was frozen in her mind. He was impressed with her and she was going to Mars. Once he was out of sight she stopped to catch her breath and her heart was really going. She had seen Brez. No matter what else was going to happen with this contest she got the feeling she'd leapfrogged the callback and had made the finals. She didn't know who to tell. Her instinct was to call Brian Clark, but she remembered she was trying to give him distance. She wanted to tell Erin but didn't think Erin would really understand how big of a deal this was. If she explained it to someone they might not get the significance. Brez had a look like she'd given him an idea. It was really Kevin who had given him the idea, and she wanted to call him and thank him, but she didn't have his number. She could ask the Findability operator, but didn't even know his last name. She held her phone, scrolled through her contacts, and called her ex-husband, Ronny.

"Hey, Ron."

"What's up, space cadet?"

"It's not funny," she said. "I'm really serious about this. And I need something from you."

"The hard-shell luggage?"

"I'm advancing. I really have a shot at it. And I need you to take Erin for a while."

"How long of a while?"

"Maybe two years."

She hated to ask him. She hated acknowledging the tenuous

connection to this man she never should have married. She knew why she did, she couldn't take the marriage back, but she was still unable to live entirely independent of him, which was how she felt on most days.

"We'll need to work out child support," he said.

He was supposedly doing just fine. She had never asked him for a dime to take care of Erin. She knew she made a lot more than he did, no matter how well off he was, and so the arrangement seemed right. But now he was asking for money.

"How much?" she asked.

His figure seemed high. Really high. Only she didn't care. She remembered the look she had gotten from Brez, she felt like she was going to be famous, and so the money was nothing. She also knew that if she tried to negotiate with Ronny he'd raise his number.

"How soon can you take her?"

"I'll be out there at the end of the month."

She wished it didn't have to be this way, she felt like she'd betrayed her daughter, but she really needed this for herself. Going to space was something she didn't even know she wanted. Now she wanted a seat on the Vulture XIV more than anything she'd ever wanted in her life. Ronny could have her money.

Later in the day, there were more members of the family in red "First woman on Mars" t-shirts and Peg was meeting and talking to people who would have never come up to her before. All these men recognized her as the first woman on Mars, the subject of the t-shirt they were wearing. And Peg realized there was an aspect of the job she'd missed out on. A lot of these men were friends: they played video games with each other after work (or during work), they went out to movie premieres, comic-con conferences, or even out for a drink. The one thing the Findability campus didn't have was alcohol. So they sometimes went off together, and Peg was meeting people for a change. It occurred to her that while the other introverts were able to bond over projects or common interests, she mostly kept to herself because she hadn't overcome her shyness. And because she was a woman, all the other introverts clammed up in her presence.

She wasn't Claudia, she knew that, but she did have that effect, and she hadn't learned to use it to her advantage. She wanted to go out for a drink with Claudia, to cement their friendship, but she didn't even know if Claudia drank. And how would Claudia take the t-shirt? It seemed kind of bold. They were in competition as far as that went, and Claudia might not like it.

She saw Claudia jogging on the track, and to her surprise, Claudia was wearing one of the red t-shirts. Peg was really amazed to be supported by her number one competitor like that. Then she realized that if Claudia had one of the t-shirts, there might be confusion about who the first woman on Mars really was. She wished Kevin had been smarter about that, but knew he was probably handing them out, and no one, not one of the men here at Findability could ever say "no" to Claudia. So there she was rounding the track at a phenomenal pace and all the men watched her and stared at her boobs as they bounced around in her athletic bra, and they gave her the thumbs-up for the t-shirt, Peg's t-shirt. Peg wanted to tell them all it was *her* t-shirt.

So she started to jog and before long, she caught up to Claudia, and Claudia looked genuinely happy to see her.

"Nice shirt," Peg said.

"Really smart," Claudia agreed.

Peg relaxed a little as she pumped harder trying to maintain her pace. Claudia couldn't have gotten more than one of the shirts. So she couldn't wear it every day as Peg could. She'd have to wash it every night, which she might do, but it just didn't seem likely. Of course, nothing could stop Claudia from printing up her own tees.

"I saw Brez today," Peg said.

"I had a meeting with him," Claudia said.

"Today?" Peg said, wondering if Claudia's meeting was pre or post t-shirt. "You know him?"

"As well as anyone can know him, I guess. We work together sometimes."

"Wow," Peg said and she wished she could take it back. Claudia apparently didn't think of Brez as such a big deal. But he was a big deal. There was no denying it. "What kind of work?"

"We go over the numbers," Claudia said. "I'm a statistician."

"Oh right," Peg said. "I think I knew that." But she didn't. She really didn't know anything about her new friend. She imagined that maybe Claudia was too important to go to Mars. They would need her. Of course, by that logic, Brez couldn't go either. And Brez was definitely going. "Have you met the supermodel?" Peg said and she felt stupid as soon as she said it. She knew the supermodel had a name, a name as sexy as Claudia.

"She's the hostess whenever he has cocktail events at his house. So yes."

"You've been to his house?" It didn't seem possible.

"It's not as big as you'd expect."

"But pretty big?"

"Just not as big as you'd expect."

And then without even knowing she was going to say it, maybe because all the men at the gym were staring at them as they went around the track, maybe because the approving glance from Brez made her bold, she said, "Do you want to go out for drinks?"

Claudia seemed surprised at this. She took a good look at Peg. "Okay," she said. "But you should know; I already have a girlfriend."

"Oh, I didn't..." Peg said.

"I didn't think you..."

"I mean, I'm not..."

"I knew you weren't, but then..."

"Okay," Peg said.

"Tonight?" Claudia said.

"Okay."

And they continued to jog in silence. Peg had no idea that Claudia dated women, or that she would think Peg had asked her out, or that she might accept. And then Peg realized Claudia really did have one up on her, because first lesbian on Mars was way better. So much better. Peg suddenly wished she hadn't called Ronny because this whole thing was clearly Claudia's, but it was too late. She'd offered Ronny the child support, which he really seemed to want. She'd have to break it to Erin sooner or later. Just not tonight. Because tonight she was going out for drinks with Claudia.

And Peg got a bit of a thrill. All these men who looked at them—and it wasn't just Claudia, they looked at her too—they didn't know Claudia was unavailable. Forever unavailable. And they *were* friends. Peg had a lesbian friend.

When Peg ran out of astronaut pies she descended deeper into her order. What could she have been thinking when she had put "French fries with ketchup" in her Internet shopping cart? She had wanted to try everything and she was resolved to only eat out of the tubes for as long as she was in the contest. Perhaps the better question was what were the astronaut-food-chefs thinking when they puréed the fried potatoes and stuffed them into tubes with a dose of ketchup that didn't do anything but color the stuff pink. Lycopenes, she reminded herself. There were lycopenes in ketchup and whatever it was lycopenes were good for, an astronaut might need that. Sailors would eat lemons, which was no easy feat, because on the salty sea they needed vitamins, and sailors were called "Limeys," since back then they called lemons "limes." Luke warm and puréed or not, French fries was the most American food she could think of. Were they trying to make the astronauts feel at home or make them homesick? The puréed fries were like oily mashed potatoes with a burnt aftertaste. They did not go down well. There was oatmeal, there was rice and beans, there was polenta. How bad could they be? Cheese and spinach ravioli, meatloaf, chili, scrambled eggs. Some of the foods, though mashed, weren't entirely puréed but left chunky whenever possible. There were cold soups. She had bought a lot. And yet she was going through it all so quickly. She tried the carrot soup (awful), she tried the bread pudding (anything with cinnamon and brown sugar was good), and she tried the grilled cheese (a mistake). She hadn't been on the astronaut diet for very long and already she was craving solid food. The solution was more pie. She was going to try to eat what she had, but she would need more pie.

In her cube she spent the day looking around for astronaut memes. There weren't as many as she'd expected. She supposed all the space-hype had long waned by the time the Internet had come around. There were basically two kinds of space-memes: science fiction in its many forms, including costume-play; and UFOs and aliens. She didn't have a solid opinion about aliens. She'd never seen a UFO but supposed it was possible. She had a latent fear of being abducted but knew it was probably an abstract twist on her fear of home invasion. There were women who were raped in their own homes, in their own beds, the doors and windows of modern American homes not really fortified against an invader, with only the illusion of safety. With an alien, however, there was no way of keeping them out. They could teleport through walls, paralyze the abductee, communicate calming thoughts telepathically, and fly them up for a lab procedure only remembered later via hypnosis. If Peg was given a choice, that was clearly the preferable home invasion experience.

However, any of the E.T.s that had been photographed looked faked to her. There was an aspect to living flesh that was recognizable, and the large-headed Grays with the deep glassy black eyes, though they sometimes gave her the chills, they never looked convincing to her. With the ubiquity of cell phone cameras, she wondered why we hadn't captured that many more pictures of them. The only answer, it seemed, was that the number of people faking the photos and videos had remained about the same. Maybe she would ask Claudia about that, Claudia the statistician, a good-enough statistician that she had met personally with Brez.

As practical-minded as Erin was, she also tended to believe all kinds of stuff, and Peg felt responsible for the drift. When Erin was six Peg had told her there was no Easter Bunny. Peg had gotten her an iPod, an impulse buy, something more suited for Christmas or her birthday, and Erin had said, "The Easter Bunny got me exactly what I wanted!"

Peg wanted credit, offended that Erin hadn't yet figured it all out, and she made an abrupt attempt to dispel the bunny myth: "How do you suppose a bunny buys stuff? How would a bunny keep track of all those kids? We're not talking candy here. This bunny apparently went into a store and bought you an iPod."

"He probably has a database."

"He? How do you even know he's a he? 'Bunny' is pretty vague."

"He was at the mall," Erin said.

"That was a guy in a costume. It might have even been a woman in a costume. I bought the iPod. It was *me!*"

"I don't think so," Erin had said. "I got this from the Easter Bunny. It was in my Easter Bunny basket."

Thinking back on it, Peg was sometimes surprised at how worldly Erin appeared to be, yet, every now and then this idealistic little girl broke through. Peg hadn't taken her to church since she and Ronny split, and she knew that was something that would happen again if Erin went to live with them. Erin was still malleable, except with respect to the cultural myths that lacked empathy. She wasn't swayed by patriotism as an excuse to go to war, or any cover story for the homeless or the second-class status of immigrants. Erin really cared about people and so she was ripe for a religious conversion. It would mean a confrontation in Peg's future that she wasn't quite prepared for, because Peg didn't know how she felt about God or Jesus or any of them. She really liked the idea of an afterlife, and of an intelligent purpose to the universe, which for her was the best reason to be increasingly convinced there was nothing. She wasn't interested in passing her pessimistic worldview down to her daughter, but she also didn't want Erin brainwashed, so they didn't talk about death or religion, and Peg consigned it to the part of her consciousness where she buried her least favorite thoughts and memories: her first boyfriend, a guy named Wilson who went by Willie; the years of her adolescence that spanned eighth grade through tenth grade; and the time in her early twenties when she had gone outside naked to check the mail, with the intention of popping out and popping in, only she'd locked herself out, and there was no good way to cover herself and no one she saw would help her. She knew the hour-and-a-half before she finally decided to toss a rock through the window of her own apartment would have gone much smoother if she were slimmer and more attractive. This was many years before she got the job at Findability, and no one would have ever thought to compare her to Jodie Foster then, at least not anyone who had lived on her street.

Death was kind of like that for her, a reality that she didn't think about because, in it's finality, her thoughts didn't matter. Death would happen, and that would be that. Religion, likewise, with a few exceptions (she kind of liked the Dalai Lama, she loved Mel Gibson's

The Passion, and she had far too much patience for the Mormons and Seventh Day Adventists who came door-to-door) was a cultural practice constructed with the focused intention of covering up death's utter lack of mystery. She wanted to believe there were religions that were more than just Band-Aids for the inevitable despair—that they helped the poor, that they uplifted the spirit, and that they gave us a connection to a civilized past—but the donations and the tithing got in the way for her. So many churches were so rich in resources and yet there were still homeless and poor people, and those turned away for being a little too human.

Peg hated all of that, preferred to deny it, but whenever she and Ronny went to Beneficent Trinity, the hypocrisy dragged her down until she was less of a believer than when she'd gone in, and she didn't like to be reminded of her growing certainty of the ugly overarching truths: money was wasted on cathedrals and candles, people knelt down to lift themselves above everyone else, they didn't think of themselves as sinners no matter what, and the money they gave, if they had it, they were buying off guilt and purchasing a fake ticket to a nonexistent eternity. She hated coming out in that mood, but Ronny liked to go, and he was usually more kind to her afterwards, so as soon as they were done, and she'd put the uncomfortable thing out of her mind, and they had gone out to brunch together, and she loved brunch, Ronny might hold her hand across the table, and so he was still a romantic, and he might still love her that way, and she went to Beneficent Trinity for as long as he looked at her like that afterwards. And she hated to admit it, but Erin was going to fall for it wholesale.

8

Dave and Buster's was a Chuck E. Cheese's for grown-ups. Claudia suggested it for the happy-hour specials. Despite the assault of noise and light from all the video games, Peg felt immediately at home there, like a sports bar for introverts. At the very least, Dave and Buster's wasn't the kind of place where men in suits who smelled like cigarettes would try to buy them drinks. If she met a man there, Peg decided, they could play a few rounds of skee-ball or mini-golf, and that would take the edge off, and they wouldn't be stuck on their bar stools making small talk.

Peg was still wearing the t-shirt, and people looked, which made her more self-conscious than at Findability, where everyone knew just what the shirt meant. Here the t-shirt made her an oddball. She sat at the bar and waited for Claudia. She was nervous, surprised at herself that she'd asked another woman to go out for a drink, and she'd only ordered a glass of water. She wanted to hear what Claudia said about what their best drinks were. She wanted to flip through the drink menu with all the brightly lit blender drinks, but didn't want to draw the attention of the bartender, a guy who seemed too eager, and would probably be more at home in some other kind of bar.

He leaned in when he talked to Peg, "Add a dollar to any of the specials to upgrade to top shelf. You strike me as more of a drinker than a gamer, am I right?"

"I'm meeting a friend."

"The more the married-er."

Peg laughed though she didn't think he was funny. She didn't even know what his remark was supposed to mean. When he turned to fill a glass of beer at the wall tap she saw where he'd tried to comb over a bald spot where his hair was thinning. He had to get out of here. Though she didn't know him and only projected her own anti-social leanings on to him. She decided this job was killing him, and he needed something where he wasn't always on his feet chatting up strangers for tips. She wondered how many times he had fed that line to a woman sitting there by herself. He had seen her t-shirt but hadn't said anything. Probably he couldn't think of anything funny about a woman on Mars, and so he went to his old standby line.

When he came back, she said, "What does that mean, *married-er?*"

"Oh, I..." and all his confidence suddenly washed away. "I guess I see people come here for affairs. Not that I meant you. I just, I misspoke."

"But there are a lot of people around," Peg said. "this bar is kind of *public*, right? Families and kids and people on first dates?"

"Hiding in plain sight," the bartender said, and he winked. Peg felt like she had learned something. She looked around with this new wisdom but didn't see anyone who appeared to be meeting a paramour. And maybe that was it. Maybe Dave and Buster's was a great cover-up and the perfect establishment for cheaters to carry on affairs.

When Claudia came in the door Peg waved her over, the two of them in their matching red t-shirts, and Claudia smiled. As soon as she was settled on the stool next to Peg, the bartender came over.

"I didn't know what to get," Peg said.

"Two frozen orgasms," Claudia said.

"I didn't see that on the menu."

The bartender worked the blender, which wasn't far enough

away, and with all the noise, Peg and Claudia had to shout to have a conversation.

"Love the t-shirt," Claudia said pointing at herself then Peg.

"I'll look stupid when they pick someone else."

"Nonsense," Claudia said. "You're having fun wearing it."

"You must be used to the attention," Peg said.

"Why do you say that?"

"Oh come on," Peg said. "You must know the way they look at you."

"I need a shirt that says, 'I'm gay!'"

"Why don't you?"

"I've never felt comfortable saying it. I was married before. And I was good at being married."

"So what happened?"

"I really am gay," Claudia said, "though it feels funny saying it. Even now."

Peg was self-conscious, because they were shouting at each other. Then the bartender poured their drinks into curvy woman-esque daiquiri glasses with long straws and they both took a headache-inducing draw.

"No one knew?" Peg said.

"Everyone knew."

"And you met someone?"

"That was it."

"Your typical cliché divorce story?"

"I wish it weren't," Claudia said.

"But you're happier?"

"It's like being married all over again, so there's that. But yes."

"The Montessori teacher said you took your kid out," Peg said. "Was it for the contest?"

"It was for my ex. He got married again and he has this idea that his home is a stable environment."

"Is it?"

"Depends on your definition of stable. His wife doesn't work, so she's always around. If I was a kid it would drive me crazy."

"Your kid is still young, right?"

"Brent is seven. He likes having three moms."

"Oh Jeez."

"I was okay with him having two moms, when Brent stayed with us. So I guess it's fair."

"You didn't fight him?"

"Are you kidding?"

"This is California."

"Everything depends on the judge. You'd be surprised."

Peg finished her drink and she poked her straw around at the last of the crushed ice in the bottom of the glass. Thanks to the bar noise she wasn't self-conscious about the loud slurping sounds she made as she finished the last of her drink, and she pushed the glass forward to get the bartender's attention.

"The teacher told me you took your kid out too," Claudia said. "Was it the contest?"

Peg nodded.

"Really? Why?"

"A single mom with a kid?"

Claudia understood Peg's meaning, but was unconvinced: "Brez is progressive. I don't think he'd let that sway him."

"That may be true," Peg said. "But I've got to get through human resources. Someone there will screen the apps."

The bartender came over and Peg ordered another round. Claudia's glass was more than half-filled, and she shook her head "no." The noise from the blender was back and they were shouting again.

"I haven't given her up yet," Peg said. "But I talked to my ex and he agreed."

"I'm sorry."

"What about you?"

"It's so quiet now," Claudia said. "Brent's always been around. He's been a part of everything. I feel like without him, we're headed for a breakup."

"I'm really sorry."

"Stop apologizing," Claudia said. "Maybe it's for the better."

"Is that why you're going to Mars?"

"*You're* going to Mars," Claudia said, and Peg was surprised and excited.

"Oh come on."

"I mean it. You've got this wrapped up."

"But you already know Brez. Why wouldn't he pick you? You're better at everything. And gay. You're like a P.R. jackpot."

"Not for the middle of the country. And his knowing me is not a plus. People tend to look better on paper."

"I don't look good on paper."

"Sure you do," Claudia said. "I can help you. I'm good at it."

"Do you honestly believe I'll win by resume padding?"

"It's a job application. They'll ask for more materials in the second round."

"Are you giving up?"

"I'll apply," Claudia said. "And I'll be the first to congratulate you when you get it."

Peg could not believe it. Here was a woman she thought of as totally put together and one hundred percent more competent than she was. And yet, she was telling Peg that Peg had a better shot.

"Everyone successful," Claudia said, "everyone who has ever gotten anything—they had help."

"Even you?"

"Especially me. I've had a long string of older men who were interested in me and who helped me."

"You used sex to get ahead?"

"Sex appeal. There's a difference."

"I need to lose weight."

"I think you are beautiful," Claudia said. "But it wouldn't hurt to lose weight."

Peg had downed both of the large frozen drinks so that she felt tipsy, and she was suddenly wondering about calories. Each of those things was probably equal to a meal. She felt terrible about the way her butt hung off the barstool. She hated herself for eating so much pie. She looked down at where her glass met the bar napkin and she slowly turned the drink stem between her fingers.

"It's okay," Claudia said. "I can help you. Meet me at the pool tomorrow. We can start slow and ease you into a good workout."

So fitness was going to matter. Of course she should have

known. Maybe Claudia was wrong. But she knew in her gut, in her ice-cold but alcohol-warmed gut, that this was something Claudia was most certainly right about. She flexed her abs as she sat and listened to Claudia talk but her mind was elsewhere. She wanted to get off the barstool and go jog. She wanted to try to lift something heavy above her head. She steadied her breathing and inhaled deeper to work on her lung capacity. Then she realized she hadn't been supportive enough of her new friend, who, despite the way she looked and the way she carried herself, must have had her own insecurities.

Peg surfaced from her breathing and flexing exercises while Claudia still talked, and Peg blurted out, "Of course you'll win! I'd pick you in a minute!"

Claudia was taken aback, but after the initial surprise, she was won over and said, "Thank you."

Peg said, "Kevin would make t-shirts for you too."

"I've got one," Claudia said.

"With your own saying."

"But what would I?" she started, but quickly understood. "You really think so?"

And Peg was beaming. She knew she might be ruining her own chances, but she felt good about being able to help her friend, and that was the best part of all of this. Peg was now absolutely sure that Claudia was her friend.

Convincing Kevin was easy enough. Like all the introverts at Findability, if there were ever anything geeky and fun and all they had to do was pay for it, cost was never an issue, and Kevin was more than happy to get the t-shirts. The next morning he showed up with a box of purple t-shirts with the saying, "First dyke on Mars." Peg knew dyke was offensive, but if Claudia was going to come out to everyone, she was also reclaiming the term that she'd often seen on the Reddit boards, to teach all the introverts a lesson.

Kevin was already wearing one, and since he knew Peg's size, he handed her one too. Like magic, Brian Clark appeared in her cubicle two seconds before she changed t-shirts, and his presence gave her pause. She was wearing her red t-shirt, "first woman on Mars," and they had decided on purple so Claudia's shirts would stand out, after first considering some of the other available shades of red.

"It's not me," Peg said to Brian Clark. "But my friend. I'm just the woman on Mars. I'm not the dyke."

"I know," Brian Clark said. "But you're wearing one right?"

Brian Clark took off his own red t-shirt and put on one of the purple ones. He did it quickly while noticing how Peg watched him. She'd never seen him with his shirt off and he did have baby fat but he wore it well. He didn't have defined muscles but also didn't have a paunch. Brian Clark looked respectable with his shirt off. Peg was surprised to see that he looked healthy, and she would have to admit, with less of a weight problem than she had. They made contact and she felt the way he looked at her was with an unspoken anticipation. She took off her own red t-shirt but didn't put on the purple one. She looked right at Brian Clark and moved a step closer to him, her purple shirt there on the desk.

"Where do we go from here?" she asked.

"Brian knows a guy who can get you the astronaut suit," Kevin said.

"Really?" Peg said. She could hardly believe it.

"Will he get in trouble?" Peg said.

"No one's ever been fired," Brian Clark said, and he shrugged his shoulders. She knew he was right. But Findability was extremely protective of their research and development.

"I could try one on?" Peg said.

"We were thinking you could go for a walk in it," Kevin said.

"In the food courts," Brian Clark added.

"We'd hand out freeze-dried ice cream," Kevin said.

This idea was even better than t-shirts. She hugged Brian Clark with all her might then moved to hug Kevin, except that Brian Clark didn't let go. He held her tight for an uncomfortable moment, and when he let her go she put on the purple t-shirt and hugged Kevin too. They both left to hand out the t-shirts and once she was alone and slumped in her office chair, Peg realized she had a problem.

A big problem. She liked hugging Brian Clark a lot more than she liked hugging Kevin, and the only uncomfortable part was that they were here at work and Kevin was with them. If they'd been alone that would have been it: all her resisting for all these years would have been for naught. Peg only now realized she had feelings for Brian Clark at the very moment she had pushed him away. And her pride wasn't going to let her do what was probably best for both of them. She was going to keep this secret to herself, not even telling Claudia, and while she might take off her shirt in front of him again, in fact she was sure she would, she would do her best to keep him at arm's length.

On the moving walkways Peg felt awful. She wanted to tell everyone that she wasn't the dyke and that dyke was a term she would never ever use. She was an enlightened and tolerant liberal and the only thing that kept her from saying anything was that if she took the time to tell everyone she wasn't the dyke, she might come off as too apologetic. "I'm the woman on Mars," she wanted to say. "Not the dyke." And so she rode around embarrassed and all the stares had the opposite effect of the stares she'd gotten just the day before that made her feel like she was winning.

Then she saw someone else who wore one of the purple t-shirts coming toward her on the opposite walkway and he gave her the thumbs up. She nodded and tried to smile and really really wanted to shout, "I'm not the dyke!" She supported the dyke. She was a friend to the dyke. She *loved* the dyke. But she was, alas, not the dyke.

And as if it had been scripted, as if it were both the worst and best thing that could happen to her, on the opposite moving walkway coming toward her she saw Brez's entourage, one of them wearing a red "First woman on Mars" t-shirt. Brez saw Peg, their eyes locked, and Brez nodded approvingly. After years of working at Findability, she had, out of some stroke of amazing luck, run into Brez two days in a row, and he had seen her. Now, she was horrified to understand, he had probably thought of her as a dyke and as someone who would use the word "dyke." She wanted to bury her face in her hands but realized she couldn't. She was winning, despite herself, and she would just have to accept his mistaken assessment of her as he raised his arm and he also gave her a thumbs up.

Back in her cubicle Peg sent Claudia an instant message: "Have you seen Brez today? Did you have another meeting?"

"Those are only once a month, or once a quarter, depending. Why?"

"I just saw him again and I was in your t-shirt, which he now thinks is my t-shirt."

"How funny," was Claudia's reply. "I can't even come out."

"So I just came out?" Peg typed.

"Yes, I think you just came out."

"Great," Peg typed. "No offense, but I have a hard enough time getting these geeks to talk to me. I was just trying to be supportive."

"Thank you," Claudia replied. "I think. Probably Findability shouldn't be your dating pool anyway."

When she got home Peg forgot she was still wearing the purple t-shirt and Erin looked at her a long time, and said, "Is there something you want to tell me?"

"Oh, this," she said when she realized Erin was referring to the "First dyke on Mars" business on her t-shirt. "I made a new friend."

"Oh, really."

"You may have seen her," Peg added. "She's really beautiful

and confident."

"And a dyke?"

"We don't use that word."

"*We?*"

"Oh, *I'm* not a dyke. I'm being supportive."

Erin stared back, unsure of what to say.

"If I get this," Peg said. "If they pick me."

"I know," Erin said.

"You know what?"

"I'll have to go stay with Dad. I've already thought of that."

"Are you okay with it? Because if you're not I'll drop out. I'll quit."

"It'll be fun," Erin said. "I'll be the new kid at a new school, *whose mom is an astronaut!* It might even get me a boyfriend."

"Well, now, I don't think," Peg started. "I don't."

"I'm eleven," Erin said. "I'm nearly twelve. I'm nearly a teenager. I may as well explore the fairer sex."

"*You* are the fairer sex."

Erin raised an eyebrow, "Depends who's doing the looking, right?"

"You're too young to date."

"That'll be up to Dad, won't it?"

"You're absolutely right," Peg admitted. "And you're going sooner than later."

"How soon?"

"End of the month."

"*This* month."

"I need to concentrate on this contest. I have to be able to devote all of my energy...

"To sucking down Tang and tubes of meat pudding?"

"It's more than that."

"You're sending me off to live with Ronny and Cecelia? No fucking way!"

"A minute ago you were more than happy to go."

"That was if you won. You didn't tell me you wanted me to go, like, right now."

"I'm telling you."

"No."

"I'm sorry," Peg said. "But we've decided."

"Without asking me?"

"I wanted to make sure it was okay with your dad first."

"Are you kidding me?" Erin said. "Of course it's okay with them. They fucking love me."

"It's true."

"Is it your new girlfriend?" Erin said. "Is she moving in? Are you testing the waters?"

""I'm really not gay," Peg said. "You know me better than anyone."

"It makes a lot of sense," Erin said. "It's not as far fetched as you're making it sound."

9

In the morning, Peg knew she would probably undress again to put on the spacesuit, and so she dug through her drawers for her best lingerie. She had a black see-through lace bra with matching thong that Ronny had gotten her for their second Valentine's as a married couple. She'd put on weight since then but not in those specific areas, so she was sure they would still fit. What she was less confident about was how she would look in them. She slipped them on and stood in front of the full-length mirror in her room. She sucked in her belly and turned sideways. Her bust-line looked good but her thighs were large. Her stomach passed for respectable as long as she continued to suck it in, and she was free of a double chin as long as she kept her head level. She raised her arms and flexed her biceps, which showed muscle, but below, in the triceps-region, flab hung down. She was getting there but had a long way to go. She knew, however, that Brian Clark would not miss the chance to see her put on the spacesuit, and she knew that seeing her nipples through the lace and the suggestion of sex that her Valentine's costume would invoke—Brian Clark was going to get hard, and he would be beside himself with embarrassment, and she would enjoy every minute.

Erin popped in to tell Peg they were running late and she caught her mother checking herself out in the mirror. The made eye contact in the mirror and Erin pointed and shouted, "You have a girlfriend! I knew it!"

"It's not for anyone," Peg said. "I wanted to feel sexy. It's okay to feel sexy."

Erin stood there with her arms crossed and she shook her head. She was upset about Peg sending her away and entirely convinced that her mother was dating a woman.

"This is why you took me out of school? You didn't want the kids to make fun of me because of my dyke mom?"

"I'm sorry, but it was really only ever the contest."

Peg got dressed as quickly as she could, which was a lot easier these days, since she wore a t-shirt and jeans, and she put on one of the red t-shirts. As long as people were going to question her, and as long as Erin was still living with her, Peg was going to wear the red t-shirts.

On the moving walkway, there were coworkers who wore the red t-shirt and coworkers who wore the purple t-shirt, and she noticed, here and there, how there were other women who worked with her. They didn't wear the t-shirts. In fact, it seemed like they made a point not to wear them. They were well-dressed, in tailored business suits and expensive shoes. Each of the women Peg saw this morning looked professional, serious, and really great. Peg felt sexy, with the secret knowledge of what she had on under her t-shirt and jeans, but then she saw how these other women were really pulling it off and apparently having it all. They were like a women's magazine's version of feminism: powerful, smart, disciplined, sexy. These women were not the usual geeks and nerds of the Findability family, and Peg wondered if Brez had been sneaking them in when she wasn't paying attention. And she hadn't been paying attention. This job was the beginning of her personal decline: when she mostly stopped reading, when Ronny started losing interest in her, when she became more of a mom and less of everything else. She was occasionally aware of her own slip, though the job at Findability was rare and a reward for anything intellectual or creative she had ever done, as payoff, as proof of self-worth, and as her publicly lauded identity. Before long Ronny had stopped bragging about her job, though he kept spending her money. And then she was the one always telling the people they met where she worked, and she waited a beat for them to wow, then she went on and on about how great it was. And it really was great. Except she lost her husband, and she let herself go. And until now, being there had pretty much been the same from day to day.

In her cubicle, she sent Brian Clark a text to let him know she was there and he texted back that they had the spacesuit and were on their way. She slumped in her office chair and felt dumb. The other women were younger, smarter, better-looking. She shouldn't have toyed with Brian Clark like that. It was rude and she just might make a fool of herself. There was no reason that he couldn't go out and pursue one of those women. What had he seen in her anyway?

And then he was at the threshold of her cubicle in the red t-shirt, and he was with a friend of his from Launchability who seemed even more of a dork than Brian Clark. She kept up her composure through introductions, and she thanked the man who laid out the spacesuit in its complex parts. Peg disrobed slowly, her heart not really in it, and Brian Clark gasped when he saw her. The guy from Launchability became visibly shaken. So that maybe she did still have something, and her spirits rose.

The suit had a metal frame, with coiled arms and joints, like Robby the Robot, each piece snapped on and locked with a twist. The suit was bright white, and accented in Findability blue, with the Findability logo emblazoned across the chest and the Launchability logo alongside the NASA logo on each upper arm. The suit was impeccably clean, and new, and Peg got the feeling no one had ever worn it, perfectly her size, as if it had been made for her. The helmet was a silvery glass globe loaded with speakers, microphones, electronic sensors, and LCD displays. The whole get-up was like a superhero version of an astronaut, like Buzz Lightyear, and Peg got the impression that it maybe even came with a cape.

The man knelt in front of Peg and held up the pants for her to put on. He tried to do so without lifting his head, but the weight of the space pants prevented this and he found himself blushing and staring right at Peg's lace panties, merely inches away. Peg took the pants and tried to put them on, with Brian Clark holding on to one side. She had to lift her leg high to get in, and all the movement caused her thong to slide and expose a patch of pubic hair. The man from Launchability closed his eyes and held them shut, though this rendered him awkward and unhelpful to Peg, who was in the pants, but didn't know what to do next. With the man kneeling, eyes closed, he was effectively not there, and Brian Clark grew bold; he leaned forward to kiss her. Peg recoiled, not exactly repulsed by the idea of kissing Brian Clark, but she was surprised by his sudden gesture, so that she fell over with the pants on, and because of their weight, she couldn't get back up.

The sound of the suit hitting the ground woke the man from Launchability out of his bashfulness and he was suddenly able to help her and get her into the suit the same as if she were a man. He snapped on the arms and the helmet, and he powered on the life support. She breathed through the ventilator, her vital signs were monitored, and the temperature inside the suit was kept an even sixty-eight degrees. She took a few steps, the boots heavy, but the man reminded her the gravity on Mars would be half that of Earth, so she wouldn't become as easily fatigued, and besides, he told her, she'd be coursing with adrenalin.

"There's adrenalin?" she asked.

"You'd be on Mars," the man reminded her.

"Right," Peg said. And she remembered. She walked out of her cube and over to Kevin's. She imagined the office full of cubicles and computer stations and the blue carpet dissolved away as she saw before her a gravelly vast rust-colored desert with a pale yellow sky. She was walking on Mars; she would walk on Mars.

Kevin applauded with delight when he saw her, and he dug out an extra large red t-shirt to put on over the suit. He patted her on the back, which she didn't so much feel as sense. And she was on her way, lifting one leg at a time and breathing heavily and loudly, which she was sure everyone on the floor heard. They came out to see her and her coworkers were smiling. She had come here and worked alone in her cube for years and years, but they knew her now, and seeing her in the suit made them happy.

The man from Launchability followed behind with a walkie-talkie, and he spoke to her, "How's it feel?"

"I'm doing it," she said.

She maintained a forward momentum to the bank of elevators, where the man from Launchability ran ahead of her to press the down button, and they all entered the elevator together: the man, Kevin, Brian Clark, and Peg, the astronaut. She had ridden these elevators countless times but felt different in them, in the airtight suit, and as she descended she imagined going down to the surface of the dusty planet. Normally, in the elevators with men, she could sense them either noticing her or ignoring her, but the suit was a like a protective shield. Brian Clark and the man from Launchability knew she was in there in her lace panties and bra, but in the suit her femininity was shielded and fortified. And when the elevator doors opened, she imagined the opening of an airlock and she ventured out into the long hall like she was stepping into a hostile oxygen-free atmosphere.

She didn't dare step onto the moving walkway but continued her Frankenstein gait down the middle of the carpeted hall, with her compadres keeping their distance behind her, for maximum effect. The introverts who passed on the moving walkways pointed and stared. They talked about her, and they stepped off the walkway to come over to her. A few wore the red t-shirts and some wore the purple. They stared with the giddiness of teenagers in the presence of R2D2, and with the scientific curiosity of serious men at work. Peg could hear them, from a microphone that picked up the ambient crowd noise, though she was otherwise sealed inside.

"Where's the power source?"

"How does it heat-transfer?"

"What's the PSI?"

"What about gamma rays?"

The man from Launchability stepped up to field questions, with a circle formed around Peg. She turned and turned to look at them and she lost her bearings so she stopped. She wasn't sure from where she'd come, or where she was going, but she wanted to walk, so she took a step and the circle of men around her followed. She continued forward and ignored their questions, until the man broke in on the walkie-talkie to tell her she was headed for a food court. She hadn't known where she wanted to go, but this was good, it was more open, with the family coming and going, and if she wanted she could sit on a chair. The mention of food made her wish she'd brought a few tubes of pie along. There were large zippered pockets all up and down her legs, and she supposed she could fit a lot of food in there. What she was unsure of, was whether or not there was some kind of feeding system for when she had the helmet on. Because she'd surely get hungry out there on the surface. And hopefully, they'd thought of that. Which led her to her next thought: could she expel? She didn't remember being fitted with anything, so she decided not to. Though once she'd thought of not being able to go, it made her want to go, and she now imagined the expanse of the Martian surface as one with no bathroom.

She walked faster and the circle of men around her dissolved into a general crowd as she recognized the food court at the end of her building. It always made her hungry to be there at lunch and she realized this was the first time she was able to walk through without smelling the stir-fry and pizza slices. She saw the food under lamps at the kiosks, but it had no power over her. With no wafting tempting aromas it was much easier to continue on. There was a new crowd of men following her, and so the same questions repeated, until she heard Brian Clark ask a question, and he used the man from Launchability's name: "Tim, how much does one of these suits cost?"

"This is a prototype, and we paid $325,000. If we put them in production the cost will come down, but not a lot. It's the batteries, the electronics, the personal cooling system, the customized oxygen tanks, the airtight, insulated, pressure-safe, puncture-resistant, reflective fabrics. It all adds up."

"Tim," Peg said. "Can I pee in here?" and she heard laughter.

"I didn't bring the excretion system. Can you hold it?"

"Just checking. But there will be one?"

"I'm wearing one right now," Tim said.

"Guide me," Peg said, and she lumbered toward a moving

walkway. She'd gotten up the confidence and Tim counted down the approximate number of steps left as she approached. With a slight jerk, she was on the walkway and moving swiftly along. She noticed the crowd trying to keep up as they walked down the carpeted hall, and she turned around to see a long line of the men on the walkway behind her.

She was separated from Tim, Kevin, and Brian, but Tim reassured her, "Right behind you."

In the next building her crowd met another, smaller, better-dressed crowd, and she soon realized, for the third day in a row, that she was about to run into Brez's entourage. This time Brez came right over and followed as she moved on the walkway, until she stepped off, which tipped her balance and she fell into his arms. She righted herself, lurched forward, and eased back into her Frankenstein lilt. Brez was really interested in her now, and it was apparent he had come out of his office just to meet her. Someone had noticed the hubbub and had gone up to tell him, and here he was, directly in front of her and smiling as he stared at her in the helmet. He was walking backwards, keeping right in front of her, so she stopped, and he stopped. Tim came up to Brez and handed him the walkie-talkie.

"*I* haven't even tried on this version," Brez said. "How's the air in there?"

Peg didn't know what to say. She was glad she was isolated from Brez by the separate atmosphere of the airtight suit, because language failed her, the words caught in her throat. She lifted an arm and gave him the thumbs-up, which delighted him.

"I've seen you before," Brez said. "But we've never met. I'm Maxim," and he held out his hand for her to shake, which she missed, but he caught it and moved her weighted arm up and down.

"I'm not a," Peg started to say, but then she stopped. She couldn't say "dyke," to him, especially in front of all these people, and it wasn't just men, she realized there were other women in the crowd. She felt dumb that she would even bring it up. But she didn't want him thinking something about her that wasn't true, and it wasn't true. Looking right into Brez's piercing blue eyes was an experience that reassured her of her attraction to men beyond a doubt. She felt the temperature rising inside the suit and the cooling mechanism kicked on with a low hum. "I'm Margaret Myers," she managed to say. "*Astronaut* Margaret Myers."

"The first woman on Mars," Brez qualified. He was still shaking her glove.

"You can call me Peg."

"Nice to meet you, Peg."

And because she didn't know what else to say or what else to do, she started walking again, and Brez stepped aside. Tim, Brian, and Kevin followed, and it seemed they would follow her anywhere, with or without the spacesuit. As she neared Building Sixteen, she remembered she had told Claudia she would meet her at the pool at lunch, and it was past lunch. She had just made a woman-friend and had already stood her up. She felt bad but also knew Claudia would understand. She was wearing the spacesuit and she'd gotten to meet Brez. All at once she remembered there wasn't a way to text or email from inside the suit—at least she didn't know of a way. She'd left her Findability Phone back at her cube and wouldn't be able to work the touchscreen in the gloves anyhow.

She pushed through the double doors and up the stairs to the pool area, which didn't smell like chlorine and wasn't any warmer. For her, the changing environments looked, smelled, and felt exactly the same. There were a few men and women swimming laps, with the lane markers in the pool, and Peg soon spotted Claudia, who kicked furiously and charged forward with a stroke that created a wake. She flip-turned at the far wall and surfaced and swam back as Peg walked up to the edge of the pool, at her lane, and Tim shouted into the walkie-talkie, "Don't! Please don't!"

Peg stepped forward and sank, surprised that this end of the pool was at least six feet deep, and she stood there, completely submerged, as Claudia swam right for her.

"We haven't tested in water yet," Tim shouted. "The electronics are quite sensitive. You'll ruin everything."

The phrase, "You'll ruin everything," struck a chord with Peg and she remembered her mother. Peg wasn't exactly raised to be a confident child, and she was always made to feel that everything that went wrong for her mother had been her own fault. She was terrified, when she and Ronny divorced, that Erin would be left with the same feeling. And when she and Erin were living in the house by themselves, Peg went out of her way to make Erin her friend, and Peg kept all of her negative and depressive thoughts to herself. Peg suspected Erin knew she was unhappy on the inside, despite her keeping up appearances, but it was something they never talked about. And now Peg was feeling like that sad and lonely girl again. And though he didn't mean to, Tim had made her feel that way. Whatever chance Tim may have had of asking her out or of even being her friend was greatly reduced. She would hear him talking to her as her mother had from then on in her head. That critical, accusing voice wasn't likely to go away.

"I'm sorry," Peg said. "I'm sorry."

Claudia swam up. She laughed under water so that bubbles rose from her smile, and Peg felt better. And she smiled back. Claudia floated in front of her in a sleek Speedo and mirrored goggles, with her long auburn hair flowing off of her like flames. She was muscular and posed like a superhero frozen in an action frame. She was beautiful.

"It's okay, Tim," Peg said. "The suit passed. Water-tight and fully functional."

"I'd feel better if you came out," he said.

"Yes, of course," she said, but she walked along the bottom of the pool toward the deep end. She saw how there was a ladder that went down one wall all the way to the bottom of the deep end, so she could climb back out whenever she felt like it. The pressure from the weight of the water made her lighter, and it was more like walking on Mars.

"How much air have I got?"

"There's a feedback display on your inside left forearm."

Peg looked to see a small screen lit up with numbers and it worked just fine underwater.

"Which one is air?"

"It should be counting down, in hours and minutes."

Peg walked down the steep slope of the pool into the deep end. She walked over to the middle, near one of the drains, and she lay on her back, looking up. According to the wrist gauge she could stay down there for seven hours. She looked up at the surface of the water and at the refracted lights on the ceiling. Once Tim realized she would be on the bottom for a while, he stopped calling her name, and all was quiet and calm. Claudia had gotten out of the pool and had gone back to work. There was one man swimming laps, but he did ten down-and-backs and he climbed out too. After a while, Peg wasn't even sure Kevin, or Brian, or Tim was up there anymore. She was sorry about Erin. She didn't want to give her up. But she was going to Mars. Here she was breathing underwater at the bottom of a pool in California. And soon, sooner than she could fathom, she was going to be in this same suit, and on the surface of Mars.

10

That night at home, as Erin sat with the laptop and Peg stared at the TV without really watching, she got a text from Claudia.

"When I said meet me at the pool, that wasn't what I had in mind."

"Pretty cool, huh?"

"You are well on your way. Did Brez see you?"

"I think he came down *just* to see me."

"OMG!"

"I know."

"You're the one."

"YOU are."

"I don't know," Claudia responded. "I think I need to stay. For my girlfriend."

"She doesn't want you to go?"

"She says she does. But she's so beautiful. And restless. She wouldn't be here when I got back."

"Are you kidding? You know how many women would wait for an astronaut, just to be married to an astronaut?"

"Not mine," Claudia replied. "Does that make me the jealous

type?"

"You're talking yourself out of this. You should go."

"I don't think I want to go."

Reading this really surprised Peg. She was sure, with the exception of Kevin, that everyone at Findability wanted to go. And she thought about her own feelings. Did she really want to go? She would miss Erin. She would feel bad about leaving her with Ronny and Cecelia. And their church. And her new school. And if she died and left Erin without a mother. But she remembered the look on Brez's face and the calming solitude of being in the suit. She thought about the near impossibility of the little girl her mother had berated and blamed, of the girl she had been, little Margaret Myers, small on the inside too, all grown up and really doing something. She would be Margaret Myers the astronaut, the *famous* Margaret Myers. She really wanted this, for herself but also to prove herself to Erin, to Ronny, to Brian Clark, and to her dead mother.

She turned on the caps lock and typed, "I WANT THIS MORE THAN ANYTHING I HAVE EVER WANTED EVER." And then she thought, almost immediately, that it was stupid of her to think Brez might pick her. He had a supermodel girlfriend and a billion dollars. He owned the rocket and the capsule and the launch pad. Why would he want to take her with him?

And then came Claudia's reply, "You'll be the one to go and I'm going to help you."

Erin scrolled through text on her laptop and clicked from page to page. On the TV interior decorators from some stupid redecorating show yammered on. Everything was the same as any other Wednesday, but Peg felt incredible. She had the sense that she could walk outside, climb the long zigzag stairs up the launch tower to the Vulture XIV capsule and rocket away. Mars was within reach, and she would go. And when she came back, she could have everything.

"Oh my God," Erin said, and she turned her laptop around so Peg could see.

There was a paparazzi photo of Brez's girlfriend leaving a Starbuck's and she wore one of the red "First woman on Mars" t-shirts. It was an extra-large shirt that was hitched on one side like a short skirt, with a thin black belt to give the shirt a waist. She had on large dark sunglasses and her bright red lipstick, with her black hair pulled back, a casual messy look, like she'd just gotten up though by the angle of sunlight in the photo it was clearly late in the day. Peg sat there in one of her own red t-shirts, amazed at how much better the supermodel looked in hers.

"How did you get her to wear that?" Erin asked.

"I don't know," Peg said, and she realized the message was generic, that the supermodel didn't necessarily support Margaret Myers on Mars, as the first woman, but *a* woman. And then the horrifying thought crept up on her: what if the supermodel was in the running to go? There was the rumor that she was somehow employed by Brez, but would he do that? Would he go through all this trouble to set up a contest just to pick his girlfriend? He could take her if he wanted; it was his money. Letting her be in the contest would be nepotism and the publicity could backfire, right? Peg wasn't sure. The supermodel obviously generated a lot of publicity by just buying a cup of coffee. Putting her on Mars would blow up the tabloids forever and ever. Peg took the laptop from Erin, cut-and-pasted the address of the web page, she emailed it to herself, then she opened her own laptop and sent an instant message to Brian Clark: "Have you seen this?"

His reply came back almost immediately: "That's good, right?"

"Is she in the contest?"

"Don't know."

"Can she be?"

"Maybe."

"Did Kevin give her a t-shirt?"

"He's given everyone a t-shirt."

"She's wearing *mine*. And she's a woman. Who might go to Mars."

"This can only be good," Brian Clark said. "It could catch on."

"You're probably right," she typed. "Erin was pretty excited."

"It *is* exciting," he agreed.

She stared at the picture a little longer and couldn't grasp what Brian Clark saw in her. Comparing herself to this woman in the same shirt made Peg feel like she wasn't even the same species. And the supermodel was who America would want to watch floating weightless inside a space capsule.

"I guess I wished I looked more like her," Peg typed and she immediately regretted sending such a revealing and personal instant message to Brian Clark. She'd given him an opening.

"I think you are beautiful," came his reply. "I don't even see how she's all that attractive."

"?????" was all Peg could come up with for a response.

"She looks ridiculous. Like she's homeless and starving and someone put the t-shirt on her out of pity."

"Now you're being rude," Peg typed.

"He's right," Erin said, who could see the conversation from her vantage point next to her mother on the couch. "She's not all that great. All hype."

"If you win this contest," Brian Clark replied, "and you will: Brez is going to fall for you, and this sad skinny girl just might lose her boyfriend."

Peg knew Brian Clark was biased, but now he was either lying to make her feel better or he was insane. There was no way she and Brez...just no way. She'd never even be able to fantasize about something like that; it was absurd.

"Would that make you jealous?" Peg typed and it was by far the most flirtatious thing she had ever communicated to Brian Clark, so she turned the laptop to keep Erin from reading.

"I'd understand," he responded. "But I'd never get over it."

And Peg could feel herself blush. No one had ever been so forward with her, not Ronny in the early days, not anyone. She didn't know what to say back. The cursor blinked and she had to type something. He'd finally poured himself out to her, and courtesy demanded a reply. If he was with her and they were alone—she was so flustered by his attention—she would let him. But she had no idea what to say. After an uncomfortably long while she typed, "How sweet!" which was noncommittal, yet acknowledged how important this moment must have been for him. And the cursor blinked, and he didn't reply back, and then he signed off. She felt bad letting him down like that. Despite what she'd told the chip architects the other day, she really wanted Superman, and what they had said about Lois

Lane was probably right. She wouldn't have settled down with Clark Kent. Not in the 1930's, and not today. She'd have risked it all for the man of steel, and while she didn't believe a word of what Brian Clark had told her about her chances with Brez, now she at least felt like she could admit that maybe he was the only man she really wanted.

Because Peg's laptop was synced with her work computer, her iPad, and her Findability Phone, she saw that a meeting had been scheduled this morning, and that it was with Brez. She had already put on one of the red t-shirts and now she had no idea what else she might wear. She loved the freedom of getting up and putting on the same t-shirt every day, though it had only been a few days, but she could easily project this look of hers in perpetuity. Except not today. Not if she was meeting with Brez.

She frantically stood before her closet and slid business suit after business suit along the hangar rack, disgusted with herself at how frumpy each of them was. She hadn't ever really cared about her looks, which she took as an introvert trait, though maybe that was an excuse. She wished she had the flair, like the supermodel, who knew how to make the t-shirt look good. She stood paralyzed, with no options. She also couldn't stall, because it was time to leave, so she put on her best pair of jeans and one of the t-shirts, and she hoped that her not really giving a shit was a strength that Brez would recognize, and the t-shirt, which he was well-aware of by now, was maybe what he expected her to wear anyway. The first woman on Mars wouldn't get so worked up over something so silly, now would she? The first woman on Mars would walk right into Brez's office and take charge. She didn't feel at all like that, but she hoped by the time she got to campus that she would look less like a ghost.

"You're freaking out," Erin said.

Peg tried to tell Erin what was up, but it wouldn't come out. The best she could muster was, "He wants to see me."

Erin shrugged her shoulders and shook her head.

"The guy," Peg said. "The one."

"Your boss?"

This word worked for Peg and she qualified, "My boss's boss's boss's boss."

"Maxim Brez? Mr. dating a supermodel? Mr. Findability?"

Peg couldn't actually say "yes." Her mouth formed the word but her throat froze up. She looked at her daughter and she nodded slowly.

"Is this it?"

It couldn't be it. It was too soon to be it. There was no way this was it. She had no idea, and so she turned and left the house.

"Text me!" Erin shouted after her. "Or send me an email! Or better yet, call!"

The waiting room outside Brez's office seemed small to Peg. After all, there were times when he probably met with corporate representatives flown in from all over, with their legal teams. There were seven leather loungers, scattered magazines, a medium-sized fish tank, and a flat screen that played the Findability Channel with the sound muted while a thin young dapper male assistant beyond a glass partition bobbed his head slightly to what sounded like The Grateful Dead, the music instrumental, looping, and with a protracted crescendo. He pointed at a speaker in the ceiling and said, "Egypt '78, at the Pyramids of Giza." Peg flipped through a *New Yorker* without reading as she watched this young man reminisce over something that happened before he was born. She watched the door to Brez's office and imagined him absorbed by monumental decisions, reserves of money crashing like waves after each "yes" he signed off on. Did the supermodel come see him in there, or did he go to her?

Without warning, Brez entered the waiting room from the same door Peg had come in. He saw her and said, "Oh good, you're here."

His assistant held open the glass door, and Brez held open the door to his office for Peg to go on in.

Brez's office had a conference table, a bank of computers along one wall, and a bay window with a good view of the Findability courtyard and the surrounding parentheses. Brez's workstation was a presidential desk littered with screens, Brez in a tailored suit that fit so neatly it made him look shorter than Peg. She stood in the middle of the room, unsure of which direction to go, her hands behind her back. She should have brought a briefcase, just to have something to hold on to. Brez sat at his desk facing the conference table. He indicated an open chair Peg plopped down into. She looked up at him. He was quite near. He seemed happy to see her.

"Let me tell you what this is about," he said. "I thought we were doing okay, but I want to do the right thing."

He walked over to the conference table and reached into the middle where there were stacks and stacks of folders. He patted the tallest pile and said, "All these boys want to go to space. We've been hiring more women, but if we send up one we recently hired it'll look fishy. Which leaves us *this*." He lifted a folder and handed it to Peg. "Go ahead," he said. "Open it."

Inside were the applications of fewer than twenty of the women who worked at Findability with start dates and some kind of ratings system of relevant qualifications penciled in at the top. She saw her own application and her rating looked pretty good. Her name had been circled and there were three emphatic asterisks in the top-left corner.

"Before yesterday," Brez said, "you were middle of the stack."

Brez pulled up an image on one of the computer screens on his desk. "Today," he said, "you are our number one candidate, and leading by a mile."

"Because I'm a woman?"

"Because of this." The page was a technology blog Peg recognized, one of the ones that had scooped Findability stories weeks before they went public. The headline said, "Findability Picks Woman Employee," and there was a short looping video of Peg walking toward a camera in the spacesuit. There had been lots of people filming her on their phones, so there was no telling who leaked it, but the image was good enough that Peg was recognizable.

"I don't see why that would get me the position," Peg said. She had the sinking feeling he was trying to get her to admit to taking the spacesuit for a walk without his permission.

"There's also this," Brez said, and he pulled up an image of Drew Barrymore on another screen, Drew wearing one of the red t-shirts that said, "First woman on Mars."

Brez scrolled down the page to a still image of Peg in the spacesuit.

"The celebrity blogs and the tech blogs are putting these two stories together. Everyone is asking who you are. When it gets to this point, I like to give them what they want."

"Do I have the job?"

"I want your permission to release your name to the press."

And I want to know if there is any reason why you might not want to go to Mars. If there's anything about you that I should know."

"I have the job?"

"It would be counterproductive to pick another woman at this point. So you're our guy. Can you think of any reason why we shouldn't select you to go?"

Peg didn't know if it was physically possible to faint sitting down, or if it was simply safer. But she felt like she might. She looked at the grainy candid photo of Drew Barrymore and at the looping video of herself clumsily treading toward the camera phone. She looked at Brez, who was there in the flesh, as he would be for two years, in a high-tech tin can as they sped toward a giant rusty rock. She couldn't think of any reason why she shouldn't go. There was Erin but her care had already been arranged. Ronny might make trouble as he thought about extracting money from her, but she wasn't going to let him stand in her way. There was the time she shoplifted an extremely expensive jar of cellulite cream, but that was fifteen years ago and she'd paid the fine. She was even allowed back in the store, though she avoided the makeup counter on principle.

"Is there anything *you* want to tell *me*?" She asked.

He asked, "Can you keep a secret? You will need to keep a lot of secrets."

Peg was feeling much better about her position vis-à-vis Brez. The blood returned to her head and she grew bold. "What should I know about you?"

"There are questions about my citizenship," Brez said.

Peg didn't understand why that might matter. Everyone knew he was born in Russia but had been in the U.S. since he was a teenager. Last year he brought more to the American economy than General Motors. No one was going to kick him out.

"My partner in this," he began.

"NASA?"

"It's very important to them that the first person on Mars is an American. We want you to be more than the first woman on Mars. We want you to be the first human on Mars."

"One small step?" Peg said.

"Yes."

Peg got the feeling there was something really wrong with what he was saying. He was the one who was special, who had worked all his life and continued to set new goals. This was his. She'd had childish fantasies about going up in a rocket but never in a million years would have thought they'd select a woman to be the first to set foot on the planet, especially not her. She didn't deserve to go. Kevin would love this twist, a perfect subversion of the patriarchal order that had persisted in the silicon age. She wished she could get behind those chip architects on the moving walkway again to tell them Lois Lane wasn't interested in Clark Kent or Superman. Lois was oozing with super herself. Peg wanted to call Erin. To go out for sushi and announce her big news as they ate crunchy shrimp rolls. What she wanted most was to call Ronny and Cecilia to tell them they could suck it.

"I have a trainer and an adviser," Peg said. "Can I say anything?"

"Absolutely not. We act like you're hardly in the running until we announce it, so the press feels like they scooped us, and they will love us for that. It will be smooth sailing for you from then on."

"I'm not very good on camera," she said.

Brez looked over at the looping video of Peg walking in the spacesuit and the camera zoomed in on her positively beaming inside the glass globe helmet.

"You look good to me," he said. "Just be yourself."

"Have you selected the rest of the team?" Peg said.

"Down to a handful of alternates."

"Do they know?"

"They know they are going. They know each other. But they don't know about you."

"Can I know about them?"

"You'll meet them soon enough," Brez said and he picked up another folder from the table.

He set down headshots one at a time from the folder and said, "The pilot; the co-pilot; the physician-microbiologist-dietician; the linguist; and of course, myself, the programmer."

What would her own title be, she wondered. How would they sell her as valuable to the mission?

Six astronauts, she thought. *Linguist?* she thought. Why would they possibly need a linguist? Had he been someone, like herself, who was good P.R? Was he a black linguist? No, the crew was all their laid out in headshots: white, white, white, white, white, and Brez, also white. They were men, all of them young good-looking wildly successful men. Six white men and herself rocketing off to Mars, together in a capsule, a supposedly big capsule, but together, in close quarters, for two years.

Peg took a tube of pie from her jeans pocket because she felt suddenly hungry, but she didn't want to seem rude, so she offered it to Brez.

"Cherry pie?"

Brez, having been up there, was not one to turn down astronaut food. He squeezed out a large dollop and nodded in appreciation.

"Finish up this week," he said, "then we send you to Groom Lake to train."

"Astronaut training?"

"You tell everyone you're off to Launchability, Huntsville. You don't have to say why. It's going to seem like we're filming a movie," he said. "But only because they want to see how it looks."

"Why is there a linguist?"

"For contact."

"Martian contact?"

"They want to be called Trafalmadorans. They will meet us in space. We have an alien weekend, we get an exchange of technology, and we never talk about it."

"Or what?"

"The Trafalmadorans have this telepathic chip, or crystal. I don't know what to call it. But it works."

"Devices that respond to thoughts?"

"It's better than that."

"And what could we possibly give them?"

"They like maps."

"Maps?"

"They have an interest in food," Brez said. "We could bring along some really nice cookbooks."

"Can't they just use the Internet?"

"We print up a line of the "first woman on Mars" t-shirts. Push them out there with just the catchphrase and no graphic. I like this. We're good. We'll talk again next week at Area 51."

On the way home she called Ronny. She had to share with someone.

Ronny said, "I drew up a contract. It spells out the terms of our arrangement. She's yours, but for two years you can't take her back. You get visitation, but for two years you don't tell us how to raise her. You send checks and you butt out."

"I can't visit. I won't visit. I'm going to Mars."

"You're talking to a lifelong Lottery player," Ronny said.

"They have you to thank for keeping them solvent."

"You need to sign the papers in front of a notary," he said. "Full temporary custody. And I'll need it by the end of the month."

"I won, Ronny. I'm really going. I need you to take her next week."

"Once you sign, there's no turning back. Two years."

"I really won," Peg said. "I'm telling the truth. I'm going to Mars."

"We don't have to argue anymore," Ronny said. "We've moved on."

Peg realized, despite her promise to Brez, that she could blab all she wanted, because anyone she knew wouldn't believe her anyway, except Erin, who had drawn her own conclusions. Erin had a Findability Alert set for Mars news and so she knew what Drew Barrymore had worn, and she knew her mom had gone for a walk in one of the spacesuits. There were celebrity gossip websites that revealed Peg's name and they were calling her the 'speculative' winner. Erin already believed, so when Peg told her about her meeting with Brez, Peg started off by saying, "It was just like you said. I visualized winning and now it's happening."

"Aren't you shitting your pants?" Erin said, "You're actually going?"

11

At Dave and Buster's Peg had brought along her resume because any excuse she gave, Claudia countered with eager helpful enthusiasm. So they sat at the bar together, sipping frozen orgasms, and Claudia said, "there's got to be more than this. *Before* Findability, I mean. What else have you done?"

"I made some web pages but that was the nineties. If they're still around, they've been redone by now."

"But you were in tech," Claudia said. "And we can call it 'coding'."

"I used templates," Peg said. "It wasn't exactly coding."

"It wasn't exactly *not* coding."

"This isn't going to matter," Peg said.

"It *matters*," Claudia said. "This will be a highly competitive pool. We've got to make you look good."

"I don't look good," Peg said, and she wished her new friend were going instead. She wanted to tell everyone she knew that she was going except Claudia. She dreaded telling Claudia, who had pulled up her own resume as an example of what someone else might look like, and she was amazing. She'd worked at big-time universities and had very important positions at the Office of Civil Rights, at the Rand Corporation, Nielsen, and Southwest Airlines. Time sped toward a grand injustice where Peg would be selected over this much more qualified and incredible woman, and she got the sense that her winning was going to jeopardize their fledgling friendship.

"Another drink?" Peg said. She sipped the last of her own, Claudia's still half-full though most of the blended ice had melted.

"We need to work on this," Claudia said. Peg hoped to make eye contact with a couple of guys who would send over drinks, but it was a Tuesday, and the Dave and Buster's wasn't as bustling as last time.

"Pinball?"

"I'm serious."

"I don't feel comfortable lying," Peg said.

"Everyone does it," Claudia said. "It's not lying."

"We're both out without our kids," Peg said. "I just want to have fun tonight."

"The appearance of a work ethic is really important," Claudia said. "Whoever goes is pretty much on the job twenty-four seven."

"Brez works really hard, doesn't he?"

"You're changing the subject."

"Why doesn't he take his girlfriend?"

"Are you kidding?" Claudia said.

"I'm serious," Peg said. "Tell me."

"He's not married to her," Claudia said. "He's a man. He's thinking that if they break up he's stuck with her for two years. If he's smart, he'll pick someone he finds entirely unattractive."

"I wouldn't say that," Peg said, and she frowned.

"If he picks a woman, he'll respect her, but never in a million years would it be someone he might sleep with."

"He might," Peg said. "Those kinds of things can be unpredictable."

"No, they're predictable," Claudia said.

"You don't think I'm attractive?" Peg said. "You think I'm ugly?"

"We're talking about Brez," Claudia said. "You're not his type."

"How do you know?" Peg said. "And what about you? You like girls."

"I'm just not," Claudia said. "I'm in a relationship. I don't really look around."

"Everyone looks around," Peg said.

"I'm not attracted to you," Claudia said. "It's nothing personal."

"But it *is* personal."

Peg remembered how Claudia had come out to everyone in the company with her purple t-shirt. Peg decided that Claudia, despite all her "help" and her declarations to the contrary, thought for sure she was going to win, and one of the reasons, maybe even the biggest reason, was because Brez couldn't screw up and sleep with her, even though she was gorgeous.

"Last two people on Earth," Peg said, "are me and Brez. Which of us do you shack up with?"

"I'm really not attracted to you," Claudia said. "I knew it would come to this eventually."

"You'd pick Brez?"

"*You'd* pick Brez," Claudia said. "Me? I'm a lesbian."

Peg understood that Claudia deserved to go in so many ways, and she wouldn't be able to take losing, and they wouldn't be able to stay friends, if that was even what this was.

"Play some darts with me or something," Peg said. "Or I'm leaving."

"No hard feelings? I'm only being honest. I don't want you clinging to false hope. It is never going to happen between us."

"My ego can't really take it right now," Peg said.

"You've got a shot at this contest," Claudia said, "You really do. Just not with this shit resume."

Most of Erin's clothes had been packed up and boxed, and so Peg also boxed up her own. Brez had moved quickly, had wanted her to go out to Area 51 ahead of the announcement, to begin their training that was like making a movie, and she was to tell everyone she was at Huntsville.

Erin was leaving and so was Peg. The house that had meant everything to them, where they had always lived and where Erin had grown up, would soon stand empty. Peg couldn't bring herself to rent it out or to sell it. She was thinking of asking Brian Clark to house sit, which didn't seem like the right thing to call staying at her place for two years, but she liked the idea of him there. He would say "yes," she was sure, and it would be easy enough for him, since for as long as she'd known him he'd lived alone in a two-bedroom apartment.

"First woman on Mars" t-shirts popped up everywhere. The court of public opinion wanted a woman on Mars.

Peg stood at the threshold of Kevin's cubicle. His t-shirt said, "Team Batman," and he sat at his computer working, his Bowflex collecting dust since he'd given up to become Peg's astro-coach.

"How far along are you?" Kevin said.

"I won," Peg blurted out. "I'm going."

Kevin made a sour face, not really processing what she'd said. "I meant in your reading? How many have you read?"

"I haven't read anything," Peg said, and Kevin crossed his arms.

"We were starting with Bradbury, then Heinlein, then Arthur C. Clarke, Azimov, Rodenberry. *Hitchhiker*. And Octavia Butler! Why didn't we start with Octavia Butler?"

"I'm going," Peg said again, and the news sunk in. Kevin wasn't yet smiling but he looked at her unsure of what to think.

"Brez is sending me to Huntsville," Peg said, "*wink-wink: 'Huntsville.'* I won't be around soon and I really want to thank you."

"Are you really?..." Kevin couldn't say it out loud, but Peg nodded vigorously, so he got up and squeezed her with everything he had.

"We won one!" he said. "We finally won!"

"*You* won it!" Peg said.

Kevin sat down and shook his head in disbelief. "I was sure they'd pick one of the pretty ones."

"It was just like you said," Peg said. "Brez is one of us deep down inside and he hasn't forgotten where he came from. He's a nerd like us. He's rewriting the narrative."

"He said this?"

"He said I'm going."

Kevin mimed zipping his lips shut, and he said, "You *have* to read those books."

"I'll be gone for two years. I can load up the Kindle."

"Wonder how they'll explain you to the Masons," Kevin said.

"You believe in that shit?" Peg said.

"Kubrick, Arthur C. Clark, Neil Armstrong, *all* of the astronauts, and the head of NASA, all of them Masons, I could keep going."

"What do Masons care?"

"They're archivists," Kevin said. "What did you think they kept in the stone temples?"

"Documentary films?"

"The Masons keep everything. Except every once in a while they conduct a burning ceremony."

"You know this?"

"I've read it in the underground journalism from eyewitness accounts of anonymous sources. And you know who else is one?"

"The Pope?"

"Mr. Findability," and Kevin pointed his thumb at the ceiling, to indicate *upstairs*.

12

At home, Erin and a well-groomed man in a black suit sat at the kitchen table across from each other, at their respective laptops. His black hair was combed over, stiff, and off center. He wore a toupee, black tie, dark glasses indoors, and his white skin was unnaturally shiny and pale.

"I'm sorry I forgot your name," Erin said to the FBI guy, who closed his laptop and stood to greet Peg.

"Agent White," he said. "Am questioning for background check. You signatured."

Peg pointed at Erin, and said, "She's a minor. You need my permission to talk to her."

"We were paused in activities for your return," Agent White said, and he sat down at his laptop, opened it, typed notes, his hands in fists, his thumbs pointed down to make the keystrokes. "Is this the often-time of your return?"

"No, this is not the often-time."

"When did you office leave?"

Peg wondered if he already knew. If he had been watching or if he was tuned in on her.

"I already told him," Erin said. Peg had called to say she was meeting Claudia, and she wondered what Erin had said to the man about Claudia, Erin suspicious of her mother's new friendship.

"Please to describe your political believings?" the agent said.

"Commie Pinko," Peg said, but the agent didn't so much as crack a smile. He sounded Slavic to her and she was curious how an immigrant could wind up in the FBI. She was uneasy around him because she realized she'd thought he was speaking but she was really listening to his voice in her head. When he spoke, his mouth was open, but his lips didn't move.

"That was a joke," Peg confirmed, and he nodded, but he continued to type with his thumbs. "I'm not a Commie Pinko." She was tipsy from the frozen orgasms.

"Have you made party contributions in these five years?"

"Humane Society," Erin said.

"And the...which ones were they?" Peg said. "Not the Mormons, but the other ones? Some church thing. They don't believe in blood transfusions?"

"Are you having religion?"

Peg and Erin looked at each other. Erin was curious to hear what her mother would say, and hoped she wouldn't joke her way through it.

"Atheist," Peg said. "Mostly."

"Mostly of an atheist?" the agent said.

"I don't believe in any of them," Peg said, "but I've changed my mind before."

"Approximate age of onset of atheist?"

"I remain undecided."

"Having of guns?"

Peg shook her head. She was hungry and tired. She responded to the rest of his questions with a flat "yes," or a flat "no." When he was done he closed the laptop, got up to leave, and thanked her on the way out. Agent White was trying to mouth the words now, at least, but his mouth didn't match up. Erin had ordered a pizza earlier and Peg took a piece out of the fridge and stood there chewing.

"The U.S. government is interested in your personal religious philosophy," Erin said.

"I wish I had better answers for them," Peg said.

"Me too," Erin said.

"What did you tell him?"

"Stuff about you and Dad. Stuff about your job. Stuff about your patience or lack of patience."

"How did I rate?"

"You're a good mom. We both decided so."

"You told him you're off to stay with your dad?"

"Don't worry," Erin said. "I told him about the Ronny and Cecelia situation. He wrote it all down."

Peg realized, as she stood there, that she was chewing solid food. She'd broken her own rule without thinking about it and she would have to be better, more vigilant. She was an astronaut in training after all.

"Is it me," Peg said, "or was he really strange?"

"I hate to break it to you," Erin said, "but everyone you work with is strange."

"But I mean really strange."

"He was French or something."

"Did he tell you that?"

"Wasn't it obvious?"

Peg took out a second slice of pizza and chewed. Erin had good taste in pizza. She'd gotten a wood-oven-broiled margarita, and it was delicious. Peg was going to miss chewing. It was so simple and kind of disgusting if one focused on the saliva and the mechanics of mastication, but she enjoyed it and before she was done with that slice, she told herself yes, she would have one more.

In bed that night, Peg dreamed she was falling. She wore the red t-shirt and nothing else and there was no wind, she couldn't breathe, but she felt gravity pull at her gut as she fell and fell, surrounded by utter depths of blackness.

She heard Agent White's voice but didn't see him. There was

100

no anything anywhere. He said, "Weightlessness," which he chanted at intervals like a mantra. "Weightlessness." His strange accent made the word sound foreign, but Peg experienced the feeling of falling more intensely with each repetition of the word.

Peg was distressed and she cried out, "I'm falling!"

Agent White drew out the word, emphasizing the windy breathiness, "*Whhh-eight-lesss-nesss.*"

There was nowhere to fall to. Nowhere she fell from. *Wheightlesssnesss.*

She heard the awkward rhythm of his thumbs hitting his keyboard, Agent White typing at his laptop, but she couldn't see him. Her stomach was full and she sank into darkness, pulled down. She became aware of her body in bed, she slipped in and out of consciousness, but she was too heavy to move. She gathered all her will, opened her eyes, rolled over, now awake, and she stared up at the ceiling. In the darkness she imagined stars, a bright glittering endless field of stars. She was tired and she wanted to sleep, but when she closed her eyes the stars were projected on her eyelids. She thought about Agent White and felt he had really been with her, disembodied but in her room and in her dream. When she had met him earlier in the evening he had looked odd, acted odd.

"What does FBI stand for?" she said aloud.

She heard Agent White speak clearly in her mind, as if he were in the bed with her, "First Brainwave Intercommunication Agent."

Peg was wide-awake at this point. She sat up in bed, and said, "Is there a *second* brainwave intercommunication agent?"

And she heard his voice: "Please hold unknowns for reference in cosmos. There is a promise us." Agent White's phrasing was increasingly unearthly. She couldn't place him: not Russian, not French.

"I am of good anticipation."

The alarm clock on the night table shined three in the morning and though Peg was tired there was no way she was falling back asleep.

"I'd like to revise my position on atheism," she said.

"Truth-ness was the correct response."

"I don't want to die."

"We are also inclined of this disposition."

"Do you have a body somewhere? Was the Agent White in my kitchen a robot, or a vessel? Where are you?"

"End brainwave intercommunication. Goodbye."

"Seriously?" Peg said.

There was something bigger than NASA, Masons, and Findability. She didn't know what search terms to try, but she pulled up Findability. When none of her searches retrieved satisfactory results, she did something she never did: she pulled up Bing to try the same searches.

The local library made drop-offs at Findability, so Peg wanted to read sturdy library-bound hardback versions of the books Kevin recommended. She felt guilty about blowing off her work: true, her "work" consisted of surfing around the Internet, but she was supposed to be doing it. Her pathways were tracked and the programmers tried to translate the ways she searched into their logarithms.

There were searches that were yielding conspiracy theories and Peg got stuck in that loop. She wanted to know about Masons, NASA, Kubrick, and all the rest. Before she was even at it a few hours one of the mathematicians came to her cubicle to check on her.

"We're monitoring your searches with interest," he said. "I would recommend that you go no further down this path."

Which was okay with Peg. She didn't like the way some of the videos made her feel. They all seemed to have the same synthesized organ and deadpan delivery. Reading science fiction for the first time, there were things the stories made her wonder about: the atmosphere of Mars, the evolutionary advantages of monogamy, the trajectory of Halley's comet, the long-term effects of synthetic testosterone, the order of naval military ranks, the bends, relativity, time travel, black holes, lasers, radio waves, magnetic interference, Planet X, Alpha

Centuri, backgammon, and the flight of eagles in pressurized suits, in low-gravity low-density atmospheres. There was plenty she could continue to search for. She really enjoyed letting her mind wander out into space. Reading science fiction made her terrified and excited about the journey she would soon embark upon. She'd gotten into the habit of listening to audio books over the years, only because she was always doing other things: driving, making dinner, loading the dishwasher, surfing around at Findability, and she'd missed reading.

She immediately knew why all the grown-up boys at Findability wanted to be astronauts, because they had spent their adolescence in these books, where men could be lone idealists and adventurers, where perfect egalitarian societies existed, where theoretical science was made real, where evil was embodied in grotesque humanoid species, where women were subordinate crew members, and beautiful, and young. Science fiction was an imaginative realm of, by, and for boys. When there was a female lead it was always for titillation, with futuristic sex, and women's liberation was actualized as galactic promiscuity. Many of the novels were thinly disguised wish-fulfillment boner fantasies for fourteen-year-old boys unable to get their hands on a *Playboy*. And this was probably why her coworkers were all so excited about "the first woman on Mars." Regardless of their attraction to Peg, all the men at Findability—with the exception of Kevin and Brez—were probably reminded of residual teen-sex fantasies whenever they put on the red t-shirt. And as much as she'd always wanted to be that woman, the one they were shy about, the one they stared at, Peg wasn't comfortable with the obvious sexism of damsel-in-distress tales set on intergalactic spaceships. And maybe this is what Kevin wanted her to know, because he was excited about her subverting the archetype. Had there been women who had gone on Joseph Campbell's Hero's Journey? She didn't know. And so she set off on another Findability search to look for answers.

Brian Clark popped up on her screen with an instant message. He had sent her a link to one of the celebrity websites, which, when she clicked on it, she saw a photo of Brez himself in one of the red t-shirts. So he had worn one. For Brez this was calculated. He was fueling the media speculation and building up to his big reveal. As hard as it was to believe, Peg really had won.

"Get over here," Peg typed. "I have to tell you something."

He must have messaged her from his phone, because almost as soon as she turned around, there he was at the threshold of her cubicle. They both wore the red t-shirts and maybe it was the suggestion of sex from the science fiction novels, or maybe it was because she hadn't seen him for a few days, but she suddenly had the urge to undress him and take him in her arms. He wasn't bold, or all that good-looking, or a standout in any kind of objective way, but he was hers and she wanted him.

"I met with him," she said.

"Wow!" Brian Clark said, and he moved toward her. He expected her to get up and embrace him but she stayed in her office chair. "You've really got a chance!" And then he didn't know what else to say, so he stood there, close to her, in her personal space, but neither of them reached out for physical contact.

Peg stood on her chair to look around the office, she sat back down, and she lowered her voice. "I'm not supposed to tell anyone," she said. "But I've already won. He picked me."

"I knew it!" Brian Clark whispered as enthusiastically as he could without raising his voice, though he betrayed his disappointment with a fake smile. Despite his enthusiasm for the good luck of his friend, Brian Clark couldn't fathom a future with Peg absent.

"I'm going to be gone a long time," she said. "I want to try something."

She reached up and took his hand. He blushed. He was confused.

"I want you to take me out on a date," she said. "A real date."

"Yes," he said.

"Don't go crazy or anything," she said, "but treat me like a woman and we can get a room, and we can do it."

He was blushing. He was confused.

"I'm not your girlfriend," she said. "It's just the one time. I really like you, but it wouldn't work out."

"Then maybe it's better if we don't."

"Are you fucking kidding me?" Peg said. "Did you hear what I said?"

"My heart."

"I am offering you a no-strings-attached night. Do you know how many men would jump on that?"

"And afterwards?"

"We go back to being friends. Or not friends. Or whatever we are, because I'm going to be gone for two years anyway. We'll see where we are when I get back."

"You'll be famous."

"If I don't die."

"With incredible men vying for your time."

"Do you want me Thursday or not?"

"Of course."

"Then ask me out."

"Do you want to go out?" he said. "On Thursday?"

"Out where?"

"On a real date. With kissing and falling asleep in each other's arms."

"I'd love to," Peg said.

13

At the pool in Building Sixteen, Claudia and Peg rested at the end of their lane and Peg wanted to crawl out and give up exercise for good. Claudia looked back at her through mirrored goggles that made her an unrelenting bug-alien. Claudia was in her element in the pool: she was strong, sleek, fast. Her flip-turns were perfect and she lapped Peg on every set, which made it so Peg barely got to rest before she had to push off the wall and swim again.

"Last set?" Peg said, hopefully.

"We're not even halfway done," Claudia said. "We've got a set of 200s, a set of 100s, a set of kicks, and then 50s."

"You said you were easing me into this."

"We'll be up to a full workout by the middle of next week."

"A full workout for you might not be a full workout for everyone."

"You're not trying."

"I need to tell you something."

"Shoot."

By this point, Peg was completely won over by Brian Clark's suggestion that the desk-bound geeks at Findability were already conditioned to the stationary work of riding in a space capsule, and she didn't see that working out would bring her anything other than fatigue and sore muscles.

"I'm being sent to another office," Peg said. "Next week."

"Which office?"

"The one in Huntsville."

"Launchability? You got a job at Launchability?"

"I've been trying to find a way to tell you. I'm not supposed to tell anyone. But I didn't want to just up and leave. Your friendship has meant a lot to me."

"What's the job?"

"They're trying me out."

"For what?"

"For the thing."

"The contest?"

Peg didn't answer. She wanted to nod but couldn't. She wished there were a better way to break it to Claudia.

Claudia repeated her question: "Is this because of the contest?"

"I never in a million years thought I would win."

"You *won?*"

"I'm going to Huntsville."

"Did you win?"

Peg closed her eyes and moved her head up and down. "I didn't mean to," she said. "But yes, I'm going."

"Fuck," Claudia said. "Fuck, fuck, fuck, fuck, fuck." She took off her goggles and threw them so they hit the wall and she slapped her hand against the surface of the water. She was crying.

"I'm sorry," Peg said, and more than she had wanted to hug Brian Clark, she wanted to embrace Claudia. "I'm really sorry."

Claudia covered her face with her powerful hands, embarrassed that she had broken down in public. "It's not you," she said. "It's the patriarchy. I shouldn't have come out. I should have just let them think I was ready and willing as I always had."

Peg embraced Claudia, amazed at how solid she was. She could hardly believe how unfair it was that Claudia hadn't been selected. She doubted her sexuality had anything to do with it, but she couldn't be sure.

"I'm sorry," Peg said. "It should have been you."

"I know."

"But you're happy for me, right? And we're still friends?"

"I'm upset with myself," Claudia said. "How could I have believed any differently?"

"But you're happy for me?"

Claudia opened her eyes and stared at Peg.

"You can hardly make it down and back. You can't do a flip-turn. You look like you're going to pass out even now."

"It's true, I'm not as athletic..."

"*As* athletic? You're not athletic at all."

"We knew there was no physical compon—"

"I'm taller than you and smarter than you. I have more experience than you. I'm kinder than you. I outpace you in every way except for procreation and docility."

"I don't think that's really..."

"I shouldn't have gotten my hopes up," Claudia said.

"I can talk to Brez," Peg offered.

"*I'm* the one who knows him."

"But maybe he would listen to me."

"What could you possibly tell him?" Claudia said.

"I'll think of something."

"All because of a fucking t-shirt," Claudia said and she slapped the surface of the water again.

"That was Kevin. That wasn't me."

"None of it was you," Claudia said. "You just followed everyone else's advice and fell right into it."

"I'm not arguing with that."

Claudia pushed Peg away, and she held up her hands to indicate that she didn't really want to be consoled. She took a deep breath, put her goggles back on, and she took off swimming. Soon enough she was back at Peg's end of the lane. She swam hard into the kick-turn, pushed off the wall with her powerful legs, and torpedoed away before she surfaced and pumped her arms with a quickly measured and graceful stroke. It was clear to Peg that Claudia was done talking, at least for now, so Peg crawled out of the pool and took her towel with her into the locker room. She felt terrible about Claudia but very good about giving up lunch-hour workouts.

On the drive home Peg saw a man she was sure was Agent White, who walked on the sidewalk and looked up just as she recognized him. She saw him again in a boxy black eighties Ford LTD sedan, and he turned his head to look at her just as she passed him. He stood on an overpass and stared down as she zoomed below. She was afraid to turn around or to look in the rearview. She was certain he was behind her, or maybe in the back seat

"What do you want?" she shouted. Her windows were up, the air conditioning blasted, and she was glad no other drivers noticed her agitated state.

"We have a promise us," she heard, and she didn't like Agent White talking to her again as she was on her way home. She turned on loud music, something from one of the college stations that played classical music, an orchestra in the middle of a dramatic symphony, and Agent White's voice was heard over her speakers, "I am of good anticipation." And: "End brainwave communication."

She worried about seeing Agent White again as the days wore on, especially tonight, when she had a date with Brian Clark. If Agent White popped up, she knew she couldn't deal with him, with either of them. She decided to wait until she was at Area 51 to really ponder what Agent White's appearance meant, and where she hoped maybe someone would have answers. She remembered what he had said to her in the waking dream, "Please hold unknowns for reference in cosmos," and she couldn't tell if she were simply remembering his voice or if he was talking to her. She looked at herself in the mirror, in a dress, with her hair styled and she wore lipstick. She had lost weight and Brian Clark was very lucky because he was going to get the best version of her. She saw her brow was furrowed and realized she was puzzled by Agent White's use of the phrase "hold unknowns."

"Hold them?" she said to herself. She tried her best to calm her mind, because she certainly didn't want Agent White chiming in, especially not now that she was nervous about her date with Brian Clark, who would be over to pick her up. Yes, she was holding her unknowns because she didn't know what else to do with them. Her trip to Mars was either the absurd will of a pranking goddess, or her trip to Mars was entirely a combination of luck and circumstance. Why hadn't any of the other women of Findability attracted attention to themselves in some similar but wholly original way? Was Brez really out to right the wrongs of sexism or was it just a matter of trying to make the company look good? And Agent White: had he somehow influenced her selection? Was Agent White's return a product of stress and something else within her that she didn't want to confront?

It dawned on her to ask Erin what she thought. She had met Agent White and knew how peculiar he was. Peg hadn't told Erin about seeing him again, and maybe Erin had seen him again too.

Peg went downstairs where Erin sat on the couch with the TV on and her laptop on her lap.

"Wow, Mom," she said, when she saw the dolled-up version of Peg.

"You're on your own tonight," Peg said. "We're staying out."

"I know," Erin said.

"How did you know?"

"Lover boy has been lighting up your phone."

Peg lifted her phone from the end table to see that Brian Clark had been sending text messages. He told her he'd confirmed their reservations, that their room was the honeymoon suite at The Hilton, and that he'd bought her a corsage. Was that stupid? She didn't have to wear it? He shouldn't have bought it. He was nervous and Peg was flattered. There was nothing he had said that couldn't have waited until he saw her. The promise of sex had him going crazy and he didn't know how to act. He was trying to be his old self, who did text her a lot, though he should have known to leave her alone so she could get ready.

"Remember that FBI guy?" Peg said.

"How could I forget?"

"Has he followed you or anything? Has he turned up in

dreams?"

"Why?"

"I'm curious."

"I know what this is," Erin said. "He's a 'Men in Black'."

"A UFO agent?" Peg said.

"People believe they're extra-terrestrial."

"Would explain things."

"You saw him?"

"Pretty sure."

"He's recognizable."

"I hear him sometimes. In my head."

"*You have an implant!*" Erin said and she stood up on the couch and waved her mother over. Peg bowed to let Erin run her fingers over her head, to examine her scalp. "I don't see anything."

"Maybe it's been there a long time. How would I find out?"

"You can ask them at Huntsville. Maybe they can X-ray you or something."

"You can't tell Ronny and Cecelia but they're sending me to Area 51," Peg said. "To learn about aliens."

"Learn what about them?"

Peg's phone vibrated as another text from Brian Clark came in. Erin looked down at the phone and said, "I've got to get ready."

For as long as Peg had known Brian, she had never gone for a ride in his Audi. He held the car door for her and shut it once she was inside. For a second, before he walked around and got in the car himself, her heart lifted. She had asked him to act a certain way and he was doing it. She decided to go ahead and wear the corsage, a white lily that was heavy and threatened to flop over, but the gesture made her feel special. She would see him again, probably, before she left, but the date was supposed to be a celebration of her departure.

Brian was a careful, confident driver. He positioned the Audi so cars couldn't cut in front of him and he consistently surpassed the speed limit by four miles per hour.

"I feel like we're going to the prom," Peg said.

"I wouldn't know," Brian Clark said.

"You didn't go?"

He shook his head.

"Probably you were in love with some girl all through high school and were best friends with her but never said a word about liking her the whole time."

"Are you making fun of me?"

"Am I wrong?"

"She went with someone else but kept me in the loop," he said. "I picked out her dress. What about you?"

"I got asked but I said 'no'."

"Why?"

"It just seemed like a night for all the jocks and cheerleaders while the rest of us watched."

Peg was breaking her astronaut diet for their date, but when he told her where they were going, she felt better. This was his idea of a romantic dinner but it was also food that could fit in a tube. The restaurant was candle-lit, with fondue pots cooking over Sterno flames at the tables. The diners were paired off with bowls of diced bread and trays of splayed fruit slices between them. The vittles themselves were humble, more like appetizer trays, so maybe it was the pastel enamels of the pots, the decadent long narrow fondue spears, the champagne pairings, or the omnipresence of the thick hot pungent sauces—because Peg got the impression that everything about the place inspired baby-making. They were led to a table and Brian Clark pulled out her chair for her. The gesture was simple and perhaps clichéd, but in the moment it worked on her.

She ordered champagne right away and by the time the first course arrived she was a little buzzed. Brian had parked on the street and the hotel was just a few blocks away. Brian matched her glass for glass and by the time they were alone they would be drunk and inhibition-free.

"Are you nervous?" Peg asked.

"About us?" he said. "About later?"

"I haven't changed my mind."

"Are we supposed to," Brian Clark said, "*talk* about it so much?"

"Why not?"

"If some things are better left unsaid."

"It's been since Ronny," she said. "Are you surprised?"

"I think I knew that," he said, "but it's like riding a bike, right?"

"I'm *not* like a bike," Peg said.

"I just meant..."

"It's okay. How long has it been for you?"

"Two weeks," he said without skipping a beat.

"Wait, what?"

"Ten days exactly."

"I thought," Peg said. "I mean you've been *pining* for me."

"I have," Brian said. "But there's this woman in my building."

"Are you dating her?"

"Not exactly."

"You got lucky?"

"You could say it like that."

"Here I was feeling sorry for you."

"You and I weren't going anywhere. You made it obvious."

She reached over the platter of splayed apples and pears to take his hand and to salvage the date. "A girl wants to be the only one. Let's forget about her."

"You're going to Mars," Brian Clark said. "You can't be nervous about being with me compared to that."

"I don't *have a date* with Mars."

"Am I doing okay?"

"This is nice," she said.

When the platter was taken up and the cheese pot disassembled and carried away, the chocolate was brought over by a different waiter who moved awkwardly and placed the next round of items on the table clumsily, so that the pot nearly tipped over and he caught it and held it, though Peg and Brian were sure he couldn't do that without burning himself. He wore dark glasses inside the restaurant and his toupee slid around with each exaggerated gesture. He didn't speak but appeared to be concentrating on a memorized set of instructions. The new waiter was Agent White, and Peg suddenly wanted to leave.

Brian Clark sensed her discomfort, and once the waiter was gone, he said, "Do you know him?"

"He's just so *odd*," Peg said.

"Suppose they get Swiss immigrants coming over for jobs?"

"You think he's Swiss?" Peg said. "Why would they come here? Don't they pretty much have it made?"

"I don't know," Brian Clark said. "He's not from around here."

"Do you believe in UFOs?"

"I suppose so," he said. "I don't know."

"Can you get the check?" she said. "Can we go?"

"Is there something wrong?" he said. "Don't you want to try the chocolate?"

"I made you a promise," she said, "and I want to go."

Brian Clark waved over the first waiter, settled their bill, and they left.

On the street Peg was suddenly anxious. Fundue wasn't in a bad part of town, but at night all the banks and lunch spots were closed, and the downtown was nearly deserted.

"Put your arm around me," Peg said, wishing they didn't have to walk now that Agent White was around. The rhythmic clack of Brian Clark's heels on the sidewalk echoed off the tall empty office buildings and announced to anyone in the vicinity that they were there. Peg listened for Agent White's shoes as Brian Clark lackadaisically swung the carryout bag with what was left of their champagne. They went through the revolving door of The Hilton together and at the desk, they checked in, the two of them kissing as they rode the elevator up to their room, Brian Clark clutching a key card. Peg caught a glimpse of her distorted reflection in the polished brass panel of the elevator. She looked good but desperate. She should have begun this with Brian Clark long ago and held out for more dates. And here they were. And she liked kissing him. And she wanted him.

In their room he uncorked the champagne and poured out the last of it into two water glasses. Peg was undressing, and she pulled back the covers of the ornately made bed where she sat and she kicked off her heels. Brian turned on the TV and flipped through the stations for music: 90s, 80s, 70s, Solid Gold Oldies, Jukebox Oldies, Smooth Jazz, Jazz Classics, Latin Jazz, Tejano, Maximum Party, and finally settling on R&B Hits. Peg was naked and pulling him onto the bed and the music didn't matter. Except it did matter. When he had set down the remote Marvin Gaye was on the channel but by the time he had his shirt off it was Michael Jackson, and the mood just didn't seem right. He reached over to change the channel with the remote but hit the bedside alarm clock and somehow managed to set it off, so the buzzer repeated its insistent staccato beep until Brian Clark climbed out of Peg's embrace to go turn it off, with the TV on Adult Alternative and the caption said it was Lana Del Ray, he settled back in bed, and Peg was on him.

"Should I?" he said. "Do you want to me to?"

Peg didn't reply.

"Should I put on a...?"

Irritated with him, Peg said, "What? What is so important?"

"I brought protection."

"We don't need it," Peg said. "Just pull out. Can you do that?"

"I think so."

"You'd better."

And they both leaned in too enthusiastically so that they bumped heads, with Brian's forehead hitting Peg in the eye, and she sat up.

"Why is everything so difficult with you?" she asked.

"I didn't know it was," Brian said.

They were naked and under the covers. The lighting in the room was harsh. He got up and irritated her further. He pulled the bedspread up over both of their heads so they were smothered in each other and in darkness. He felt her hand on him and she guided him toward her. They moved together and as simple as that, what Brian Clark had longed for, for years, was an actuality. He ran his hands over her and breathed deep to take her in. He rolled his full weight onto her.

"I do like sex," she said.

He mouthed the words, "I love you. I love you."

And she didn't say it back but just once, she said, "Yes."

From the airport terminal Peg could see the pyramid and the sphinx at the edge of the Las Vegas strip. She was met by a plainclothes guard, who escorted her past the rows of slot machines to the main ticketing area and to the curb outside where a commuter van picked them up and rode them out to a separate terminal. In the waiting area she got the impression everyone was military: government employees or contractors. She was surrounded by the serious and muscle-bound conservatives who knew how to cash in on the security state. They all wore badges and only talked to each other when they were paired off. Mostly they paged through portfolios or typed on laptops. Whoever they were, this wasn't the Findability family. On the departure board was the designation KXTA, with two flights per day, and they were leaving momentarily. Peg's Launchability escort left her and no one seemed in charge until a flight attendant logged in at the desk and spoke over the PA, "We'll be boarding the Janet for The Ranch in fifteen minutes. Please have your credentials out."

She sat down and waited. She wanted to send Erin a post card from Vegas. She wanted to gamble. The vodka was wearing off and she felt tired. She had hoped she could nap on the plane, but she was on her way to Area 51, with no idea what was in store for her, and so there was no way she was going to be able to sleep.

She didn't wear the red t-shirt, but she felt underdressed in jeans and a polo. She didn't have a badge, so she shrugged her shoulders, but the flight attendant knew who she was and waved her through. On the plane there were no seating assignments and she took a window seat near the front of the mid-sized jetliner. She tried not to look at any of the men or women who passed her on their way to their own seats, but one asked, "Is anyone sitting here?" and what else could she say?

There were no magazines in the seat pockets, and there was nothing on her laptop that qualified as entertainment, so she took out her Kindle, just to have the appearance of having something to look at. She flipped through the titles: *Fantastic Voyage, Rendezvous With Rama, R is for Rocket, Planet of Exile, Left Hand of Darkness*. She tried to imagine her own space epic, but couldn't think of a title that would star the thoroughly average Astronaut Margaret Myers. She had won the lottery and was going along as a space tourist. All these people on the plane with her, they did the real work. She doubted anyone knew who she was since Brez was waiting for her return to make the official announcement. But this was real. She was going to Area 51 to train, she was going to Mars, and she was in a plane full of very serious well-paid conservatives.

The man in the seat next to her held a white Stetson in his lap and an iPad. He had gray hair with a ring across his brow from wearing the hat. He was in a bolo tie, he was tanned, he wore a light gray suit, and cologne, and his mustache was thick. He looked at Peg who buckled herself in and she pretended to read from her Kindle. She felt like the conservatives owned this whole experience and the man with the white Stetson would be the one to show her around.

He said, "First time to The Ranch?"

"Is it obvious?"

"None of the stuff they say about it is true."

"I'm an astronaut," Peg said, and she said it confidently, and it felt good.

"Who did they get?" the man said. "Spielberg? James Cameron? JJ Abrams?"

"The rocket is real," Peg said. "They film because they want to see what it looks like."

"Your secret is safe with me."

The flight attendant made her final rounds and she reached across to shut the blind on the window Peg looked out of.

In the mess hall at Area 51, Peg sat at a table with Major Tom, the Vulcan XIV mission pilot and commander, and Shirt, her master sergeant who was a woman. On Shirt's tray was the evening meal, some kind of hamburger pasta and a salad. Peg and Major Tom both went through the cafeteria line without placing anything on their trays, Peg with her tubes of pie, and Major Tom had brought his own food as well. Once they were seated, Peg reached into the deep pockets of her fatigues and selected rum raisin pie for fortitude and a key lime for finish. She placed the tubes on her tray. She waited to see if either of the men was going to make a show of praying before they ate. She had seen it happen here at Groom Lake with some of the Air Force guys. Peg wasn't unthankful. She felt uneasy over the probable non-existence of the recipient of the thanks. Shirt ate the meaty pasta with a tablespoon while Major Tom took out portions of nuts and dried fruits that he'd rolled up tightly in plastic baggies, a quirk that gave Peg the impression that Major Tom had been or maybe still was someone who smoked a lot of pot. She looked around at the people eating in the mess hall and tried to assess them but soon gave up. There were too many buzz cuts, which disguised the true natures of the men. At Findability the ones she suspected of smoking weed on weekends could have been pretty much everyone. When singled out, each eccentric introvert could easily give the impression that yes, here was another pothead. The majority of the Findability family, however, though they liked their coffee and their wine well enough, were sober, though not because of any ideological stance or reverence for the law. They were a community of nonconformists and Peg had never once seen a member of the Findability family pray or even hesitate before eating.

Major Tom lined up his nuts and raisins so he could easily count them, and he made a note of his intake, to the nut, on a small spiral pad he kept in a shirt pocket.

"I see what you're doing," Major Tom said to Peg. "That's smart. I like it. Me? I'm trying a more traditional approach."

"You count them?"

"I need to know how many to bring. How many to eat at each meal. How many calories I'm getting. But it's never the same. I like to mix it up so I get different combinations."

He picked up two hazelnuts and a blend of dried fruits, with a dried cacao bean, set them in front of Peg, and said, "Try this. It's my space mix. It's delicious."

Peg looked at the pile of nuts and raisins like he'd asked her to eat a monkey. It was solid food as far as she was concerned. If she was going to live on tubes of pie, she was really going to live on tubes of pie. But she was a captain and he was a major. She wasn't sure if he'd ordered her to eat the nuts and raisins, or if he had to actually say: "I order you to eat these nuts and raisins."

She was saved from her dilemma when Captain Nick walked by and set a red apple on their table.

"This is what I'm going to miss," he said. "Two years without biting into an apple. Go get you one. There are bushel baskets over by the salad bar."

Peg nearly got up, but then she remembered she and Captain Nick were the same rank, so she didn't have to do what he said.

"I'm bringing dried apples," Major Tom said.

"I think it's best to leave our diets up to NASA," Nick said.

"They said I could bring mine," Tom said.

Shirt nodded to confirm what Major Tom said, and she nodded at Peg, who also wanted to bring her own food.

Major Tom pointed a thumb over at Peg, and said, "She's going to live on pie."

Captain Nick smiled, leaned forward, and said, "After two years of pie, she'll be sweet and delicious."

He was being playful but his flirting made Peg uncomfortable. There was the potential, Peg realized, of not just a love triangle on the Vulture XIV but a love hexagon. The possibilities were boggling, and she went down the line of men, and tried to imagine whether or not she'd lock herself in a compression chamber with any of her crew mates. Her list included the famous film director, Brez, the guy she sat next to on the flight in, and Shirt, yes Shirt was a woman, but Shirt was also a sergeant, so Peg imagined she could just order her to spend the night. She was not at all interested in Captain Nick, who was her age but gave the impression of a creepy uncle. No to the two mission doctors, especially Dr. Lex, because a Ph.D. isn't the same. There were lots of Ph.D.s at Findability who weren't going around calling themselves doctor. Dr. Leonard made her think of Leonard Nimoy, who would bleed green, and his hands were cold. And no to Major Tom, who was a very good-looking kid. But he was sometimes dumb, and Peg couldn't get past that.

Would she have wanted Brian Clark in the capsule with her, maybe a museum version of the capsule they could sneak into, defile the captain's chair, and then leave? But no way would she want Brian Clark in close quarters for two years, especially with other men around. He was a nice enough guy; he just tended to automatically subordinate himself to other men, which she didn't like. Honestly, it bugged the crap out of her.

Neither of the astronauts reached for the apple, so Shirt took it and had a bite.

"He's right you know," Shirt said. "Being gone two years is one thing. If the coin lands tails."

"If the coin lands tails?" Tom said. "I'm the pilot of this mission."

"By no fault of your own," Shirt said, and she covered her mouth with her hand so she wouldn't spit chewed apple, "anything could go wrong."

"I might get me one of those," Tom said, and he turned around to see where the bushel baskets might be. He stood up and asked Peg, "You want one?"

Peg shook her head. She didn't really know the reasons she did the things she did. She just knew that eating an apple at Area 51 felt like a bad idea. She also decided that even if the pilot was a major, he hadn't talked to her like he expected to boss her around.

Major Tom returned with two red apples anyway. He set one on the table and said, "The Red Planet," and he bit into the other.

"If that's the Red Planet," Captain Nick said, "then Earth's halfway to Las Vegas."

"Where do we land?"

Major Tom picked the apple up off the table and rotated it

until he recognized their landing site.

"Here," he said, and he pointed at the apple, between the North Pole and the equator.

"Oh shit, I ate us," Captain Nick said looking at the core of the apple he held in his hand.

Peg felt the crew was joking around enough she could ask them about her implant. She hadn't seen Agent White since she'd arrived at Area 51, and she didn't know if the military base had some kind of protection, or if Agent White had just been away. Surely there were other implants in other women all over the globe. It was the only way Peg could reconcile Agent White. He was amassing an army of women. He couldn't have picked her alone out of the millions. She couldn't be both an atheist and the chosen one. What did he mean by "a promise us"? She was anxious about the possibilities.

Instead, Peg said, "Where do they keep the aliens around here?"

There was a pregnant pause. Shirt turned to Peg, and said, "On your two year mission, you will encounter humanoid creatures from another solar system. Our mission is peaceful, and these Martians will give us aid."

"Martians?" Peg said. "She said *Martians*."

"They refer to themselves as Trafalmadorans."

"Why the secrecy?" Peg said.

"As long as there is at least a question about who is in charge," Shirt said, "then we are in charge."

On the sound stage, in the cockpit of the Launchability Mars Lander (LML) simulator, Major Tom was given the okay to turn off the autopilot and make his descent under emergency protocol. Brez was in the seat next him, with Peg seated behind them, as an alarm buzzed insistently with red lights flashing. There was limited visual perspective of the surface of an enormous bright green globe that spun slowly, Ping-Pong balls fastened to it in a grid to sync with a computer-animated map of Mars. The LML was itself suspended on a rig and hung from a tall crane. The lander lowered toward the giant green ball and Peg felt dizzy. The view offered by the windows of the LML was disorienting. Their actual Mars descent would be made on autopilot, and this rehearsal was an emergency landing. They filmed it like a movie. They wanted to see what it looked like.

Captain Nick, who observed from the ground, and chimed in over the radio, said, "You're coming in too steep. You need to pitch."

Tom reacted nervously with the joystick that seemed to fight him and the LML simulator wobbled.

"Coming in too fast. More thrust."

The computer simulator also spoke, with a feminine robotic voice, "Landing site out of range. Scanning for alternate landing site."

"What now?" Tom said.

"Let the computer do its work," Nick said.

"The Kobayashi Maru," Peg said, and Brez laughed. He'd gotten her joke and he'd laughed. She was in the back of a tin can falling to her simulated death and incredibly happy because she'd made Brez laugh.

"Alternate site at mapped coordinate points 25.2 kilometers West South West."

"Twenty-five kilometers?" Tom said.

"It's not far," Brez offered.

"Keep it level," Nick said.

"Fuel reserves critical."

"We've got a ton of fuel," Tom said, pointing at the gauge.

"You're burning too fast," Nick said. "We'll need to take off again."

"Fuel reserves critical."

"Can we shut that thing up?"

"You need to make your descent."

"Hold tight," Tom said, as if this were the real thing.

"I want a fucking parachute," Tom said.

"This is live TV," Nick said.

"They can fucking bleep me out in live TV," Tom said.

The green globe filled the porthole and they were going to crash. Peg didn't think that would really happen, since this was a simulator, but before she could really prepare herself there was a collision, the LML smacked into the green globe, displacing Ping-Pong balls and scraping off green paint. Because the LML was suspended from a crane, it swung back, then hit the globe a second time.

"You're all dead," Nick said. "Heroes for all time."

Tom threw his hands in the air, "This is bullshit!"

"Want me to show you how it's done?" Nick offered.

"I would *love* that."

But the Mars Lander was lowered, the astronauts climbed out, and Peg felt good to be on the ground. Later they would watch the footage of the landing with the CGI spliced in and it would look convincing. She hated that there was footage of her death, especially since Shirt had threatened them at lunch the other day when Peg had asked about UFOs and aliens.

Captain Nick gave it a shot and crashed into the globe. Brez tried and he crashed into the globe. So that everyone but Peg had tried, and landing the LML was like a carnival game. It seemed rigged. They were doomed to failure. NASA could combine today's footage into a realistic and dramatic crash landing reel.

During one descent, Brez lost total control of the LML simulator as Peg sat quietly behind the two men. She watched as they planted their feet, strained against the joystick, and crashed repeatedly into the big green globe.

To rub in how bad their landings were, one last descent was filmed on autopilot. The feminine robotic voice narrated as it performed the perfect landing with ease, ending with: "Surface contact. Launchability Mars Lander has landed. Congratulations, you are the first astronauts on Mars."

Part 2

1

There were days when an unmarked white sedan was parked on Peg's street. They never broke down the door to haul her away. Mostly, she kept to the couch. She took the remote and surfed up and down the channels until Ronny found something he wanted to watch.

There was an armed guard at the Launchability gate who had orders not to let her leave, but she said, "What are you going to do, shoot me?" And she drove through the gate with a company car.

The Vulture XIV had returned to Earth orbit 609 days ahead of schedule with the living quarters not yet jettisoned. The astronauts were strapped in and wearing jumpsuits with inflatable life preservers over their shoulders. The living quarters were ejected, communications with Huntsville established, and the Vulture capsule moved into landing position, a controlled fall at descent angle, from a mere fifty miles out.

They stared at the control panels, with nothing much to see through the porthole windows except the sky that went from space-black to bright blue, until parachutes were deployed, the end of weightlessness.

"Vulcan," the voice from mission control said, "Navy helicopters have your position and are being dispatched."

"We've had an onboard tragedy," Major Tom said. "Maxim Brez was lost in space."

"We'll prepare a report with your debrief."

"Splashing down in three minutes," Captain Nick said.

"Helicopters will arrive in ten."

"First contact has been established," Dr. Lex said.

"Fantastic," another voice on the ground said. "We'll cover that in debrief. We're very interested in the technology exchange."

Peg hadn't expected the whole capsule to be submerged but the porthole window went dark again, and the quick change in pressure triggered the inflatables, which brought them bobbing back up to the surface where they got out of their seat restraints as quickly as possible. The door was opened, warm sea air rushed in, the first air they'd breathed that hadn't been canned since they'd left. The ocean was choppy, waves lapped into the open capsule, and there was an urgency they hadn't felt during most of the trip. The command capsule that had been their refuge and their home was in danger of sinking with them inside if they didn't get out fast.

Peg experienced a moment of panic when she couldn't get her shoulder restraint to disconnect. All the other astronauts were milling about, and they watched her, and she realized they were waiting for her to exit the capsule first. She got free and stood up, finally on her way back home.

"Really, you guys?" she said. "Women and children first?"

No one said anything, but they did wait for her to climb up and out before they left the capsule themselves.

Peg jumped into the inflatable raft that bumped to-and-fro on a short rope, and once they were all safe on the bright yellow circular island, they cut the rope, and before the sailors in helmets with dark visors descended on them one at a time from the helicopters to lift them up and away, Peg tossed two of the three Trafalmadoran gifts of technology into the sea. She kept the memory glass they had given her packed away in her duffle, with an iPad cover on it.

"We went to Mars to get those!" Captain Nick said.

"I know what *you* did!" Peg said. "So shut the fuck up."

Aboard the troop helicopter, everyone wore respirators and the mood was somber. Maxim Brez's absence would be felt by the world. The astronauts were flown to an aircraft carrier where a prefabricated house was set up on deck, where they lived until they got to Northern California, where the whole structure was lifted by a helicopter and flown to an area on base.

They slept in bunks and lived in close quarters all over again, expected to stay out of the public eye for as long as the mission was supposed to have taken, and while they had gravity, TV, the Internet, solid food, and hot showers, Peg knew, cramped up with these men, these murderers, that she would soon go mad. She used the Trafalmadoran glass by remembering what using an iPad was like, so that it appeared, at least in her own mind, to look and act just like one. When the generals came on the TV screens to ask questions and to feed the astronauts the officially sanctioned story, Peg told them there had been no exchange of technology. They had given her three telepathically controlled handheld devices and she had given them her Kindle with the Merriam-Webster's Dictionary on it, but what she told the generals was that the Trafalmadorans had only given them the Pythagorean theorem. The generals didn't doubt her version of the exchange and none of the astronauts ratted her out.

To Peg's surprise, quarantine only lasted two weeks, after which the astronauts were transferred to their own apartments at Launchability, where, while they were still expected to keep a low profile, they could sometimes wander around the Huntsville campus. And on a day two months later, when Peg had had enough, she helped herself to the keys of a Launchability campus car and simply drove away. The guard at the gate didn't know who Peg was or why he had orders not to allow any of the five special guests to leave. He put it together over the coming days, when he saw her picture in the news, and the knowledge terrified him. If he told his story, he might end up dead. Yet, what he knew was all he could think about and he wanted very badly to confide in someone. Margaret Myers wasn't in space but on Earth, and he had seen her, and he had let her drive out the front gate. He had no choice but to keep quiet.

When Ronny wanted to go out, Peg took the family to Dave and Busters where she stayed away from the bar but played the video games, which never lasted long, since they were designed to eat credits, and Peg would sometimes hide in a bathroom stall. She tried wearing sunglasses and an Angels cap when she went out, but that drew attention. One night a man approached to ask if she was an actor.

Months went by and she took up Internet poker. She played a massive role-playing game where she was a wandering magical elf. She bought vintage board games on eBay but could never convince anyone in the family to play. Ronny and Cecelia would drag Erin to church and Peg didn't intervene. She tried to meditate while they were gone, except she couldn't keep it up because she was afraid meditation would invite Martian contact. She got a new Kindle and she downloaded and read some of the books from Kevin's list.

She went for long drives up and down the coast where she parked and waded into the water. She always wished she had brought along a kite but would never remember until she was already out on the sand. She would eat a sno-cone. She would pick up shells and colorful pebbles and put them in her pockets.

She filled the closet in the guest room with Christmas presents, and then when Christmas came, everyone but Ronny was embarrassed by how much Peg had spent. She had organic groceries delivered and she'd taken to cooking elaborate vegetarian recipes with moderate success. Ronny humored her, but the absence of meat in her dishes made it impossible for him to be enthusiastic about anything she had made. She kept returning to Findability, but only to use the pool. In her cap and goggles—and she had lost weight—she was confident that no one, not even Claudia, had recognized her. She had to go out in public in disguise, but Peg finally felt good about her body, and she was glad she wasn't recognized, because she had run out of ways to fill the time at home.

On the day of the Mars landing, she went out to the grocery store to get snacks, and when she got home, Ronny was making popcorn. Once again, she was on the couch that she had paid for, with Erin, Ronny, and Cecelia, in the house she'd bought after the divorce.

Cecelia and Ronny seemed really happy to be there. They'd made themselves at home, and when Peg moved into the guest room, they continued to sleep in her bed. There'd been no discussion about their moving out, and Peg was starting to think she didn't want them to go.

Kevin and Brian Clark were the only ones she had told about the device the Trafalmadorans had given her, and they had given it *to her*. On the TV, newscasters babbled on about the details of her approach and descent and Peg learned things about the Vulture XIV, about Launchability, and about Maxim Brez, that she hadn't known.

Erin sat with her iPad as they waited for the big moment and she texted her friends, who also watched. Erin pulled up the Findability Map of Mars and she scrolled around the surface to where her mom would soon land. Peg lifted the rectangular Martian glass, disguised by the iPad cover, and she looked through it at the astronaut, Brez, on the TV screen. Through the glass she could see how driven he was, and that, even when she sat next to him, or when she had talked to him, he hadn't really paid attention to her. The glass showed her Brez's true nature: how he'd been more focused on Mars than on any of the people around him.

When the TV camera cut to a viewing party with the supermodel, Peg wished she hadn't seen her through the glass, because there she was, with the familiar caption, "girlfriend of Maxim Brez," and she looked equally determined. Peg felt bad about eating Brez and her heart sank. She wished she had gotten to know him better while he was alive, but she knew now that wouldn't have been possible, and it wasn't her fault. Major Tom and Captain Nick were selfish in their collusion, but Peg understood that maybe they had made the right choice, if there was such a thing. The supermodel was glowing. Some time in the next year she would learn that Brez was dead—and after the initial shock—she would wear her mourning well. Peg realized that life would go on for all of these people, that they'd been brought together out of circumstance, and that her own trajectory had brought her back here.

"What's that?" Erin said.

"It's a new app," Peg said, but Erin didn't buy it.

"Are you senile?" she said. "That thing's not even an iPad."

"I'll explain later," Peg said, and she looked through the glass at the room where they had watched so much TV. She looked through the glass at Ronny and remembered when he was young. She had loved him then, and supposed she still loved him, though no longer in a way that consumed her. She remembered her first impressions of Cecelia, how pretty she was. Cecilia's looks had really gotten to Peg, but that all seemed so long ago, and maybe it was. They were together for reasons none of them wholly understood, and Peg was the provider. Whatever else might happen to them from here on, they were going to be okay, because Peg would always have money.

"The anticipation is killing me," Cecilia said. "What did you say when you took that first step?"

"I don't know," Peg said, and she really didn't. There were different versions of Peg's big moment on film and Peg had no idea what would be broadcast.

"Just tell us," Cecilia said.

Peg was hungry and the popcorn was surprisingly filling. She wished the Martian glass could show images from her future, but even if they knew how to do that, they may have known she wasn't ready.

Brez counted down their descent from two miles out, and Peg waited, with the rest of the world, for the moment when the LML would touch down.

2

In the briefing room there was a Thermos dispenser of coffee, a half-filled box of donuts, and a basket of fruit. Peg took out a random tube of pie from the pocket of her fatigue pants, which turned out to be lemon meringue, a favorite, and they sat at a table together.

"I don't know what you know about this rocket," Captain Nick, the copilot, said.

"At Findability we joke about them. We call them Vultures."

"Whatever anyone tells you about safety, once the launch sequence has begun it's my job to disable any and all abort mechanisms."

"Shouldn't that be the pilot's decision?"

"I am a pilot."

"You're the co-pilot."

"The pilot isn't going to pilot any more than I am. He *can* pilot. Same as me. But there is nothing manual about this launch."

"Except the abort mechanism."

"Which I will disable."

Peg tried to imagine the PR disaster of Brez incinerated in fiery failure. Then she remembered her own skin.

"What is it you want me to know?"

"When we go up it's going to feel like dying. From inside the capsule we can't be trusted to know what's going on. We won't be able to see, let alone read any of the instruments."

"So why put an abort sequence in?"

"The engineers. They mean well."

"I understand that this is dangerous," Peg said.

"Before we got okay-ed for this mission," Captain Nick explained, "each of us was asked if we would volunteer for a one-way trip."

"Did you?"

"We did. All of us except Dr. Connery, the linguist."

"What was the game plan?"

"The mission would be dependent on periodic supply drops supplemented with a mobile lab to grow an edible yeast, at first, with an eventual hydroponic garden."

"You'd be the Donner Party."

"Failure was imminent."

"Ours is not a one-way trip."

"There is the potential it may become a one-way trip. Escape velocity of Mars is more than twice that of the moon. And *a lot* farther away."

"You'd eat the linguist?"

"He's really more of a mathematician. Have they shown you his 'language'? In its written form it's like computer code with Latin thrown in. And 'speaking' it is like playing one of those dancing video games."

"Why is he going?"

Captain Nick stared at Peg. "You know what linguistics is, right?"

Peg stared back.

"To talk to them," Captain Nick said.

"*Them?*"

"How did you get on this project?"

"I won a contest."

"I'm not sure 'win' is the right word."

"Fill me in."

"I'm supposed to talk to you about the flight," Captain Nick said, "the take off, the cruise, the landing. It's straightforward and we will rehearse. The rest of it I'm leaving to the others."

"Do they live on Mars? Are they Martians?"

"I don't think they *live* anywhere. But they have a presence there."

"Why are we going?"

"Ask your billionaire boss. Forward progress of humankind? Because we can? I don't know."

"Why are *you* going?"

"I'm a pilot."

As the sun made its descent, Peg walked over to the dining hall in one of her red t-shirts, not to eat, but for something to do. Captain Nick had described the mission, which was a grander repeat of the Apollo program, with some of the components reverse-engineered from museum pieces. There was a line for mess, uniformed men paired off at the long tables, and the plainclothes contractors mingled in amongst themselves. Peg got a vision of her high school, with the jocks and the pretty girls sitting together, like the nerds might somehow envy them, when really the introverts like Peg were infinitely more interested in their own kind. She saw how the contractors were more animated in their conversations, that they sometimes wrote on napkins, their brains engaged and working out problems, their scientific curiosity put in service for their country. For weapons, Peg remembered. This was a military facility built for the purpose of the violent domination of other peoples. She wondered what the relationship with *them* was, and if there was the potential for that kind of confrontation across such vast cultural, cognitive, and spatial distances. For all she knew there was already a war going on and she'd just been enlisted.

She picked up a tray and looked around for Shirt or Captain Nick to sit with. The red t-shirt drew attention, just as she'd expected, and a huddle of mathematically-gifted men waved her over.

"You're our girl!" one of them said.

"The astronauts have arrived," said another.

She sat with her tray and took out a tube of chocolate pie to give her something to do with her hands.

"Tell us your name, darling!"

"Captain Margaret Myers," she said. None of the men saluted, which made her more at ease. She supposed they were like her, uncomfortable with enforced authority, though maybe she only got salutes when she was in uniform. The men introduced themselves and their occupations: particle beam architects, aeronautical engineers, programmers, theoretical physicists, jet propulsion technicians. They were enthusiastic about her and also wanted to know what she did. What had been a comfort to her in recent years, simply saying "I work at Findability," was now a liability, because surfing the Internet, for the folks around here at least, hardly counted as qualified.

"Are you a pilot? Do you fly the ATFs?"

"No, I'm not a pilot. I've met the pilot. The co-pilot, actually."

"You're a scientist? A geologist?"

"I *like* science. But I don't *do* science."

"So what do you *do*?"

They wanted a handle, a way of understanding her.

And so she said it, for lack of anything better to say, "I work at Findability."

"Are you a programmer?

"A mathematician?"

"I work with those guys," she said. "But no."

After a silence, one of the men at the table with her finally said, "Did you just write a really good essay, 'Why I want to go to Mars'?"

This also wasn't true, and she felt she was being made fun of. She couldn't fly a plane, or design a plane, or even really explain why a plane didn't fall out of the sky. She had a general understanding of the concept of lift, something to do with the shape of the wings, but she would have been just like any of the men of the Wright Brothers era, trying the damn things out one flop after another. She knew that wasn't how things worked around here, not in the Air Force, not at NASA, and not at Launchability.

"I'm here," Peg said, "because I'm a woman."

They'd seen her t-shirt and understood the historic significance. They were men who worked almost exclusively with men, and they had somehow managed to suppress that reality as they invited her to their table. Sure, there were other women who were flown out to Area 51—but those women had very specialized duties and weren't of the class of scientists seated at the table with her. They were lab technicians, office assistants, nurses, and instructors. They were laundresses, psychics, telephone operators, and like Shirt, liaisons and chauffeurs. She'd seen women here, but Area 51 was a boy's club. The men were running it.

And none of them knew what to say to her. They each had a tale of reverse-discrimination where some highly qualified friend of theirs had been in the running for a prestigious job at a research one university, only to lose out to some woman. She'd just told them she was a diversity-hire, and they could hardly believe it. Here she was before them, and they'd wanted to root for her, to be able to say they'd met her, but now they'd felt kind of cheated.

"You always wanted to be an astronaut growing up?" one of the men offered.

"No," Peg said. "I didn't."

None of them was eating anymore, and she picked up her tube of chocolate pie, untwisted the oral dispenser cap, and squeezed the tube from the bottom into her mouth.

"Surely, you have," another said, and he searched for the word, "...skills."

Peg turned the word over in her head. What had counted as skills at her job at Findability was not at all what counted as such in the bespectacled eyes of these men.

"I keep to myself," Peg said. "I read a lot. I listen. I do my own thing and I've never really fit in."

They warmed to her. While they had been so extremely successful as to not really think of themselves as nerds anymore, they identified with what she'd said, though they were still slightly uncomfortable with the unjustness of her being the one to go, because technically, none of the traits she had just named really qualified as "skills." She squeezed more of the tube of pie into her mouth and swallowed. She wished she had Claudia there to pluck the one thing from her weightless resume that could convince them she belonged there. But Claudia had had an equally flabbergasted reaction.

"I'm riding the pendulum of human history," Peg said. "I'm the answer to millennia of sexist discrimination. I'm a quota."

"Feminism!" one of the men said, and he wagged a finger at her. "Why didn't you just say you're a feminist? An academic? We get it. We support it."

But feminism wasn't Peg's skill either. She was a woman and she hated sexism, though she was certainly not an expert in her hate.

"Is there a black guy?" one of the men said, which elicited groans but also lightened the mood.

"I don't think so," Peg said. She realized she was going to have to do better with her own backstory, because very soon Findability was going to expect her to talk to the press and explain her leapfrogging her way into the position without admitting how poorly qualified she really was. I have a good constitution and a high threshold for pain, she told herself. I'm kind to most people in most situations. I'm an underdog, and underestimated, but I've been known to come out on top. She understood that none of this would sound very good if spoken into a microphone, but it made her feel a lot better.

And then she finally hit on her answer, the one that worked on the geek elite here at Area 51, and the one that would work on the American people: "I'm here because Maxim Brez chose me. I wasn't privy to the hiring process, so you can ask him about that, but I'm going to assume I was the best woman for the job."

And saying this made it true. And so she was.

3

At night, in her dorm room, Peg stared up at the dark ceiling and thought about Brian Clark. She would have liked to have him there with her, despite her nonchalance about their non-relationship, and despite his presence surely crowding her out in the military-issue single bed. She wanted to call him, but couldn't stand the thought of the telephone operator logging her passing whims in some register that would be archived. Occasionally, she had thought of her abstinence as a strength, not getting too bound up in the sexualized trivial media culture, though she considered it her job to know the ins and outs of every major sex scandal: women teachers in their thirties sleeping with the teenage boys who had been their students, congressmen sending photos of their genitals over the cellular networks to their mistresses, celebrities making the rounds with public snuggling caught by paparazzi and breakups acknowledged on Twitter. Everyone on the web either seemed to be having sex, commenting on sex, or motivated by sex. In the same way Internet trolling revealed the worst of what was inside us, the all-pervasive emphasis on inserting penises into bodily cavities made us exactly like all the other vertebrates: base hominids, *homo eroticus.* Coitipods.

Fuckbots.

Only now that Peg had had sex again, she remembered sex, and she missed sex. Not so much the awkward stumbling procedures Brian Clark or Ronny had performed on her, but their needing her, and their believing she was preeminent.

Here she was unable to sleep at night, in a room alone, extremely self-conscious of having her activities monitored, and without unfettered access to the Findability search engine.

And so this was the thought she hadn't quite prepared for. She was going on a space journey and she wasn't going to have access to Findability search for two years. When she had a question about something she was just going to have to turn it over in her mind until she came around to her own answer, however satisfying. Or, she wondered if she would be able to send search suggestions to Ground Control? Or—and she couldn't quite accept this—it was possible, probably even probable, that there were going to be times, maybe even *lots* of times, when she was going to have to be okay with not knowing. And eventually, she might even get used to not asking unanswerable questions anymore. But then she relaxed, and she realized she would only be gone two years, and two years was going to be worth the unimaginable experiences she would have. Findability would be there for her when she came back. Though when she came back there might be whole new search algorithms or a brand new search engine from some other company to pop up and replace her good old friend. She didn't like the idea that Findability might somehow fall behind and lose a grip on their total search dominance. She had maybe always intuitively understood that there would come a day when people would stop saying, "Findable that," or "Just Findable it," but she had never dreamed she'd spend two whole years away and a slow steady decline would appear to her, because of her absence, as sharp and immediate. And she wondered if Brez was prepared for that too. Probably not, given his pride in the company and his swagger, the same swagger he brought to Launchability. She'd trusted him. She believed in him. But he was human, and his human endeavor couldn't continue unchallenged indefinitely.

Only she stopped thinking about that, because she imagined comforting Brez, and she was touching herself again, without abandon this time: *Brez, Brez, Brez, Brez*. And she came much sooner than she'd anticipated. She wondered why she'd never thought to imagine herself with him while she was doing that. And she supposed, pretty sure of herself, that she would from then on. She also realized that masturbating in space wouldn't be the same for her as it would for the men. Yes, she'd still need to find privacy, but there was no blast-off, so she could go right ahead.

She felt relaxed. She stretched out, rolled over on her side, and fell right to sleep.

Peg got into the jeep with Shirt and the co-pilot, Peg in the backseat this time. They drove along the landing strip and over to a large hangar. Shirt drove inside the hangar, around a cargo plane, and to a freight elevator in the back. The chain link gate was open, Shirt drove onto the elevator platform, climbed out of the Jeep, closed the gate, and hit the button that began a long descent.

"Was an old tin mine or something out here," the co-pilot said.

"We're not going into the mine," Shirt clarified.

They passed lights periodically in their slow fall down the shaft and Shirt turned on the lights of the jeep. Peg tried to imagine how deep they'd already gone, but lost her bearings. Long after she'd given up anticipating touching down, the elevator finally slowed and came to a stop. Shirt opened the chain link gate, climbed into the jeep, and drove along one side of a painted yellow line that proceeded down an enormous cavernous tunnel. Peg felt like they were driving too fast. They continued as the tunnel opened wider and there were spotlights trained on a life-size diorama with a crew working around the perimeter. When they pulled up and parked Peg recognized that the center of activity appeared to be a movie set, with the Launchability Mars Lander, or LML plopped down in the middle of an expanse of rusty sand. A few of the men wore the spacesuits—and with the exception of Shirt and two other assistants they were all men. She saw a short man in a spacesuit that she was sure was Brez.

"Let's get you suited up," Shirt said, and she led Peg and the co-pilot over to a rack of hanging suits. They passed a prop box filled with Styrofoam Mars rocks that looked very realistic, each with a letter stamped on its level-bottom for its placement on set.

Peg was self-conscious about the lack of a curtained-off dressing area and she looked around. She was disoriented by the size of this mammoth chamber and no one seemed to be looking at her. So she pulled one of the suits from the wrack, nowhere near as heavy as the one she'd worn at Findability. She laid it on the cement floor, and she stripped down to her bra and panties. She was able to get the pants on herself, which made her suspicious of the authenticity of the suits.

"Shouldn't this be heavier?" Peg said to shirt.

"We're just getting you used to the idea of them."

Peg pulled on the top of the suit and fastened it all together with Velcro, which was not airtight. The co-pilot came over and helped her get her helmet secured and she returned the favor. The two of them faced each other, reflected in the mirrored visors of their helmets, and they didn't look too convincing, like Halloween astronauts. But Shirt came over and turned on a fan in each of their backpacks, and each suit puffed out like it was pressurized, and then the suits looked more realistic.

"Try the comm-link," Shirt said.

"How do we do that?" Peg said, and her voice was broadcast out of a small, concealed speaker in her chest.

"All you do is talk," Shirt said.

"Testing 1,2,3," the co-pilot said.

Once they were suited up, they went over to meet the others. Peg exaggerated her steps because of the bulk of the blown-up suit, with the co-pilot stepping along beside her. Peg was a little confused about all of this, and she was unable to hide her unease. It wouldn't really matter since no one would be able to read her expressions for as long as she wore the mirrored helmet. She spotted cameras on rigs, with cameramen and a man walking to-and-fro who seemed to be in charge. One of the spotlights was moved closer to the LML and one of the assistants took out a tape measure to check the distance.

Peg and the co-pilot instinctively went over to where the other astronauts stood around, and Brez lifted the mirrored visor of his helmet, so that he was facing Peg and she saw him through the tinted glass, and he said, "Glad you made it."

"What is all of this about?" Peg said.

"We're just running through some lines," Brez said.

"Why are we making a film?"

"They want to see how it looks," Brez said.

Peg got the sense that how it all looked was going to be more important than anything else. In the distance, black curtains were hung. They tested different filters on the spotlights, with one assistant walking around and taking readings with a photometer.

"Let me introduce you to everyone," Brez said, and Peg lifted her mirrored visor so the men she was about to spend two years with would get a good look at her and know she was the one who'd been chosen to be first on Mars.

"You've met Captain Nick," Brez said. "This is Dr. Kyle Leonard, chief scientist and a specialist in microbiology." Dr. Leonard lifted back his mirrored visor for an introduction, and Peg saw an older man with jet-black straight hair and he wore glasses inside his suit, a bit of the mad scientist look about him. He nodded toward Peg but didn't smile, and he didn't extend his gloved hand. She imagined him running a battery-powered shaver over his face in the morning, and she remembered that in space there would be no morning. She didn't like the way Dr. Leonard looked at her, she felt she was being examined, and all she'd eaten was pie. She knew, probably no matter what, that there was no way he'd allow her to continue to eat like that.

The linguist was a Dr. Connery, who was shorter and fatter than the rest, with dark circles under his brown eyes, his thick black hair shaved down to a half-inch regulation high-and-tight. He extended a hand.

"Call me Lex," he said, and Peg would swear he squinted when he looked at her, like he'd seen her before and was trying to recall.

Finally, there was the pilot, easily the most charismatic of the bunch, with penetrating blue eyes, sculpted chin, reddish-brown unruly hair, and probably no older than twenty-six.

"Major Tom," Brez said, provoking smiles all around.

"Tom Lancaster," he said, and he shook Peg's hand firmly.

"I don't know why we all need to be here," Captain Nick said. "Since a few of us aren't going down in the lander."

"This is our first day of shooting," Brez said. "We all need to be here."

"You'll be talking to us over the comm-link," Major Tom said.

"I'm familiar with the mission protocol," Captain Nick said.

"Let's meet our director," Brez said, and he waved for the astronauts to follow him along the edge of the set, through the red sand, but presumably out of the shot. The director faced away, in discussion with one of the assistants who looked down at a schematic on a clipboard. Brez placed his gloved hand on his shoulder, and the director turned around.

"We're setting up the shot," he said, with a distinctly British accent. "We'll be ready for you in just a moment."

"Ridley," Brez said. "These are your astronauts." They each raised a gloved hand to say 'hello.'

"Astronauts," Brez said. "This is our director."

The director gave a wave and a bow then went back to his conversation with the assistant.

Lex said, "Is that?"

"Yes," said Major Tom.

"Are you sure?" said Lex.

"Yes," said Brez.

"Are we faking the aliens too?" Captain Nick said a little too loudly because the comm-link broadcast his voice and the director heard him, turned to look, and came over, clipboard in hand.

"We are not faking *anything*," the director said. "We are running over these shots so that we will have footage if we need it. You are going to Mars. You, and you, and you, are going to walk on Mars. I'm just here to get it in the can in case the cameras fritz in your amateur hands. In case your work isn't good enough for the historic record. I'm here to teach you technique, and we're all here to get it right. We merely want to see how it looks."

"That's what I thought," Captain Nick said and he took a step back.

"We won't be needing you in this shot," the director said. "The rest of you go over your lines."

A gaggle of assistants handed out scripts, but instead of checking her lines, Peg took in the scene. Around the perimeter were uniformed men who observed, uniformed men with scripts and microphones. On the other side of the set as the costume area was a makeshift commissary with catered food and chairs and tables. Peg didn't see anyone except Brez and herself who seemed to be from Findability or Launchability, but she couldn't be sure. After a few minutes, it became clear to her that whatever the director was doing was going to take a long while, and she went over to the catering area.

There were trays of warmed fried chicken, trays of donuts, and trays of turkey sandwiches. She wasn't about to eat any solid food, or anything for that matter, since she was comfortable in the helmet and couldn't exactly unfasten it by herself. She sat at one of the empty tables and took off the gloves, which let the air out of the suit, and the pressure from the fan in the backpack blew out of the open holes at her wrists and over her hands.

Shirt came over and sat with her.

"I heard some of that," Shirt said, "and I want to be clear that we are not faking anything. However, people will only believe what they can see. We want them to believe what they can see."

"But we're not faking it?"

"Unofficially," Shirt said, "if you die in transit Margaret Myers will still be the first person on Mars. Because of what we're doing here today, your place in history is secure."

"If I die in transit who comes back?"

"You don't," Shirt said. "But we disclose the tragedy *after* we run the landing footage, mourn you as a national hero. Is this okay with you?"

"I don't know."

"Well, please please please be polite to the director," Shirt said. "He has some say in all of this. If *he* doesn't like you, you can be replaced."

"I'm getting that," Peg said. "Once you've got me in the can you don't need me."

"The mission will be a success," Shirt said. "However, there are unavoidable risks. I'm sure this is no surprise. We'd love nothing more than to keep you around."

"I should go over my lines."

Shirt said, "No changes to the script without direct consent of the writer."

"Which one is he?"

Shirt looked around. "Over there. In the Buddha t-shirt, ripped jeans, and sandals."

"A hippy?"

"I don't think so," Shirt said, still looking around. "I think it's more like he doesn't make very good money."

"Where'd they get him?"

"A teacher or something."

The writer stood with a Styrofoam cup of coffee, his other hand in his jeans pocket. He was dressed just as Shirt had described and he looked like a tourist. If he had written the script and maintained creative control, he didn't project that kind of authority. Peg got the feeling that when it came to delivering the lines, any of them could say anything that came off sounding natural, and the writer wouldn't complain but would stand at the periphery in awe of the Hollywood process in motion.

Peg set the script on the table but couldn't turn the pages without flipping through them because of the vortex of wind at her wrists where she'd taken off her astronaut gloves.

"You can read off cue cards if you don't know the lines," Shirt said.

Captain Nick came over in his spacesuit and sat with them at the table. He held a clipboard, had kept his gloves on, and was having trouble gripping the pages with the gloves.

"This is what you should pay attention to," Captain Nick said.

Peg took the clipboard and the wind at her wrists fanned the pages. It was the mission log and she put on one glove, so that she was able to hold the pages down with that hand. Peg was overwhelmed at how detailed the procedures were, timed to the minute. She saw her name in there with the others, and it appeared she would be constantly at work. She hoped she could live up to whatever Brez saw in her but felt that if she didn't that would be his shortcoming. Hadn't he known she did next to nothing at Findability? If he'd only asked around about her, or taken a quick glance at her Internet log...

Brez came over and sat at the table, so there were four of them, three astronauts in their spacesuits and one disciplined capable master sergeant in her uniform.

"What do you think of all this?" Captain Nick said to Brez.

"We are going up into space," Brez said. "When you see the Earth at night, with thunderstorms, or the Aurora Borealis, this will all be worth it."

"We need to be going over the mission," Captain Nick said. "Instead of the Hollywood guy, we should be getting directions from an experienced astronaut. Someone who's been up."

Peg pointed a thumb at Brez to indicate that, yes, he had been up there, and yes, that made him an experienced astronaut.

"Right," Captain Nick said. "No offense."

Peg found a single page in the middle of the mission sequence that was not at all like the pages and pages of timed directives at the beginning middle and end of the document.

"Have you seen this?" she said to Captain Nick.

"It's a very long cruise," he said. The same single page of activities repeated for 345 days. They would coast silently toward Mars with friction-free, gravity-free momentum, with the occasional flight path adjustment or communication with Ground Control, but on their own and with nothing to do for hundreds of days that were exactly the same.

"We'll have a lot of time to ponder the blue ball of the Earth," Nick said. "Out there among the bright stars. We'll have a lot of time to contemplate it."

"With no Internet," Peg said, and Brez heard her.

"I thought the same thing," he said. "But you won't miss it."

She remembered then, that she would be with him the whole time and it was so unbelievable that she realized she'd somehow gotten used to being around Brez and talking with him. Shirt had told Peg about the possibility of crashing into Mars, or of missing it completely, but none of that made her nervous, at least not in the same way that the notion of living with Brez for two years did. What would he think of her? He'd figure out she was ordinary, and maybe he'd regret picking her. And how would she deal with that, always wondering if he'd reached the point yet where he regretted asking her to go?

"Instead of a mission physician," Captain Nick said, "maybe you should have gotten us a mission psychologist."

"To keep us from killing each other?" Brez inquired.

"We're all adults," Peg said, though none of them seemed to have the same calm manner as Erin.

"I would remind you," Shirt said, "that under the court martial system you can face the firing squad lickety-split. No playing around."

Captain Nick pointed up, and he said, "There's no laws in space. No country. No courts. No jails."

Brez shrugged his shoulders, but it hadn't occurred to him.

Captain Nick pointed his finger at Brez like a pistol and he dropped the hammer that was his thumb.

Brez smiled back to show his good nature. He'd dreamed all this up and it was coming true. No one was going to spoil it for him.

A page came over and told them the director was ready for them, so they got up, the three astronauts and the master sergeant, and they walked to the edge of the Mars lander set. The crew had been milling about but the quiet intensity of the director had settled over them, and the shoot was business-like.

"I need my three astronauts in the LML," the director said. "Myers last. She's the first out."

Captain Nick stayed with the others who watched, and Brez, Major Tom, and Peg all walked over, their progress slowed by the sand.

"Is anyone really going to buy this?" Peg said.

"Have you rehearsed the line?" Brez said.

"What do I say?"

Brez turned to face her as he walked sideways in the suit. "You say: *Here I am! A first step, on the shoulders of human progress!*"

"That's the line?" Peg said.

"Memorize it."

"It's about *men*," Peg said. They reached the foot of the mars lander and stopped. The boom microphone was up high, out of shot, so the assistants in headphones heard the conversation and the writer was waved over.

"It's not about *men*," Brez said.

"Who are *the shoulders of human progress*?"

"*Human* progress?" Brez said.

"She may have a point," Major Tom said.

"We who stand?" Brez said.

"I don't know," Peg said. "Not that."

Peg's boss's boss's boss, for the first time, had asked for her input on a very important decision that would be identified with the company on into perpetuity, and she didn't have an answer. She had to think of something.

"I liked 'One small step,'" Major Tom said.

"We can't go with anything too copycat," Brez said. "We can't just make up a line."

"How about something like, 'I am standing on Mars!'"

"That's the unspoken message," Brez said. "Needs dressing up."

Peg said, "I'm not wearing a bra!"

"I like that," Major Tom said. "She should say that."

"No, no, no," Brez said, and he placed his gloved hands on the globe of his space helmet. His hands were nowhere near his head, but that was the gesture of frustration he was trying to convey.

"I *am* wearing one," Peg qualified. "But for the trip, for weightlessness, and for half-gravity, I think it's the right choice. I just now decided that."

"You're not saying that to the camera," Brez said to Peg. "Get in the capsule," he said to Major Tom. And Tom climbed up the ladder. Brez said, "Give the line as it was written and they can edit it later."

"I don't want that line in my mouth," Peg said.

"Okay, okay," Brez said, his gloved hand on a rung of the ladder, poised to climb up, "but we are paying this guy *a lot*, and it's best not to piss him off."

"What would Sigourney Weaver say?" Peg said. "I wish we could Findable it. I liked what you said on your televised space walk.

What you'd said about the blue ball of the Earth."

"You liked that?"

"Do you think I could say that?"

"Earth will be too far away. It won't be a ball."

"Would it work if I said *blue dot of the Earth?*"

"We'll have a lot of time to contemplate it. We can come up with one together."

Brez climbed up the ladder and he followed Major Tom inside the capsule. Peg climbed up to do the same. In the spacesuit, however, she had difficulty feeling her way up the rungs. It was harder to pull up her feet and plant them in the inflated suit and heavy boots. She couldn't look down because of the large fishbowl that surrounded her head. The gloves were bulky and she felt like she might slip and fall once she'd made progress up the ladder. The lander was tall, with rocket engines below and a cabin large enough for three astronauts. From the top of the lander, she waved at the crowd of military personnel and film professionals who waited for her to disappear into the LML, and to climb back out to make history. Which she wanted to do. She really did want to move this all along. Yet, she had no idea how she was supposed to climb into the LML with the bulky spacesuit on. The porthole looked relatively small and she had a backpack on. She looked down inside the lander, where Brez and Major Tom had strapped themselves into their seats. They looked up at her and tried to talk her through the hole, like she was a long couch being moved up a winding stairwell. And they gave her contradictory advice: to bend left, to twist herself, to go feet first, no, try head first.

Peg shrugged her shoulders, though she realized the gesture wasn't visible because of the spacesuit, so she did it again and exaggerated her shrugging by raising both arms, which nearly made her fall off the ladder, and she caught herself at the last moment.

The director took a megaphone and spoke, "What's the problem?"

The boom mic was lowered in front of her, and she replied, "I won't fit."

"Nonsense," the director said. "Those are the specs. This is an exact replica. This is what they sent us."

"I can't get in there."

"All right," the director said. "What we really need is you coming out. So stand at the top and when you hear me say 'action!' you climb down."

"You want me to climb down?"

"Climb down."

"I'm climbing down," Peg said.

"You don't have to say it," the director said.

"Okay," she said. "I won't say it."

"Go back up and try it without talking," he said. "Pause at the last rung, jump down with both feet, then deliver the line."

Peg climbed back up and looked over to where the director was. She waited for his signal. She wasn't sure where the cameras were or if she was supposed to have her mirrored visor down. She had left it up and so whatever line they rehearsed that's what they'd be stuck with, because they couldn't edit in new lines if the camera caught her lips moving. She didn't see anyone with a clapper / scene board and wasn't sure if it was okay to begin. So she counted down in her head from ten and she eased slowly toward the fake surface of Mars one rung at a time. Until she got to where she assumed the last rung should be, which wasn't there, because the ladder ended sooner than she anticipated, and she slipped and fell. She hit the sand with her back and rolled over on her side.

"I'm all right," she said. "We are on the surface of Mars. I'm just going to lay here. Can one of you guys climb down and help me up?"

The crowd waited for the director to yell, "Cut!" but he didn't. The camera kept rolling. And the crowd held it in until the end of the shot, with the camera zooming in on Peg's embarrassed face as she lay incapacitated on the red sand. But they all burst out laughing, until the director quieted them down and he told Major Tom and Brez to climb down, help her up, and plant the stars and stripes.

As the two men climbed down the ladder, Brez first, followed by Major Tom, Peg went ahead and delivered an impromptu line, "They told me to say something about progress, but it just didn't feel right, especially now."

Brez waited at the bottom of the ladder and spoke his scripted line before leaping off, "We are launching into a new era!" and he landed near enough to Peg that he kicked sand onto her.

Major Tom climbed down with a metal box with a handle that contained the flag. "Give her your hand," he said, and Brez reached down to help Peg up.

Major Tom hopped off the ladder and said, "From Earth to Mars! From Mars to the future!"

Soon all three stood, arm in arm, and Major Tom took the flag out of the box, assembled it like a tent pole, and planted Old Glory.

They saluted the flag and held the pose for several minutes where "The National Anthem" would be edited in. This gave Peg time to ponder this moment repeated on the surface of Mars. She spotted the cameras, which weren't so far away, and she imagined them zoomed in on her and all the talking heads of Earth commenting on her historic fall. Leaving the footage would be easier for her than coming up with something poignant, so she was all for it and she decided she might repeat the stunt on Mars.

Peg was tired and she wanted to go back up the long elevator shaft to her dorm. She wanted to go home. She'd gotten a glimpse of how the next two years would be and there were sure to be more surprises, Brez not exactly the genius she'd made him out to be.

"What's going on out there?" the director said over the megaphone. "Can we run through the scene again? This time let's hit our marks. And Margaret, I liked that falling down bit. Let's leave that in."

4

In the morning, in the mess hall, she wore dark sunglasses and Captain Nick came up to her in the line. There were a few midgets in the line, in their little Air Force fatigues like Halloween costumes.

Captain Nick loaded his tray with fresh fruits, and Peg said, "What gives?"

She meant all the midgets and Nick shrugged his shoulders: "Test pilots?"

"That's a lot of test pilots," Peg said.

"If they didn't spend twenty times what they could, it would hardly seem worth it."

Peg leaned in and whispered, "Did we capture a UFO?"

"They've pegged us as HBs. I'd keep quiet."

"As what?"

"Hoax believers."

"We've been filming more than training," Peg said. "What would *anyone* think?"

"Filming again this afternoon," Nick said.

"You were the one who said you would disable the abort."

"I think it's a test," Nick said. "Ground Control can still

override."

"Who's really in charge?" Peg said.

"Exactly."

Shirt came over to sit with them and the two captains clammed up, Peg red-faced.

"You're with the linguist this afternoon to go over lines," Shirt said to Peg. "Have you met him?"

"We've admired him from afar," Captain Nick said.

"What about the writer? Does he still approve line changes?"

"The writer walked out."

Peg tried to remember what the writer looked like. If she could describe him to Kevin maybe Kevin would have known who he was. She got a sinking feeling he'd turn up dead by his own hand, or killed by some fast-acting cancer.

"We're winging it?" Nick said.

"It's called improvising," Shirt said.

"I can say what I want?" Peg said.

"It's going to have to be in Pig Trafalmadoran."

Peg said, "*Pig* Trafalmadoran?"

"We don't have the mouth structure or vocal chords to speak true Trafalmadoran."

"The one I met was a telepath," Peg said.

"Mine too," Captain Nick said.

"Is he named after a color?" Peg said.

"He calls himself Agent Mortifier. The linguist wasn't alarmed by that."

"Their word for us is 'meat'," Shirt said.

"How did the linguist explain that?" Peg said.

"He believes this word is archaic," Shirt said, "a remnant from when they weren't as evolved."

"Are we filming fake alien contact?" Peg said.

"They might not look good on camera," Shirt said.

"So we're faking it?"

"I keep saying," Shirt said, "but no one believes me. We are *not* faking. This is practice. We only want to see how it looks."

Peg was driven to the dojo to meet with the linguist, who was dressed in yoga pants and one of her red t-shirts with the slogan, "First woman on Mars." She didn't know what kind of mail order was allowed here, so she assumed he'd brought it with him, which meant he'd followed her in the news. The linguist was seated, in the lotus position, but he popped up once Shirt delivered Peg and Shirt left to leave the two alone.

The linguist faced Peg, crossed his arms, and said, "How high can you kick?"

Peg stared at him. His name was Dr. Connery, but he had told her to call him Lex.

She said, "I don't know."

Dr. Lex gave a couple of high kicks. He was short and Peg decided this gave him better balance. She might be able to kick him in the chest or head, but she didn't think she could kick him over.

"A symbol is something that stands in for something else," he said. "It can be markings on paper, or sign-language formed with the body in three-dimensional space."

"Like a high kick?" Peg said and she gave it a try.

"Yes," Dr. Lex said, and he kicked back, more practiced, his foot wheeling high and fast. He wheeled his other leg just as high but in the opposite direction: "And that was 'No.'"

"I'm going to *kick* 'Yes,' or 'No'?"

Dr. Lex kicked.

"Was that one 'Yes'?"

He kicked the same kick.

"They are going to do most of the talking," Dr. Lex said.

"The midgets?" Peg qualified.

"I think they like to be called 'little people'."

"You're the linguist," Peg said. "And *you* don't even know?"

He shrugged his shoulders, and said, "It's one of those things that changes."

"You've worked with them?"

Dr. Lex kicked 'Yes.'

"So what have you called them?"

"I've been calling them Trafalmadorans."

Peg practiced her kicks. "Am I doing this in the suit?"

Dr. Lex kicked an emphatic kick.

Out in the Nevada desert, at night, with large portions of the old bombing range lit up with fluorescent spot lights, Major Tom drove the Launchability Mars Buggy with Brez next to him in the shotgun seat and Peg in the back. They drove through the paths made by the lit-up sections of the desert, and Peg saw how the Mars Buggy had three pedals—an accelerator, a brake, and a parking brake—very simple, and she was a cautious driver. If they didn't give her a turn to drive eventually, she might say something.

But they drove up over a sand bank where there were cameras on rigs, with a landed saucer craft preceded by a group of midgets in costume mulling about in the landing zone. Major Tom slowed down and waited for radio confirmation to approach. They all three decided to stay in the buggy and they pulled up until they were surrounded by them, the little people crowding the car like beggars.

Peg realized that in order to deliver her lines in Pig Trafalmadoran she was going to have to climb out and stand on solid ground. There were too many little people in front of her, so she backed up and stepped down, only to trip on one of the midgets behind her and to fall butt-first in the sand. She couldn't see the famous film director, but she heard his voice on the speakers in her helmet, in stereo, and he shouted, "Cut!"

Someone came over from outside the perimeter of the spotlights and fixed Peg's oxygen hose that had popped loose. She was helped back into the back of the buggy, and the director shouted, "Take two!"

She backed out of the buggy, the Trafalmadorans gave her space, and she performed a series of kicks, punches, and poses. She had to really concentrate to remember what she was saying. "We come in peace," of course, but in Pig Trafalmadoran it didn't appear to carry that meaning.

The Trafalmadorans performed their own series of kicks, punches, and poses back, but to anyone watching, which meant Peg, Brez, and Major Tom, it looked like everyone involved was making up ridiculous dances in some kind of contest, a few of the midgets too short and too bogged down by their costumes to do the moves effectively. They were hairless, with big black eyes and small mouths. They didn't wear spacesuits but were comfortable in their Mylar loincloths and shiny silver moon boots. When they kicked too high the make-up lines were revealed under their scant clothing. There was a zipper in the back of the headpiece, and they were supposed to remember to always face the camera.

"Can I say something?" Peg asked finally, and since she wasn't kicking or moving her arms into poses, everyone knew she was talking to the director.

"Your communications are going to be interpreted and narrated back to Earth by the linguist from the Vulcan capsule."

"He's doing a voice-over?"

"What is it you want to say?" the director said.

"Maybe I could do the voice-over," Peg said. "I could say what I'm saying as I'm kicking it."

"This is the linguist's first TV appearance since launch," the director said. "He's very excited about the scene."

"Do you think that's the right artistic choice?" Peg said.

The director paused. "I see what you're saying," he said. "We could caption his translations."

They ran through the scene again. She kicked and stomped and punched and kicked. They kicked and stomped and punched and kicked. She kicked and kicked. They kicked and kicked.

Brez climbed out of the Mars Buggy carrying a long box with a handle, like a pool cue case, which he set down, knelt in front of, and opened. The case contained an actual olive branch, which Brez took in his space-gloved hand and gave to the Trafalmadorans, who descended on, and ate, the olive branch.

Brez kicked and punched a series of poses while Peg

translated for the cameras: "They are vegetarians!"

Since there was nothing left to give them, and nothing left to punch or kick, Brez and Peg backed away until they were in the Mars Buggy. Major Tom shifted into reverse and they drove away.

Part 3

1

Peg had been in simulators, and she had worn the spacesuit, but nothing could prepare her for the intensity of the launch. Peg made a video message that was emailed to Erin right after the countdown where she admitted that even though her pendulum had swung toward atheism, she was open to the possibility of something more. While atheism terrified most people, the idea of the void was comforting to Peg. She had to clarify, in her message, that when she had said "the void," she had meant death and not space, since, in many ways, they were the same. She was sorry she hadn't been more of a spiritual guide, but she was entirely unsure, and she tended to distrust those who projected, with unselfconscious certainty, their own wish-fulfillment onto the abyss. There was no way to be sure about what had come before or what might come after. She understood how, if someone were handed more, they might not want the goodness of life to end. Or, if someone were handed less, they could be glad about the end, and might feel they were owed a reward. She supposed there were those who couldn't comprehend the possibility of utter nothingness. In her video message to Erin, Peg reaffirmed her faith in orphaned humanity, even now, on the verge of either death or the greatest experience of her life, she couldn't give credit to the invisible unknowable large benevolent entity, and she also had no expectation of being received.

All of the astronauts and their handlers walked onto the freight elevator at the bottom of the launch tower and they stood inside the elevator for too long, because they all waited for Brez to push the button—which he did, once he recognized why they hesitated—and they were sent on their way up the length of the enormous rocket. Peg looked out, the elevator surrounded by chain link and open to the air, television cameras trained on them, so no hoax believer could claim the Vulcan XIV was sent without astronauts. She got a sense of the crowds out there, many of them parked along the highways and sitting on the roofs of their cars. As they reached the top of the tower, they could see for miles. The elevator jolted to a stop, the door opened, and they turned around to face a grated metal walkway that led to the gaping porthole of the command capsule.

In Earth's gravity, and with the wind and dizzying heights, the suited astronauts moved slowly as they gripped tightly to the handrails along the way. There were men in NASA jumpsuits to help guide them along, to strap them in securely, to go through the systems-go checklists, and then to walk back out and ride the elevator down, which to Peg seemed like food for conspiracy theory, since the astronauts could sneak back out in the NASA jumpsuits. Or, if the astronauts were unable to strap themselves in or to flip the right switches while in the spacesuits, then how could they be expected to fly the Vulcan? Peg saw the logic in such a line of questioning.

Here she was with the pilot, the co-pilot, and the autopilot, but no one else, no matter what, could fly this thing. She'd seen enough movies to know the situation was ripe for an Airport '75 scenario, with one of the passengers being talked through an emergency landing. There were too many things that could go wrong. She'd allowed them to gamble with her life on the flip of a coin, and now they were counting down. *T-minus*, she could hear them in her helmet, *check, check, all systems go!*

She was strapped in facing up, like the rest, by a man in the NASA jumpsuit, very near her, and with the gravity and the way she was situated, he sometimes had to crawl over her, and she felt his weight, though it was buffered by her pressurized spacesuit. She looked up at the bank of lights and switches, and at the small swatch of the cloudless sky that her view from the back of the capsule allowed. She knew there were TV helicopters keeping their distance and a lone entrepreneur in a prop plane with a banner that advertised his crab shack. There might be a flock of starlings or some kid on the ground might launch his own model rocket. There were thousands of cameras trained on them. The last of the NASA crew left the cockpit, the hatch was swung shut, and the airlock was secured.

Whether the next few minutes ended in sublime success or intrepid failure, these astronauts were about to be propelled into history and she wished she could think of something funny, or that one of these men, any of them, would make a joke to cut through the substantial disquiet of the astronauts in the command capsule. The countdown seemed to accelerate as the moment of launch neared. Peg wanted out of her seat and off this ride. She wanted to get up and to run. She remembered the co-pilot telling her he would disable all abort functions. There would be no escape slide, no parachute, no getting out of this rocket no matter what. And as the countdown fell below a minute, with nothing in her thoughts except the present and immediate sound of each well-articulated number in the quick progression toward zero, her breathing was labored and her heart pounded.

Zero family. Zero showers. Zero coffee. Zero television. Zero weather. Zero Earth. Everything she had ever known would soon be a memory replaced by conversations with Ground Control scientists broken up by air delay and a view of the shrinking bright blue globe.

"Ready or not," Captain Nick said.

Major Tom let out a yodeling Slim Pickens scream.

Brez looked over at Peg and gave her a thumbs-up with his spacesuit glove.

She didn't know if the launch sequence started early or if it was a result of the enormous explosion that rattled up from below, but Peg didn't actually hear the word "ignition." There was no doubt that they were being propelled, that the light from the windows was shaken in every direction, and the vibrations from the rocket engines was so intense that she was sure all of them in the capsule believed as she had, that the Vulture XIV had been blown to bits and they would soon fly apart into atoms of meat and metal. But her consciousness hung on, her sight returned, she became aware that her ears were ringing, and that the launch wasn't so much heard as felt. She thought that maybe her eardrums had ruptured, and that no one had prepared her for that possibility. She had the sensation that the explosion of the rocket coming to pieces would soon work its way up to them and there was nothing they could do, nothing anyone on the ground could do but watch. And her breathing became more relaxed, the weight on her chest lessened, the dizziness in her head left, and though her vision was blurred, her retinas were still intact, her body whole, the space capsule held together, and the hue of the sky in the port windows darkened from bright blue to deep blue. And she could hear the voices in her helmet again.

The first stage burned off and they felt a hitch in their course as the second stage ignited. They were leaving the Earth's atmosphere. Peg could lift her hand now. She could turn her head. She looked over at Brez and returned his thumbs-up, and he smiled. She didn't think anyone she told about all of this would believe her when she said that everything melted away because Maxim Brez smiled at her. They were not out of danger, but soon they would be cruising, and they could unlatch their shoulder harnesses and try out zero g.

Captain Nick occasionally called out readings from the altimeter, and he said, "Welcome to space."

The light from the porthole windows had gone from deep blue, to violet, to black. Then as the rocket slowly rotated, the inside of the capsule flashed white with sunlight.

A voice from Ground Control said, "Hang tight. Entering Van Allen." Peg knew all about the Van Allen belts—the sun's radiation coursing over the magnetic fields of the Earth. The magnetic fields were what kept everyone alive on the ground and venturing beyond them might cook these astronauts to death.

Peg was anxious, unsure what to expect. They might spend twenty minutes in the radiation belts, maybe half an hour. This deadly field of energy was the ace in the moon hoax conspiracy theory: NASA realized they couldn't put enough lead on a rocket to shield the astronauts and also send it up. So they faked it. Meanwhile everyone else vehemently insisted, without evidence, that the radiation wasn't necessarily so bad. Peg was about to find out.

She tried to watch the rest of the crew without drawing attention to herself, to see how they were taking it. The linguist, the ship's doctor, and even Major Tom all had their eyes closed, so she felt less self-conscious and she twisted her body to get a better look at them, at least as much as she was able, and they all had their eyes closed tightly, like they were in pain, which was unsettling. She didn't see anything or feel anything. Then suddenly, there were sparking flashes of light. And she closed her eyes, with the flashes appearing behind her eyelids. She gripped her seat and no one in the capsule talked. She wished she could sleep through it, but there would be no sleep while radiation struck her retinas. The ship's doctor sat there unable to do anything, the same as the rest of them.

Then she heard Agent White, which surprised her: "We are a promise us."

The flashes of lightning behind her eyelids decreased and stopped. Violet light poured through the cockpit windows, and a shadow was cast over them. They sensed the contrast and opened their eyes, with a magnificent view of the Earth below an enormous wedge-shaped spaceship that absorbed the energy of the Van Allen Belts and glowed violet.

"We are meet in cosmos."

The radio in Peg's helmet crackled with static. She realized it had been a while since she'd heard any chatter from Ground Control and she didn't know if it was because of the radiation or because of the star cruiser now in their midst.

Major Tom said, "Huntsville, are you getting this on radar? Huntsville?"

Brez raised a hand to calm the crew and he said, "This is the Trafalmadoran ferry. We knew they would come."

"So *this* was how they did the moon shots?"

Brez nodded, at least as much as he could in his spacesuit.

"They faked that shit in a film studio," Captain Nick said.

"NASA really went," Brez said. "With help."

"There has been a reluctance," the linguist said, "to work with the Martians again. But we've gotten better at understanding each other, I can assure you."

The scene outside the capsule was a little too familiar to Peg, the still firing Vulture XIII; a small fish about to be swallowed by a much larger one, which she'd seen dramatized by the detailed models in Star Wars and Star Trek movies—the Trafalmadoran ship long and triangular, the surface plain, the violet glow the primary distinguishing feature. The real thing would disappoint in a movie, looking like a cheap special effect, only it was enormous and undeniably real, flying parallel to the Vulcan and closing in, a gaping rectangle in its belly, with the shadow of the Trafalmadoran vessel darkening the inside of the capsule and casting it in violet. The last stage of the Vulcan fired as it neared the spaceship, and the bay doors were seen sliding closed through the porthole windows with the reflected blue light of the rocket plume. The light dimmed as the rocket extinguished, the astronauts left in darkness except for the control panel lights, until a cabin light flickered and came on. The Vulture rotated half a revolution, the astronauts felt a sudden acceleration, and nearly as quickly, a rapid deceleration.

The static in the radio flattened to silence.

The doors of the Trafalmadoran ferry opened again to reveal a view of Earth at a distance. They were well beyond the outer atmosphere with a stunning view of home.

"Look at that!" Major Tom said.

"In all her glory," Captain Nick agreed.

The static returned to the radio, then the signal was back: "Vulcan, this is Ground Control. Once again receiving image capture from your internal and external cameras. Glad to see you made it. That's a very nice view."

"She's beautiful," Major Tom said.

"There's cloud cover, but we can see the continents," Brez said, "and the oceans."

"Captain Myers," Ground Control said, "do you have a message for humanity?"

"It's been overwhelming," Peg said. "I wish everyone could be here. Watching on a TV screen doesn't give the whole picture."

"Everyone has passed checkups with flying colors," Dr. Leonard said, which made Peg nervous, because there hadn't been any checkups. How could there have been? How many people were being paid to lie, she thought, and what might happen to her if she didn't lie too? For example, if there really was a live video feed, wouldn't they all see the capsule was no longer moving. They sat, stationary, staring out from a rectangular hole in an enormous purple spaceship.

But maybe Peg was paranoid. The Findability spacesuits were pretty advanced. Probably the ship's doctor, Dr. Leonard, had a readout of the astronauts' vital signs—oxygen intake, heart rate, body temperature—that's how they would have done it on Star Trek. She wondered about Dr. Lex, the linguist. Maybe he was paid to lie too, especially since he'd been brought along as the one to communicate with them.

"Safe travels, Vulcan. We'll check in at oh nine hundred, Huntsville," which they'd decided on to keep things Amerigocentric, with TV appearances in prime time, the rest of the world up past midnight to watch live.

Once the red light of the cockpit video feed went off, Peg expected the doors of the spaceship to slide shut again, but they didn't. The vulture hung there in its berth looking out at the big blue ball of the Earth. They'd just asked her to say something and she could have used Brez's line from his spacewalk. She had her chance and missed it.

They unbuckled, removed helmets, and swam weightless through the cabin. They were alive, with nothing to do but come down off of the adrenaline and wait. They stared out of the portholes and hours passed. They floated back to the living quarters, situated in the back like the sleeping cabin of a semi-trailer, and they wormed into sleeping bags distributed along the walls.

2

Peg hovered between sleep and consciousness. She heard Agent White's voice in her dream, but when she opened her eyes it was Dr. Lex, the linguist, speaking: "Wake up! Wake up!"

Fully awake, Peg looked at him as he floated near her, and he looked back but didn't seem present.

"Together us now in cosmos."

Peg realized Dr. Lex was channeling Agent White, who spoke to her through Lex's body.

"It's good to be here," she said.

"Your plan is ungrown."

"Is that you?"

"We speak for us."

"We're going to Mars?"

Dr. Lex laughed.

"I'm serious," Peg said.

"The distance is near," he said. "Idle moments make contact."

"Won't people see us in their telescopes?"

"Please to make contact," Dr. Lex said. "Come out."

Peg unharnessed herself and floated out of the sleeping bag.

Dr. Leonard slept soundly while Dr. Lex closed his eyes and floated unmoored in the living quarters. The other astronauts were in the command module. While she couldn't manipulate Dr. Lex back into a sleeping bag, Peg maneuvered across the room with one hand as she pulled Lex by the wrist with the other. She anchored him with a Velcro strap from one of the bags, since she couldn't just leave him asleep in mid-air where he might bump into things.

Back in the command module, Tom, Nick, and Brez were well aware that a lit-up docking tube extended toward the Vulture. They debated whether to put on their helmets, but Dr. Lex shouted at them from the living quarters, "Transit vessel laden with Earth air, as guests us," which settled it. The long lit-up docking tube accordion-ed out to the Vulture, it curled at the end like a tongue that felt it's way around the capsule until it found the pressure lock, where it sealed.

"I guess we're going aboard," Peg said.

They all waited for Brez to say something, since he had foreknowledge of this portage, but he looked anemic.

"Kyle has a microbe sensor with his gear," Major Tom said. "So he's going."

"I thought we were all going," Peg said.

"I'd elect to stay behind," Brez said, "but I'll let the major make the call."

"I want to go," Major Tom said. "You want to stay here?" he said to Captain Nick.

"I'm like Spock or something?" he said. "I'm C.O. whenever you feel like going off somewhere?"

"You could go," Major Tom said.

"Who's in charge around here?" Nick said.

"I think they are," Brez said.

"They want to meet us," Peg said.

"Isn't the linguist supposed to be communicating with them?" Nick said.

"He kind of is," Peg said.

"We all go," Major Tom agreed. "Let's wake up the sleeping beauties."

They floated back into the living quarters to get out of their suits and hang them near their respective sleeping bags. Tom roused the two doctors and Peg stuffed her jumpsuit pockets with tubes of pie.

"Not a bad idea," Nick said, and he brought along his own ration of MREs.

Nick and Tom spent a few minutes assessing the sensor readings on the control panel and they concluded that, yes, the atmosphere outside the capsule was pressurized and contained oxygen.

The port door opened with minimal pressure release and they climbed out one by one to pull themselves along the inside of the long hollow flexible tube. Peg breathed air, though the confined space felt claustrophobic, with Tom in front of her and Brez behind her. Peg had been looking forward to two years of small talk with Brez in a space capsule, and while they were still on their way to Mars, the trip wasn't going at all how she'd imagined.

"Have you thought of writing a book?" Peg asked.

She had meant the question for Brez, behind her, but Major Tom, in front of her, answered instead, "Nah, I couldn't sit still long enough for that. I'm more of a *doer*."

"What about you, Maxim?"

"I have an agent," he said. "She can get me an advance to write a book. She could even get someone to write it. But I don't have time for that."

"You don't have the time for *someone else* to write it?"

"I don't think my story's all that interesting."

"*I'd* be interested."

"Aren't those business books all the same?" Tom said.

"It wouldn't be a business book," Peg said. "It would be a biography. With personal stuff. Like how he met his girlfriend. How did you meet your girlfriend?"

"At a charity event," Brez said.

"Typical," Tom said.

"Why is that typical?" Peg said.

"He's got more money than France. He kind of has to give it away. Which becomes a full time job, *with perks*. Am I right?"

"Not more than France," Brez said. "Maybe more than Palau."

"Tell your agent I think it would make a great book," Peg said.

"She'll want to sign you too," Brez said. "Maybe your book would come first."

"*My* book?"

"She doesn't know she's a celebrity," Brez said.

"Because I'm not."

"They didn't ask *me* if I had a message for humanity," Tom said.

"What would your message be?" Peg said.

"I don't know," Tom said.

"They put me on the spot," Peg said.

"You did fine," Brez said.

"Am I supposed to come up with that shit all the time?" Peg said.

"Wouldn't hurt," Brez said.

"World peace," Tom said. "Preserve the environment. Work together as a people."

"That's a good list," Brez said.

"He was joking," Peg said. "Anything we say is going to be picked apart in Web forums."

"Think of yourself as addressing a nation of twelve-year-old girls," Brez offered. "Web forums or not, you can do a lot of good."

"What do you know about these aliens?" Peg said.

"I think they might be really large," Tom said.

Peg pulled herself out and into a chamber with a giant door that opened into an enormous hall that curved out of sight in what appeared to be a section of a long ellipse. The rest of the crew came out of the chute, stood up, and looked around. They were weightless but were able to walk, as if their boots were magnetized. Since the soles of their boots were rubber, Peg was pretty sure the magnetic effect wasn't from their NASA boots, but somehow projected onto them from their hosts.

"Artificial gravity," Dr. Leonard said.

"No, I don't think so," Nick said. "But something is holding us."

"That's what I meant," Dr. Leonard said.

"Should we walk?" Nick said.

They made their way down the long hall, their movements

exaggerated like mimes through snow.

"Is there a prepared statement?" Tom said.

"I think we see what *they* say," Brez said.

"Please let me do the talking," Dr. Lex said.

"Einstein here invented an entire inter-galactic Kung Fu language and all they do is take over his body," Nick said.

"What is he talking about?" Dr. Lex said.

"You mean he doesn't know?" Tom said.

"You've been channeling them," Peg said. "They've been using you to talk to us."

"What did I say?" Lex said. "Have you been writing it down?"

"They don't even need to do that because they can talk to us in our heads," Peg added.

"That's what *I've* been saying," Nick said.

They made their way around the hall to a transparent membrane where light refracted in a way that suggested the end of the Earth air. On the other side were creatures in what appeared to be colored plastic shells of various shapes and sizes. Some were bipedal, some looked more like walking square tables, one or two were rolling spheres, another was a tripod with a long headless neck. They walked or rolled or lumbered over to the membrane that held back the air. They stepped through, were very near, and their hard shells were see-thru, so one could distinguish a soup of various organs inside: their fluttery hearts, branching vessels of flowing fluids, a brain mass or two, other opaque or cloudy masses, and pressed up against the thick transparent plastic that contained them were eyes that blinked. If it weren't for the fact that they were animated, and that they had eyes, their animal status would be questionable. They were walking, rolling, lumbering human-sized Jell-O molds.

Dr. Leonard took out a sensor and he was absorbed in this activity, not at all concerned that his observations might be rude.

"Is one of you Agent White?" Peg said.

"*I'm* supposed to do the talking," Dr. Lex said, but then he looked stunned, like he'd been hit on the head, and his voice returned to a lower register, which made it clear he was channeling again.

"Be received of Trafalmadore," he said. "For uttered intercommunication."

"We call it 'first contact'," Dr. Leonard said.

"Happy to meet you," Tom said. "Right everyone?"

And the other astronauts joined in affirmations and good tidings, ending with Dr. Leonard, who added, "Mazel Tov," which garnered odd looks from his companions, in answer to which Dr. Leonard shrugged his shoulders and said, "Just in case."

"Which of you is Agent White?"

The plastic shells turned to face each other then turned back to acknowledge that he wasn't among them.

"He said we would meet," Peg said.

Dr. Lex went limp, which made it clear he was no longer channeling. He came to and returned to himself. He recognized what was going on and he raised his hand to Peg, to let her know he would translate.

"Where is Agent White?" Peg said.

Dr. Lex motioned to Peg, to indicate to the Trafalmadorans that Peg wanted to know something. Then he paused, unable to think of a way of conveying the idea of Agent White. He rubbed his palms together to suggest that Peg was there to meet someone, though to Peg the way Lex rubbed his palms together seemed crude and might even be perceived as violent. Or it could stand as a symbol for several other unrelated activities.

A section of the floor rose to the height of a table and hovered there, with the air membrane splitting the floating table right down the middle. The Trafalmadorans returned to their side of the table and two of them unscrewed the top off of the bright red transparent plastic shell of one of their kind, and a portion of his Jell-O body oozed up to protrude into that other atmosphere, or vacuum, or whatever was on their side, and the true Trafalmadoran color was revealed. This fellow was mostly a cloudy gray with orange eyeballs, and an orifice opened as the gelatinous mass jiggled and produced a sound.

"Will get White us," was what it said.

Dr. Lex said to Peg, "He's going to get...wait a minute, do you *know* one of these, whatever they are?"

Peg nodded like it was no big deal and the creature with the open top turned and walked over to a bright blue circle on a wall on the far side of the room. The circle shrank, then expanded, apparently in response to the Trafalmadoran in the vicinity, and the white walls of the room transformed into abstract shapes and textures, with colors shading in from below, so that the room was less an antiseptic space but becoming something else, a truly alien room. The confusion of the astronauts was apparently understood and the room transformed again, darkening, round tables rising from the floor, a crimson carpet spreading, heavy drapes dropped from the ceiling along the walls, until the room had become a restaurant.

Major Tom, Captain Nick, and Brez placed their hands, palm down in a peaceful gesture on the long rectangular hovering table, which remained unchanged. The table lengthened, so that Dr. Leonard and Dr. Lex walked up and also placed their hands on the table, but Peg stood where she was, because she recognized that the restaurant they were in was Fundue, and she was shocked. She supposed this was meant to make them more comfortable, but it was unsettling. The other astronauts were made cautious by this obvious show of technological prowess, but for Peg it reminded her of her date with Brian Clark and she felt vulnerable.

The circle on the wall became solid blue and a large nozzle descended from the ceiling. Two Trafalmadorans encased in plastic shells that were shaped like the Launchability spacesuits, one green and the other violet, came into the room with the gate of lumbering robots, and they carried a third empty human-shaped shell between them, also shaped like a Launchability spacesuit, this one a see-thru white. They unscrewed the top of the shell, placed it under the nozzle, and a gray gelatinous goo that was apparently Agent White, poured inside. Agent White reoriented himself inside the shell, so his brains and eyes floated up to the top, and the two who had carried in his shell screwed the top on. He stumbled forward, penetrated the air membrane, and he stopped in front of Peg.

"This is Agent White," Dr. Lex said.

Peg was also sure of this.

The one who had spoken, who stood over by the blue circle on the wall, and who still oozed out of the top of his own plastic shell, raised his plastic-shelled arm at Agent White, and said, "For youuuuuuuu," drawing out the last syllable as he continued to jiggle, as if unable to stop.

"He said," Dr. Lex said.

But Captain Nick shouted, "Shut up, Lex! We know what it said."

Peg and Agent White faced each other. His orange eyes blinked and he seemed melancholy, squished inside his plastic container. He looked like he needed help. He looked like he wanted to say something to her, but was afraid to in the presence of his compatriots.

The one who oozed out of the top of his plastic shell jiggled again and said, "White cook feast."

"Aren't we going to Mars?" Peg said. She sounded disappointed. She'd recently had her first date in seven years and wasn't in any hurry to do that again.

Agent White shrugged his plastic shoulders, which required significant effort from his gelatinous body inside the shell, all the while never taking his sad eyes off her. Then he turned and walked to the end of the room where he stepped through another membrane and was gone.

"He's going to cook for us," Dr. Lex said, and Captain Nick didn't say anything. Dr. Leonard turned his head, concerned, but none of them lifted their hands from the long table. He was afraid to say it, but eating food prepared by extra-terrestrials presented a significant contagion threat.

The open-topped Trafalmadoran said, "Happy giving!" The others came over and screwed his top back on. Human-shaped Trafalmadorans went in and out of the membrane in the back of the room to set the tables with plates, silverware, fondue pots, and lit Sterno lamps.

"They're making fondue," Dr. Lex said. "It's a peace offering."

"Happy giving," Major Tom said to no one in particular.

"I could use a drink," Brez said.

"I brought MREs," Nick said. "We could eat those."

"We're going to eat the fondue," Dr. Lex said.

"Fucking Swiss Martians," Tom said.

"Agent White followed me to a fondue restaurant back on Earth," Peg said.

"You made contact?" Dr. Lex said. "I'm supposed to be the one who makes contact."

"It was weird," Peg said.

"Not *this* weird," Dr. Leonard said.

"They're trying to be nice," Peg said. "We should eat it."

"That's how the Buddha died," Dr. Leonard said.

"What?"

"Findable it."

Tom said, "I'm with dimples. Let's just eat it."

The activity of the Trafalmadoran waiters slowed and they all left the room. After some time, a long plank floated across the room with a row of Trafalmadorans no longer encased in anything but they were lined up on the plank as piles of goo. The plank levitated over to their side of the long table. Trafalmadoran waiters in human-shaped plastic shells placed fondue pots down along the middle of the table, so the air membrane separated the pots, and it was clear the astronauts and Trafalmadorans would be sharing from these pots. As far as peace offerings went, sharing the same melted cheeses and chocolates was about as intimate as it could get between species, and despite the strangeness, the astronauts were all self-conscious of the weight of history.

"Are we taping this?" Brez said.

"Cameras are in our suits," Nick said, and they'd left the suits back in the capsule.

"I've got this," Dr. Leonard said, and he nodded toward the bio-sensor in his hand that was also a video camera.

"Unless that thing's HD," Nick said, "no one's believing any of this."

"If it is HD," Brez said, "they'll think we animated them with CGI."

The Jell-O creatures on the long floating plank jiggled and said, "Happy giving! Happy giving!"

The nozzle in the ceiling came toward them until it hovered above the table and it lowered to fill each of the fondue pots one at a time. There were several shades of steaming fondue in the pots in the middle of the long table, bright colors and dark colors not at all like Earth fondue.

"Smells good," Tom said.

"It does," Nick agreed.

Platters were brought over with cubed slices of bread, cheese rectangles, apple slices, and whole strawberries.

"Where did they get all this?" Dr. Leonard said.

"Happy giving!" Brez said, and he raised a piece of bread with a fondue spear, eager to be the first to partake of their offering.

Brez dipped his chunk of bread into the steaming sauce, lifted it out, put it in his mouth, chewed, swallowed, smiled, and said, "It's delicious!"

This pleased the Trafalmadorans to no end, and soon everyone was feasting. The Jell-O creatures rose up from their bench as streams of fondue shot out of the pots with the aid of some kind of artificial gravity, to be subsumed into their Jell-O bodies. They didn't need fondue spears or bread or apples, and they only seemed interested in the piping hot sauces.

"I hope," Brez said to them, "that our peaceful negotiations will include an exchange of technology," but none of them said anything. None of them spoke at all. They ate and ate. And Brez added, "Margaret here is a cultural specialist. Any questions you have about how we live on Earth, she can probably answer."

Peg blushed. And while she had eaten a few bites of the stuff it was nowhere near as good as what she'd had with Brian Clark at Fundue. She mostly pretended to eat, so as not to offend, dipping the same strawberry into the same pot over and over. She was still unsettled by the exchange with Agent White, who hadn't come back out to join them, at least as far as she could tell. And she wasn't about to ask again. She didn't like the way they had treated him. He seemed as ordinary and unexceptional in his own society as she was in hers.

Dr. Lex removed a folded piece of paper from a zippered pocket in his jumpsuit and he read to them: "On this historic day, we meet in peaceful harmony, as representatives of our planets. May we work together to promote goodwill throughout the galaxy." He looked over at Dr. Leonard's camera to make sure Leonard got him on tape. Then he folded up the paper and put it back in his pocket, satisfied with himself.

The other astronauts looked over at Peg as if they expected

her to say something too. She pretended like she didn't notice and focused on dipping her strawberry in the fondue pot until they stopped looking at her and went back to eating.

"This is really delicious," Brez said.

"It's like a curried stew," Dr. Leonard said.

"A very rich sauce," Captain Nick agreed.

"I want to thank our hosts," Brez said and he raised his spear, which had something on it that wasn't recognizable as bread or cheese or fruit.

Peg poked around in the fondue pot and dabbed at a large orange morsel that floated in the sauce, rolled over, and stared back at her with the same forlorn look that Agent White had given her. So he *was* here with them at the table, she realized. He had been poured into the pots and they were eating him. *She* had eaten him. His orange eye was in the fondue pot and staring back at her.

She gagged involuntarily, which drew attention, and suddenly all the orange eyes on the bench across from her were on her. The astronauts looked over at her too.

Peg held her hand at her throat and pretended to cough. "Went down the wrong pipe," she said. "But I'm fine."

So they went back to eating, which for Peg was a monstrous affair. There was chewing and slurping, lips smacking, the occasional muffled burp. In the other fondue pots she recognized other pieces of Agent White floating, and she decided she couldn't just let the other astronauts continue to gulp him down, but she had to say something.

"This has been fun," she said. "But we do have a schedule. We've got a year to get to Mars and every minute is accounted for. Don't we have another live TV appearance soon?"

Brez was in a trance of eating, but he looked up and thought about what Peg had asked. "No," he said. "We don't go on TV for another ten hours."

"I think it's very soon, actually," Peg said. "Thank you all for all of this. It was wonderful. But we really do have to be getting back."

Peg's attempt to salvage the last of Agent White was in vain as everyone around her scooped out the bottoms of the fondue pots. Dr. Leonard even rubbed his belly with satiated pleasure.

Peg said, "Can we go, please?"

"That friend of yours is a very good cook," Dr. Lex said, and they all sat there a while with nothing else to say, especially since none of the Trafalmadorans spoke. Eventually, after an uncomfortably long silence, the astronauts got up from the table. They slowly backed away from it. And once they had left the large room, they turned and ran back down the elliptical hall. Then they climbed, one by one, back into the chute that connected them to their ship. They crawled along its length, with heaviness in their guts, though they were once again weightless.

When they were in the command capsule, Peg said, "We ate one of them. They fed us Agent White."

"Nonsense," Dr. Leonard said, and they all seemed to agree with his assessment.

They had seen what the Trafalmadorans looked like, and hence assumed what they must taste like. While the food in the heated pots wasn't exactly fondue, it did taste good.

"Play back the footage," Peg said to Dr. Leonard.

He connected his handheld device to a computer dock with a cord, and played back his recording on one of the screens. They all watched, pleased with how they would appear decades hence, in this historic moment, even if NASA chose to classify the film and lock it away in a vault. They had made contact, and they looked stately as they did so.

"There!" Peg said and she pointed as chunks of a Trafalmadoran poured out of the nozzle that dangled from the ceiling and into a fondue pot.

"I don't know," Dr. Lex said.

"That *does* look like something," Captain Nick said.

"Play that again," Major Tom said.

Peg pointed out an orange eye poured into the pot in front of her, she pointed out identifiable organs that were slurped up by the living Trafalmadorans seated on their bench, and she pointed out the Trafalmadoran heart that Brez held up on his fondue spear as he declared it delicious.

"Okay, maybe," Dr. Leonard said.

"We're getting an exchange of technology," Brez said.

"And a ferry ride to Mars," Major Tom said.

"We ate Agent White," Peg said. "And he may have been weird. I may not have known him that well. But he was a person."

"Not a human person," Dr. Lex said.

"But a person," Peg said.

"He was thoroughly cooked," Dr. Leonard said. "Probably not a health risk."

"You really think that's what we ate?" Captain Nick said.

The film of them at the Happy Giving feast played in a slowed down loop, and now that Peg had pointed out what she knew, there was no way to unsee the gory facts of the meal. The Trafalmadorans were delighted to eat one of their own, and so were the astronauts of the Vulture XIII.

"I think she's right," Major Tom said.

"Let's get our suits on," Brez said.

"I won't be able to sleep," Captain Nick said. "Y'all get some shut-eye and I'll keep watch."

In their suits, Brez and Nick and Tom went into the air lock and they disconnected the long chute that had provided entry inside the enormous Trafalmadoran ship. And as the long coiled tongue floated away they felt a little better about their isolation in the belly of the spaceship. They could wait it out without contact and maybe even brave the Van Allen Belts on their way back. They weren't exactly in control of their destiny, but they didn't trust their hosts anymore, now that they understood what they were capable of.

3

For days they waited for the bay doors to open, so they might return to the mission at hand. What was now obvious to the whole crew, except maybe the linguist, was how much miscommunication had occurred, and this put whatever partnership had been agreed upon in question.

"How exactly," Major Tom said to Brez, "was this here cosmic taxi hailed?"

"My relationship with NASA," Brez explained, "is 'need to know'."

"You fly out far enough," Captain Nick said, "and they show up."

"With fondue?" Major Tom said.

"I should have stayed here like you wanted," Nick said.

"Well, *I* ain't going back," Tom said.

"I think we're in agreement," Dr. Leonard said.

"It occurs to me," Dr. Lex said. "That things might go better if we communicate with them in writing."

"He refuses to give up," Tom said.

"We have a lot to gain from a partnership," Brez said.

"We're not exactly on equal footing," Tom said.

"They're curious about us," Brez said. "It's not like we have nothing to offer. There seems to be something they want."

"They want to know about *her*," Dr. Leonard said.

"I for one am glad that alien friend of yours didn't go out with you for pizza," Tom said.

"Or sushi," Nick added.

"He wasn't my friend," Peg said.

"If they offer to cook," Dr. Lex said, "we've got to make sure not to confuse who is cooking with who is cooked."

"Are you blaming *me*?" Peg said.

"You kept asking for White," Lex said.

"You're the one that mashed your hands together," Peg said.

"I merely adapted a common symbol from American Sign Language."

"They're not deaf," Peg said.

"And they're not human," Nick said.

"There's a message coming in," Tom said, reading one of the screens in the control panel. "It's for you," he said to Peg.

Another screen lit up, Tom turned on the cabin cam, and they saw a close-up of Erin at her laptop.

"Hi Mom!" Erin said.

Peg floated over to the screen, and she recognized the Skype layout.

"You Skyped me?" Peg said.

"I didn't know it would work," Erin said. "I just thought I'd try."

"Did NASA patch her through?" Peg said.

"I don't think it was NASA," Tom said.

"Are you having fun?" Erin said.

"We had a long day," Peg admitted.

"But it's worth it, right?" Erin said.

"You remember that guy? He was a Men in Black or something?"

"That FBI agent, or whatever he was?"

"He died."

"How do you know?"

"They told us."

"*Who* did?"

"His...agency."

"Sorry to hear that."

"I know."

"Was he fighting crime?"

"He was more of an ambassador. He worked for the ambassador."

"Explains the accent."

"Anybody else like that ever come around?"

"Hell no."

"You'd tell me?"

"I will now that I know I can call."

"You may not be able to call. These are unusual circumstances."

"Reporters have come around asking about you," Erin said. "Ronny eats it up. He lets them think you're still married sometimes. Drives Cecelia nuts."

"Your dad," Peg said. "You understand he's not the best role model."

"How's life with Mr. Findability?"

"He's right here," Peg said. "They're all right here."

"Oh shit," Erin said. "You put me on speaker phone?"

"That's the only kind."

"How's life with all those hunky guys?"

"We're coworkers," Peg said. "It's not like that."

"You look like you've lost weight."

"I haven't eaten much the past few days," Peg said. "None of us has."

"Space sickness?"

"Kind of."

"NASA didn't pack Dramamine?"

"It's not that simple."

"Well hang in there. All the little girls down here are counting on you."

"Thanks for the reminder."

"Got to go," Erin said. "Ronny wants to go out."

"What time is it there?"

"Way past dinner."

"Don't let them bully you into eating meat."

"I can handle Ronny."

"I guess I meant everyone," Peg said, "not just him."

"Oh," Erin said, as if it hadn't occurred to her. "Really? Everyone?"

"You'll see."

"Okay," Erin said. "Safe travels."

The screen went blank. All of them in the capsule were suddenly missing their families, their girlfriends, and the comforts of Earth. To sleep in a bed. To wake up and fry an egg. To sit in a church and daydream. To drive too fast on the highway. To drink too much beer. To lay on the sofa and watch TV.

"We *do* need to eat," Dr. Leonard said.

"I might take one of them pies," Captain Nick said.

"I like pie," Lex said.

Peg flew back over to one of the storage bins where there were pies and pies and pies.

When the bay doors opened, Major Tom and Captain Nick went over the checklist to prepare to fire the engines. Everyone strapped in, and there were several attempts to re-establish communication with Ground Control.

Captain Nick proceeded to count down, but the capsule and final stage of the Vulcan shot away from the spaceship before the astronauts were ready.

"I didn't say 'zero'!" Captain Nick said.

"I didn't launch!" Major Tom said.

"Engines haven't fired," Nick confirmed.

"But we're moving," Tom said.

"We *are* moving," Nick said.

One of the screens lit up to show a Ground Control operator, who said, "Vulcan, It's good to see you."

"Good to be here," Tom said.

"Although we do not have you on radar."

"We're at cruising velocity," Nick said.

"Is that what I think it is?" Brez said.

They headed straight for a bright red star that grew into something substantial.

"Ground Control," Major Tom said. "We are approaching Mars. Please confirm."

"That explains it," the Ground Control operator said. "You are roughly 325 days ahead of schedule. You are completely off your programmed course. We have you on radar now."

"How's our trajectory?"

"You're going to want to slow down."

"We made alien contact," Brez said. "Diplomatic ties have been established."

The Ground Control operator spoke to someone else on the ground, "Vulcan rendezvous with friendlies was a success."

An old man in an Air Force uniform appeared in the camera, "Vulcan, this is General Golding. Congratulations on your historic adventure. We were a little worried."

"So were we," Nick said.

"We are still operating under assist," Tom said. "Any advice?"

"They've had a lot more experience with this sort of thing," the general said. "You are still three days out. I recommend you let them take you down. Enjoy the ride."

Three days became an incredibly long time. Despite the unpleasantness of what had happened to Agent White, Peg was grateful for the shortcut the Trafalmadorans had afforded them. She didn't know what the arrangement with them was supposed to be but understood any human-Martian relations were prone to inevitable miscommunication. Peg preferred being in the command capsule to the living quarters, because of the window portholes, though the pilot and co-pilot seats were nearly always occupied by the men. There was no piloting or co-piloting being done, but when she'd gotten comfortable in one of the seats nearest the porthole windows, Major Tom or Brez or even Dr. Leonard would rest a hand on her shoulder and say, "I'm on shift. Do you mind?"

She did mind. She was never on shift. She would sit with her Kindle and try to read *Stranger in a Strange Land*, which was pretty good, though dated. Her Kindle was the kind with the keyboard and she'd bought a clip-on LED light, but it sucked too much battery power, so she would tilt the screen to take advantage of the lights on the control panel, and that worked just fine. Then her mind would wander and the LCD black-and-white e-ink screen seemed like such a paltry thing to hold her gaze. All she had to do was look up and there were the heavens, a blanket of brilliant stars. And there in the distance mars was large and round.

When the linguist touched Peg on the shoulder and tried to tell her he was on shift she didn't get up, but said to him, "What was all that down there?"

"I've thought about it," Dr. Lex said. "It was a ritual."

"You had to think to realize that?" Major Tom said, who, as usual, sat in the pilot's seat.

"I mean it can't be a regular practice for them. Only societies under distress resort to sacrificial ritual."

"Whatever we partook of seemed celebrated," Tom said.

"Where is this line of reasoning going?" Peg wanted to know.

"I don't think we're done with them," Dr. Lex said, and he pointed out the window. "Because we're going to land on their planet. Which will be a more celebrated affair."

"Christmas comes after Thanksgiving," Major Tom said.

"What do we get them for Christmas?" Peg said.

"I think the question," Dr. Lex said, "is what do they *want* for Christmas?"

The enormity of Mars, from above the Martian atmosphere, was undeniable. Peg had seen this same view hundreds of times with the animated Launchability Maps GIF that flew from Earth to Mars and back in under a minute.

Nick said to the crew, "You three should get in the Mars Lander and strap in, pronto."

Nick kept an eye on the gauges, while the rest of the crew followed Major Tom, Brez, and Peg into the living quarters where they put on their spacesuits and floated over to the rear lock, which they opened, and climbed one at a time into the LML, where the rest of the crew followed to help strap them in. The rear lock was secured and Nick patiently waited until they were in Mars orbit, and he jettisoned the last stage of the rocket, with the LML tucked inside.

From inside the LML, Tom, Brez, and Peg were sitting much closer to each other and much closer to the porthole windows. Tom fired the engines and the LML set out alone at the edge of space.

"Can you hear me, Vulcan?" Tom said.

"Roger, Lem," Nick said.

"Can you hear me, Huntsville?"

"Begin your descent," the Ground Control operator said.

Captain Nick waited, and when there was no movement of the LML from the Trafalmadorans, he pushed a button in a panel of buttons, and the autopilot replied, "Initiating landing sequence. Prepare to land."

The LML shot forward and tilted so its main thruster and the landing appendages faced Mars. Behind them in the distance was the Trafalmadoran spaceship. Beyond the spaceship was the distant blue star of the Earth. All around was a sea of bright stars, so many that the constellations were drowned out.

"It's a shame about the stars," Brez said.

"What do you mean?" Peg wanted to know.

"We're 325 days ahead of schedule," Brez said. "The stars will get blacked out in all our footage."

"Won't that be fishy?" Peg said.

"Not in the least," Brez said.

When Peg looked out the other porthole window, it was

obvious they were falling quickly, and as many times as they'd rehearsed this landing, she hadn't imagined they'd be going quite so fast. Before she had time to mentally prepare herself, Major Tom and Ground Control were performing for the cameras. They said "check" a lot. They said, "That's an affirmative." They said, "All systems go." And Brez counted down the height of the LML, in meters, from the altimeter. Peg saw mountains, craters, dry riverbeds, pastures of boulders, and so much red sand. She wished they'd given her something to do, because she had the best seat in the house, and it scared the shit out of her. None of them acted like they counted down to the end of their lives, but Peg was perfectly aware that that was very well what the descent of the LML might mean for them.

"The autopilot is making bullshit adjustments," Tom said to Brez. "The autopilot doesn't feel right to me. I'm going to override."

"I wouldn't do that," Brez said, but it was too late and Tom was now flying the LML on manual control with the thruster and the joystick.

"Oh God, oh God, oh God," Peg heard herself say, because things went from bad to worse, and they continued to fall more quickly until Peg was screaming, not unlike her involuntary ululations during their blast off, only then the cabin vibrations were so violent no one else heard. The men all behaved with a detached professionalism while Peg's response was human.

"I don't want to die!" she said, and Brez stopped counting and looked over at her.

"Vulcan, you're coming down too fast," the Ground Control operator confirmed.

"Abort landing," Brez said.

"It's too late for that," Major Tom said.

"This isn't good," Brez said.

The main thruster was at full throttle but it was not enough. Major Tom tried to increase thrust by pointing the stabilizers down, to no effect. Then they stopped as if an invisible hand had caught them, and they landed slowly and softly. The astronauts felt a disorienting jolt, but they understood what had happened, just when they'd thought they were on their own, the extra-terrestrials intercepted and saved their lives.

"We landed," Brez said.

"*They* landed *us*," Peg said.

"Huntsville?" Tom said.

"We copy."

"Vulcan has landed."

4

When the hatch of the LML was opened, the chamber was already depressurized and there was very little gas exchange. Peg was there on the ladder looking up into the Martian sky at dusk. The end of day was selected for continued visibility and a lesser chance of a dust storm. High above, in the dark orange sky, there was a hint of blue and white ice clouds that looked like the wispy cirro-stratus clouds of Earth. The sky was too familiar and Peg, despite her excitement, because of all she'd been through at Area 51 and her status as a hoax believer, couldn't help but wonder if NASA and the Air Force generals faked the Trafalmadorans as a way of skipping out on the two-year wait and of plopping them back down in some barren cold Earth desert.

She climbed up the rungs and looked out. There were no power lines, no birds. There was no litter. She snapped a photo from her chest-mounted camera, and she lifted herself out of the capsule and down the ladder. She took her time, aware that puncturing her spacesuit would lead to a quick demise, and she savored the moment, which, with each rung of the ladder, she recognized as the real deal. This was Mars. Peg Myers was about to land her space boots on the surface of Mars.

Brez lifted himself out of the capsule and he leaned over to photograph her with his chest-mounted camera, an incredible view of this historic moment from number two. Peg looked back at him and paused to smile, then she realized she was behind the mirrored visor of her space helmet and no one would ever know what she looked like right before her big moment.

She remembered that the ladder would stop short of the surface and that the last step was a doozy.

"Huntsville, can you hear me?" she said.

There was an unexpectedly long delay, but she heard the Ground Control operator, who said, "Roger, Captain Myers."

"I might as well jump."

"That's it?" she heard. It wasn't the Ground Control operator talking, but she heard someone else in the control room remark on her choice of words. "Is she quoting David Lee Roth?"

"I believe she is."

The radio delay allowed her to take her time.

"Go ahead, Captain Myers. Everyone here on Earth is rooting for you."

She let go of the ladder and planted her feet on the red planet.

"I did it!"

"She's standing on Mars," Brez said. He descended the ladder and was soon next to her. He delivered his line, "We are launching into a new era!"

And then Major Tom came down and said, "From Earth to Mars! And from Mars into the future!"

They had a lot to do before the sun went down, with the planting of the flag and posing for each other. Peg was soon bored of them, these men who had memorized their lines and who would perform their stupid Masonic ritual before they went back into the LML. She'd seen it in the script and the mission log. Every pound of supplies had to be accounted for and here they'd brought a golden trowel. Peg wandered away from them and she walked out onto the surface on her own. Her shadow was long and she looked out toward the horizon that seemed nearer than possible. She felt like she was on the set, though there was no one but the three of them out there.

Except there were others. There sitting on a rock was a

Trafalmadoran with no hard plastic shell and it's Jell-O body seemed taller and more nimble in the Martian atmosphere. The fellow appeared to be at home and looked back at her with orange eyes. Peg waved and chose not to snap a photo. She walked back to the LML. She passed the flag without saluting, and her crewmates were doing their thing with their stupid golden trowel. She climbed back up the ladder and into the LML, though there was still another twenty minutes of daylight. She wasn't going to be able to get out of her suit alone, and she didn't want to have to deal with them. She could hear them over the radio as they talked about her.

"What's up with her?" Major Tom said.

"Women," Brez said.

Peg Myers had never been to a foreign country, let alone another continent. She had a feeling she would long to stand on Mars again once they'd left, that she hadn't quite processed the experience of walking on this soil so very far away, and that later, in her memory, she would construct a beautiful Romantic landscape, with rust mountains and pink ice clouds at dusk. She thought how foolish it would be for young girls to look up to her because she had put on a costume and had walked around. She would have bags of mail waiting for her when she got back. She had never really thought of herself as someone strangers might write to, but that was who she would become. Children would dress up as her for Halloween. She would be made into action figures, probably even Barbies. They were going to give her a medal. They would ask her questions on TV shows, and she was going to have to have answers: what was it like, were you afraid, did you get bored, did you pray, did you all get along, how did it feel to be standing there on Mars?

The hoax believers were going to pick over every detail of the footage and she would want to scream at them: "I'm one of you! I thought we were faking it too but we went there! I walked on Mars! It looks fishy, we had some help, but I did it! We made first contact with alien travelers and they gave us a ride. We met them, we talked with them, we unknowingly chewed up and swallowed one of them! But we really did go to Mars!"

Peg was going to have to live the rest of her life without being able to say this, and it would gnaw at her. She realized she was depressed because she was mourning the loss of a friend. She hadn't known him well, but he had reached out to her for some reason and now Agent White was gone. She wasn't able to fully enjoy this amazing experience because of her guilt over his demise. She felt stupid for not having known better. She'd eaten him and it was awful. How were Brez and Tom and the others able to carry on like it was nothing? She didn't want to wish them ill, but she believed in Karma and felt that lack of remorse on the part of the crew would come back and bite them. Their primary emotion during all of that was self-preservation, without a thought for Agent White. What had he been through in those last moments? He'd been put into a dispenser and poured into fondue pots. *The horror.* Peg was crying and she was grateful she was in half-gravity, because in the command capsule, in zero-g, her tears could cause an irreversible mess.

During the Martian night, Peg had calmed down and she felt camaraderie with her crewmates. They rested in sleeping bags while cameras rolled and Captain Nick flew over every two hours. With just the three of them, they couldn't take shifts like on Vulcan. They would all be needed on expedition, and so their sleep was important. Of course, they were like kids on a camp out, and these particular Boy Scouts had a girl with them.

"I don't care about your movie for your Mason friends," Peg said, "but what I don't get is why women aren't allowed to join."

"The golden trowel was simply a nod to the powerful," Brez said.

"Powerful *men*," she said. "Powerful women would tell you a golden trowel was stupid."

Brez climbed out of his sleeping bag, he opened a cabinet, and he retrieved three Thermos-shaped canisters. "We landed on Mars today. Let's drink beer."

"That's beer?" Tom said.

"It's very expensive," Brez said, "when you factor in the cost of payload."

"I like Miller." Tom said.

"We'll start with the pilsner," Brez said.

He took a plastic bag with two nozzles, unscrewed the top of the metal canister, fastened it to one of the nozzles, and poured the beer into the bag. There was jostling of the liquid and the bag filled with gas and foam, some of which Brez released through the second nozzle.

"Smells skunky," Tom said.

"It will be good," Brez said. He lifted the bag and took a swig from the nozzle at the bottom. "To Mars!"

He passed the bag to Peg, who also took a swallow, "To Mars!"

Major Tom took the bag and drank. "Let's get buzzed!"

"To the first woman..." Brez began, but he corrected himself. "To the first *person* on Mars!"

"I stepped off the ladder like one whole minute before you did," she said.

"All the difference," Brez said.

In the monitors of the night vision cameras that pointed at the horizon, they watched as a Trafalmadoran approached. It lifted up and slid along the surface, or maybe floated above the dirt, with several appendages jutting forward from the chest, one appendage holding something rectangular. The Trafalmadoran set what looked like a tri-folded leaflet on the ground in front of the ladder, and it used this same appendage to knock on one of the legs of the LML, which made a distinct repeated *tong, tong, tong* inside the capsule. Then the fellow turned and scooted away.

"One of us has to go get that," Major Tom said.

"Don't we have one of those Mars rovers?" Peg said.

"They move slower than turtles," Tom said. "Booting it up would take forever."

"I'll go," Brez said, but no one got up until the first bag of beer was finished, because opening the door meant all of them would have to put on their suits. They recognized that they'd been given a note by an alien civilization, which was of urgent importance, but all they wanted to do was stay in their sleeping bags and drink beer. They did get up, to help each other put on the suits, and Nick and Peg waited while Brez climbed down to retrieve what appeared to be a folded piece of paper.

Once Brez was back in the capsule and the door was sealed, he said, "Near as I can tell, this is a take-out menu."

"Let me see," Peg said. As a single mother with a teenager she considered herself something of an expert on take-out. The folded sheet was a paper-plastic blend, like a laminated sheet that had been printed on blue construction paper with a home computer and color printer. There were pictures of entrees, which weren't well represented because the ink blended with the blue paper. The copy was written in Trafalmadoran scribbles and hieroglyphs, which weren't arranged in rows, but in clusters, or small huddles, with the occasional English word here and there, "meat" the word that popped up most frequently.

Peg looked at the pictures and did her best to translate: "There's meat sandwiches, meat pasta with meatballs, stir-fry meat, meat dumplings, meat pizza, meat Wellington, and plain old meat."

Peg was no linguist, but she remembered Shirt had told her 'meat' was the Trafalmadoran word for 'human,' and in the blobs of hieroglyphs and squiggles, the word 'meat' was cleanly typed, always near a hieroglyph that looked like a gingerbread person.

"Huntsville," Peg said, "We've got a problem."

A blip on the radar map let them know the command capsule was passing overhead. They were on the far side of Mars and in radio silence. Everyone except one of them in the command capsule was supposed to be asleep. Major Tom buzzed in on channel two.

"Nick," Tom said, "Can you wake up the linguist?"

"What is it?" Captain Nick wanted to know.

"I'm going to give it to you straight," Tom said. "We got a note from the Martians. We *ate* one of them. And as far as we can tell, they expect the same in return."

"We have to eat another Martian?" Nick said.

"No," Tom said, "they want to eat one of *us*."

"You sure?" Nick said.

"Wake up the linguist."

"Have you talked to Huntsville?"

"We may want to keep this to ourselves."

Peg said to Dr. Lex when he came on the radio, "At Area 51, Shirt told us the Martian word for us was 'meat'."

"It's a more nuanced construction," Dr. Lex said, "but yes, this is one translation."

"Nobody told *me* that," Brez said.

"Shirt explained it away."

"We all explained it away," Dr. Lex said. "I would need to see the context to better understand the meaning."

A progress bar at the bottom of one of the computer screens let them watch as a digital photo of the menu transmitted up to the command capsule.

"Well, that's not ambiguous," Dr. Lex said.

"They set this outside the door of the lander."

Tom got back on the radio and said, "We talk this out once we get back off the rock."

"Someone volunteers?" Nick said.

"Nobody dies," Tom said. "We talk about it later."

Brez filled the beer bag with hefeweizen and they drank it. Then they drank the pale ale. They'd been on a lean diet, the cabin of the LML wasn't pressurized to sea level, and the beer made them feel better about dozing off on this frontier planet of cannibals.

Peg was up before the other astronauts, because of a scheduled TV appearance. She hoped to have her morning constitutional in private, since the process was a little more difficult for her. She never felt the momentum of sexism in the sciences more than when she relieved herself in space. The argument against sexism was that there were real differences between men and women, which was obvious to her, since the urine receptacle was designed for the insertion of a male body part as integral to the system's functionality. She kept a dry towel and a cleansing gel at the ready. There were certain unavoidable smells in the living quarters of the Vulcan, but here in the LML there was so little space to move about, and far less air to dilute aromas. She wished the Launchability engineers had thought to hang up a few of those pine-scented air fresheners from an auto supply store. The engineers concentrated their energies on the mechanics of the astronauts being able to dump their waste onto the surface underneath the LML, and it was the small comforts they hadn't considered. She was a hundred million miles away, and she missed the simplicity and familiarity of toilet paper. Out here she was constantly reminded that she was in a hostile and deadly environment. She didn't like dumping excrement onto the surface of the planet via the waste management system—it seemed disrespectful, or crude—but she had no choice.

When she was suited up, she saw in the monitors that there were Trafalmadorans out there, and she was terribly embarrassed. She reached the point where she needed assistance with her spacesuit, so she went ahead and roused Brez and Major Tom. A coincidence of Mars was that the length of a day was a little over twenty-four hours, which made adjusting to night and day on the planet relatively easy for them. Except the men were obviously tired from all they'd been through, and hung over. She was more insistent as she shook them awake, anxious about meeting the Trafalmadorans again, but also not wanting to keep them waiting.

Brez opened his eyes, happy to see her, then he remembered where he was, and their situation. They were on Mars. They were meat.

He helped her get the rest of her suit on. The two men suited up and promised to come out after talking to the cameras inside the cabin, which NASA would also want Peg to do, but once the men were safely pressurized in their spacesuits, she opened the port door and climbed out.

There were six Martians who watched from not far off. The menu was in her suit pocket, and after some difficulty getting hold of the folded laminated paper with her space gloves, she walked over to them and held out the menu, as if to give it back. When none of them reached for it, she set the folded pamphlet on the surface of the planet.

"I'm a vegetarian," Peg said. This evolution in her eating wasn't intentional, but in her stubborn refusal to eat anything but pie, the declaration was true.

They stared back, unfamiliar with the word. Surely, they had their own linguist, but she couldn't distinguish who among them would best understand her.

"I only eat pie."

There was such a thing as meat pie, of course, but she wasn't about to tell them this.

Pie was a word they understood. They looked at each other and they raised their appendages in appreciation. They locked appendages to form a kind of conga line. They surrounded her in a circle and danced around her.

"Pie!" she said, delighted that this word had made them happy.

"Peg!" Brez said to her over the radio. "What's going on out there? We're seeing a lot of activity on the surface."

"They love pie!" Peg said.

"Hang on," Brez said and he switched frequencies to talk with the crew of the Vulcan command capsule. He spoke to Peg again to tell her what the linguist had said: "Dr. Lex believes you've communicated one of the central identifiers of intelligence. You may have pleaded for our lives!"

"Agent White was intelligent," Peg said. Brez had nothing to say to that, so Peg asked, "How does eating pie make me intelligent?"

"Not pie," Brez said, "but pi."

"Huh?"

"The ratio of the radius of a circle to the circumference of the circle. It's a universal truth and an acknowledgment that you are intelligent meat."

"I was trying to tell them I don't eat meat," Peg said. "They didn't seem to understand anything I said until I mentioned pie."

Long after Peg had grown tired of them dancing around her, the Martians lifted up and floated away, until like stray balloons, they looked like dots in the sky. The rest of the day would be walking around and commenting on the experience for the video record: conducting geological surveys and taking soil samples to test for microbes. On the whole, Mars was really gorgeous, a view for a landscape painter. But up close, and if taken as the sum of isolated localities, Mars was washed out and monotonous. The day wore on and the day heated up. Peg was joined by her colleagues, who played around with a Whiffle Ball and plastic bat, which seemed a repeat of Alan Shepard golfing on the moon, and she wondered what else they'd brought: bocce balls, a tennis racquet, a football? Though when she thought about it, the Whiffle Ball game seemed about right. Playing with a hollow plastic ball and plastic bat was the height of nerdist athletics, and she imagined young Brez wearing out dirt patches in his Russian father's proud American lawn, a skinny kid with grass stains on his jeans. The suits were too stiff for them to be able to hold the plastic bat in both hands. Major Tom pitched underhand, so the ball lobbed slowly at Brez, and a couple of times his bat connected.

"A home run!" Brez shouted, and he pretended to run around bases as he skipped through the red dust in his pressurized suit.

Peg walked over to where the ball landed. She picked it up and put it in the thigh pocket of her suit. She hadn't come up with anything she could leave for Erin that would survive a dust storm on Mars, but she could give this ball to Erin, the Whiffle Ball that Maxim Brez had sent into the upper decks, aided by a thin atmosphere and half gravity.

On the third day, the astronauts wandered around and picked up rocks. They took even more soil samples. They set up a seismograph and a laser reflector. They gazed longingly at the blue star of Earth in the rusty red sunset sky, on this the last day. They had come this far and would have to go back. All they'd seen was etched forever into memory, sights they weren't likely to see with their own eyes ever again. And there was the unspoken recognition that these could be their last days, that they would never see any Earth sunsets either. They waxed romantic about space travel and about the undeniable beauty of the cosmos, of the stars and our neighboring worlds. They didn't know how much of what they said NASA would choose to air, but they talked into their helmet mics as if they addressed the world, to declare that we were not alone. They set two small Mars rovers in the dirt, turned them on, pointed them in opposite directions, and left them to snail away.

Like terrible campers they threw out all of their trash onto the surface, and shortly after sunset, when there was still enough residual light on camera to capture their liftoff, they strapped in and prepared to leave for good.

"Can we just go?" Peg said. "Do we really have to count it down?"

"I think we do have to count it down," Brez said.

"We're supposed to count it down," Major Tom confirmed.

"We could have been gone by now," Peg said.

Brez counted down as Major Tom held his hand over the big red button, Tom pushed the button, the main thruster ignited, and they lifted off of the planet.

When the LML was docked with the command module and the airlock opened, Peg was overwhelmed by the reunion with her crewmates. They were six again, and while they had a daunting task ahead, she felt closer to home. And she'd never wanted to be home more than she did after having walked on Mars.

They ejected the LML and began their return trajectory, the cramped metal hull she'd lived in with Brez and Major Tom floated away, and she felt a pang of sadness. The LML had been her only home on Mars, and it kept her alive. Looking at it head-on, the LML appeared to have an expressionless face, with porthole windows for eyes.

"Is there something," Peg said to Dr. Leonard, unsure of the polite phrasing, "you can give me to put me in a better mood?"

"Uppers?" he said, pleased to be of assistance.

"Not uppers," Peg said. "But mood elevators? Umm?"

Without hesitation, Dr. Leonard said, "Pot?" and he gave her the choice of a synthetic THC pill or, "something of the herbal variety."

"He brought pot?" Major Tom said. "Why am I always the last to know?"

"It's for nausea, space sickness, and appetite," Dr. Leonard

said matter-of-factly. "Though we don't have a lot."

"I asked first," Peg said.

The very real possibility of eating cannabis while looking down on Mars from space suddenly put Peg in a wonderful mood. All the sci-fi heroes Kevin loaded into her Kindle took themselves too seriously. She felt they'd have had a better time of it all with a Dr. Leonard around, especially since she knew about the downtime that was the greater percentage of long-range space travel that the writers tended to skip over.

"I'll have some of that," Dr. Lex said.

"It's a prescription medication," Dr. Leonard said.

"I'm space sick," Dr. Lex said. "Or whatever."

"You'd be projectile vomiting," Dr. Leonard said.

"*She's* not vomiting."

"I think we should all have some," Captain Nick said.

"How much did you bring?" Brez said.

"It's pressed into a concentrate," Dr. Leonard said.

"It's hash?" Major Tom said. "How much?"

"Nine or ten grams."

"That's a ton of hash," Tom said.

"If you smoke it," Nick said. "We can't exactly smoke it."

"No fires," Brez said. "Absolutely not."

"Do you have a vaporizer?" Nick said.

"Yes," Dr. Leonard said. "It's the most effective delivery for patients who can't keep anything down."

"We kept down a Martian," Tom said.

"Which is what I'm saying," Dr. Leonard said. "There doesn't appear to be any *medical necessity*."

"Our only way home," Nick said, "is to negotiate with cannibals who want to eat us."

"How do we agree who gets eaten," Dr. Lex said, "if we can't agree about this?"

"We agree," Tom said. "He's just holding out on us."

"All in favor?" Nick said, and everyone but Dr. Leonard raised a hand, so he turned and pushed off the wall of the capsule to float away into the living quarters. He came back with his doctor's duffle, and he set up the vaporizer to fill a large plastic bag with hash vapor.

They passed the bag around and exhaled into a respirator mask that hung down from the top of the capsule. After the bag of hash vapor went around a few times the crew was all smiles, and they forewent the respirator but blew the thin hash smoke straight into the cabin air.

"What do you know about them?" Peg asked Dr. Lex. "You've studied them?"

"Their language," he said.

"There were no punches and kicks," she said.

"No," Dr. Lex said, "I made that up."

"It wasn't very practical," Peg said. "How could you bring someone a cup of coffee and also ask if they wanted sugar?"

"Telepathy doesn't film," Nick said.

"I had to come up with something," Dr. Lex agreed.

"What else do you know about them?" Brez said.

"Did you suspect they might want to eat us?" Tom said.

"It was in their language," Dr. Lex said, "but we assumed the meanings were embedded from an earlier age, and that their culture had evolved."

"We're just as barbaric," Brez said.

"*Just as?*" Tom said.

"Oh, here we go," Nick said.

"What did *you* know about them?" Dr. Leonard asked Brez.

"For us," Brez said, "the focus was always on a technology exchange."

"What do you hope to get?" Dr. Leonard said.

"They can live in other dimensions," Brez said. "They are visitors and they don't stay long because our three-dimensional world is uncomfortable for them. That's why we meet in space."

"What have they got?"

"If we had multi-dimensional computer chips," Brez said, "it would break new ground."

"What do we do?" Peg said.

"I'm going to assume there are no volunteers," Tom said.

"I volunteer," Dr. Lex said. "The world doesn't need another language specialist. I'm not doing anyone any good."

"Don't say that," Peg said.

"He's using reverse psychology," Dr. Leonard said. "He knows he's the least valuable and he's trying to make it a strength."

"What about you?" Dr. Lex said. "We don't really need a physician around, do we?"

"Oh sure," Dr. Leonard said, "smoke all my hash and then give me up to them."

"We do need a pilot," Major Tom said.

"Unless there's a co-pilot," Captain Nick said.

"This is getting us nowhere," Brez said. "All our lives are valuable."

"Easy for the billionaire to say," Tom said.

"He's a really good boss," Peg said in Brez's defense.

"He contributes a lot to charity," Nick said. "Like *a lot*."

"What happens if you don't come home?" Tom said to Brez. "Does your girlfriend get it?"

"That's kind of a rude question," Peg said.

"I want to know," Tom said.

"It's okay," Brez said. "It's public knowledge. If I die everything goes into a trust, and my cut of the Findability money will work, in perpetuity, for the betterment of humanity."

"You're giving it away?" Tom said.

"Most of it, yes," he said.

"That settles it," Tom said. "I say he goes. For the benefit of humanity."

"I paid for all of this," Brez said. "How are you going to explain to the world what happened? I'm the one they'll want to interview after the splash down."

The living quarters grew quiet as they waited for Peg to say something in her own defense. She pretended not to notice. Then, when the tension became too much, she said, "I'm not volunteering."

"No one suggested you should," Brez said.

"I'm suggesting she should," Dr. Lex said.

"She's a..." Nick said.

"He's right," Tom said.

"I'm a *what*?" Peg said.

"Well," Nick said, "you know."

"Say it," Peg said.

"Well, we wouldn't be very gentlemanly if we..." Tom said.

"Because I'm a *woman*?"

"We're not sexist," Brez said. "But how manly would we look if we gave you up?"

"So your letting me be the first person on Mars was basically the equivalent of holding the door open for me?"

"I wouldn't put it like that," Brez said.

"But there is no way we are going to eat you," Nick said.

"*I'd* eat her," Dr. Lex said.

"Thank you, doctor," Peg said. "He's the only one on my side in all this."

"I'd eat you," Dr. Leonard said, "if there was a medical necessity."

"If you were starving?" Peg said.

"If we were starving and you also died of natural and noncontagious causes."

"Sounds pretty unlikely," Tom said.

"He's hedging," Nick said.

"There are six of us and no one wants to die," Tom said.

"You all," Dr. Lex said, "are the ones who said you would take this journey even if there was no return trip."

"We *did* say that," Nick said.

"*I* didn't say that," Peg qualified.

"I don't see what that has to do with anything," Tom said. "*I am not afraid to die* is not the same as *I volunteer to die.*"

"I thought it was the same," Dr. Lex said.

"You're taking it out of context," Tom said.

"What about the pi thing?" Nick said. "You told us she convinced them we were intelligent."

"Probably only for the time being," Dr. Lex said. "I mean we're out here on a spaceship. We're obviously intelligent."

"You don't have to know about pi to build a spaceship," Tom offered.

"You probably do," Brez said.

"We draw straws?" Dr. Leonard said.

"Russian roulette?" Tom said.

"That's offensive," Brez said.

"He's Russian," Peg clarified.

"Why is that offensive?" Tom said.

"Never mind," Brez said. "We try to talk them out of it. And if that doesn't work, we let *them* decide."

"The menu," Nick said. "If it was an Earth restaurant. Just the food itself. It looks good."

5

When it was time to turn in, Captain Nick stayed on duty while the rest of the crew was encouraged to sleep. The capsule, in the evernight of space, coasted silently toward Earth, with no way of knowing when the mother ship would return. The effect of the hash wearing off fatigued them and helped them fall asleep as they hung weightless in sleeping bags next to spacesuits tethered along the walls with them, like vacant sentinels who watched over their astronauts.

Peg fought the urge to sleep, as Maxim Brez's spacesuit seemed to stare back at her from across the living quarters, which unsettled her. There was a time not too many months ago when she would have been intimidated by Brez, by all he had and all he represented. He looked so helpless there, compared to his spacesuit that remained bulked up, despite being empty and depressurized. She floated in her bag and in the weightless atmosphere of space the arm of Brez's suit slowly rocked back and forth in a way that made it look like the empty suit waved at her. She squirmed her arm out of her sleeping bag and waved back. Everyone else was asleep, all of them wore sleep blinders, since, out of necessity, the lighting of the living quarters was dimmed, though the cabin lights were left on. Peg didn't wear the sleep blinders like the others because she didn't like the feeling of waking up with blackness and no eyes.

When she saw Captain Nick float into the room, she quickly pretended to be asleep like the others. She didn't know why she was so paranoid about him being there, but she didn't want to have to talk to him or to explain herself. It was hard to sleep in space sometimes, with all the excitement, despite her being incredibly tired. She waited a long time after she was certain Captain Nick had left before she opened her eyes again. Brez's suit no longer looked at her but it was on the other side of him and facing the wall, secured. She stared in disbelief and tried to work out whether Captain Nick's floating by could have moved Brez's suit around like that. Or she wondered if Captain Nick secured the suit for him so no one would bump into it floating around like it was. Peg didn't trust Captain Nick and she didn't like not knowing what he'd done. She should have stayed awake and let him know she was awake. Or she should have watched him through squinted eyes. Now the mystery of his appearance in the living quarters in the middle of their sleeping would eat at her. They had good reason not to trust each other after all. They were millions of miles from Earth and they'd been asked to leave someone behind.

An alarm woke them and when they floated out to the command capsule there was Captain Nick in the pilot's seat staring at a flashing red light.

"It's one of our rotational thrusters," he said. "We can do without it if need be, but we might be better off going out there to fix it."

"I'd ask you to suit up," Major Tom said. "But there's no telling how long this repair might take, and your shift has ended. Get some sleep."

"You're going out there?" Nick said.

"Who else could possibly go?"

"I've done a spacewalk," Brez said.

"We've all trained to do a spacewalk," Dr. Leonard said.

"Maybe he should go," Nick said. "Since we'll need a pilot while I'm asleep."

"I'll go suit up," Brez said.

"Don't do it," Peg said, and the weightless air of the command capsule was suddenly thick. They all stared at each other, but Peg only said, "Don't go out there."

"I'm aware it's dangerous," Brez said. "I'll take every precaution."

"He said we didn't need to fix it," Peg said.

"I *want* to go," Brez said.

"He volunteers," Nick said.

Peg said, "Someone else should go. He's too valuable."

"He *wants* to go," Nick said.

"I want to go," Brez repeated.

Peg, the doctor, the linguist, and Captain Nick all went into the living quarters and the air seal was locked. Major Tom and Brez suited up for Brez to go outside the capsule. Captain Nick climbed into his sleeping bag and covered his eyes with the sleep blinders. The rest of the crew watched on the monitor as Brez moved toward the hatch and the capsule depressurized.

Peg stared at Nick, amazed at how quickly he drifted into sleep, and then it was immediately apparent to her that something was wrong. Brez spun around as his suit leaked air. Major Tom climbed up out of his pilot's seat and while at first he appeared to try to help Brez, the thought occurred to Peg that Major Tom kept Brez from re-pressurizing the cabin. He held on to Brez, to keep him from spinning, because the leak in Brez's suit was now visible, a tear on his back near his armpit where a stream of condensed gas shot out furiously.

"He's dying," Peg said, and she noticed the slightest curl of Captain Nick's lips. He was pretending to sleep and trying very hard not to smile.

"Tom is helping him," Dr. Lex said, but that wasn't what was happening at all.

Major Tom opened the capsule door and released Brez, who was propelled into space by the ejecting gasses of his torn suit. On another monitor they all watched as Brez flailed his arms and legs outside the capsule, unable to pull himself back in by the oxygen hose that trailed him. In a matter of seconds, his arms and legs stopped moving and he reached the length of the hose, where his stiff body twirled around in reaction to the jet of air shooting out of his back.

Peg wished she were the one wearing sleep blinders, and she didn't know how she would ever again be able to sleep in the company of these men. She supposed she was saved, so long as she went along with their story, now that the only good man among them had been snuffed like a chicken on Sunday.

"Oh my God!" Dr. Lex said.

"We're going to need you in here, Dr. Leonard!" Major Tom said as he reeled Brez's body back into the capsule by pulling on the air hose. Once Brez was back inside, Tom shut and locked the capsule door, and he re-pressurized the cabin. Like a diver ascending too fast from the bottom of the ocean, in the vacuum of space, the gasses dissolved in Brez's blood would boil. He was surely a mess inside that suit, and Peg didn't want to look, but none of them could look away from the monitor, except Nick, who was still pretending to sleep when Dr. Leonard floated over to him to rouse him.

"There's been an accident," Dr. Leonard told Nick. "I'm afraid Maxim Brez may be dead."

There was nothing the doctor could do, of course, but Peg understood the importance of having the doctor along, since it was the doctor who tended to the body. Brez was put inside a spare suit with the pressure ramped up, which would serve the same purpose as cooling the body, a way of preserving him without freezing him. Brez's torn suit was reassembled, powered up so that the spot could be investigated. There was clearly a rip in his suit and the suit was pushed out into space without a tether, to corkscrew across space forever and to provide the film footage that would come to be associated with the memory of him.

Because of the high pressure inside the new suit where Brez's body lay in state, the arms, legs, and fingers shot straight out, like there was a stick-figure Brez inside the suit, and he was tethered there with his sleeping bag, because it was the best place for him. Which made Peg wish she could wear the sleep blinders more than ever, so she wouldn't have to look at him floating in the spacesuit, except now she didn't dare wear blinders out of a paranoid distrust of the pilot and co-pilot.

She was depressed and upset. She didn't have any heroes anymore. She had seen how Brez was human, even ordinary, but they killed him to save themselves and they didn't measure up to one tenth of what Brez was. Peg remembered the supermodel and she imagined that she would tell the supermodel what she knew. And she wondered what good an exchange of technology would be without a Maxim Brez to interpret and implement the alien knowledge. These pilots were brutes. They were stupid jocks. She might have to wait until they were back on Earth but maybe Leonard and Lex would back her up that the circumstances of Brez's death implicated the pilots. Although if the expectation was that they would eat him, no one was going to talk, and no one would be held accountable. The great Maxim Brez was now meat. He had volunteered up his life and they all owed him for his ingenuity and his courage. The supermodel slept in his spacious house without knowing he was already gone, and the world continued on thuggishly without the countervailing good of Brez's inheritance, with a year or more until the official announcement of his death. Peg hated the way that NASA controlled her story, and that she would be expected to play along. She'd been given a place in history, held up with a growing framework of lies. The circumstance of Brez's death was yet another lie she would have to keep quiet about.

She didn't know how long she'd been in her sleeping bag staring out at Brez's body in the spacesuit with his arms and legs straight out, but she hadn't slept and soon enough Captain Nick stood in front of her to wake her up.

"There's fewer of us," he said. "We're taking longer shifts."

She climbed out of her bag as he climbed into his.

"Everyone else is asleep?" Peg said.

"All you do is keep an eye on the dashboard," Nick said. "Anything lights up, you come get us."

In the pilot's seat Peg looked out at the dark expanse of space. She tried to make sense of all the switches, buttons, and lights of the control panel, some of which were labeled, though the labels gave very little indication of what any particular button or switch might actually do. If all their lives didn't depend on them, she would have tested them, just to see what happened. But then boredom crept in, so she popped open a compartment and took out an iPad. There were no games or books loaded onto it, all the apps scientific in nature and related to their mission. As impossible as it seemed she saw an active wifi network, which she joined, and she downloaded the Skype app. She punched in her password and loaded her contacts. She was able to discern from the app that it was the middle of the night in California, with everyone asleep, except she saw that Kevin from Findability was now in her contacts, and he was also currently online. She dialed him up and he answered.

She saw him in his room at home, which was like a larger version of his cubicle, with shelves of action figures and models of spaceships hung from the ceiling. He looked a little haggard, like he'd stayed up all night playing a video game or to bid on a rare collectible on eBay, but he smiled, glad to see her.

"You're calling me from space?" he said. "This is unbelievable."

"It's even more unbelievable than that," Peg said.

"Tell me everything."

"I think aliens are relaying this message," she said. "NASA won't even know we're talking."

"I *knew* it!" Kevin said.

"You did?"

"I suspected."

"Brez is dead," Peg said. "They killed him."

"The aliens?"

"The crew. And now we're going to have to eat him."

"Oh my God, this is juicy," Kevin said.

"It's bad," Peg said. "Really bad."

"I can't even imagine how it came to that. Your book will be amazing."

"NASA's not going to let me write about this."

"I suppose. Are you going to do it?"

"Do what?"

"Eat him."

"Of course not. How could I?"

"I don't know. It's your one chance. Aren't you curious?"

"This is Brez we're talking about here. Even if it wasn't, I couldn't eat a *person.*"

"I guess."

"Could *you?*"

"I wouldn't rule it out."

"Can you tell the supermodel? I think she deserves to know."

"No, no, no. Number one, that chick wouldn't keep her mouth shut. Number two, she wouldn't believe me. Number three, that gets NASA on *my* ass."

"What can NASA do, do you think?"

"It's not so much NASA as the federal government and connected interested parties. People disappear. People commit suicide out of the blue and leave notes with questionable handwriting. People contract fast-acting cancers."

"You're scaring me."

"Don't be scared. Just play it cool."

As if on cue, out of the porthole windows, Peg watched as the UFO mother ship approached.

"They're here," she said. "I got to go."

"Was nice talking," Kevin said. "Don't sweat it. I'll see you in two years?"

"Probably in a few days," Peg said. "They've really speeded things up."

"Oh, that's awesome!" Kevin said. "We'll have a party!"

"I'll have to stay underground."

"I suppose. Skype when you can, okay?"

Peg sat frozen in the pilot's seat as the UFO in the distance came closer and eventually completely filled the view from the porthole windows. Since none of the indicator lights on the dashboard lit up, Peg let the crew sleep.

She pulled up Findability Maps and typed "Vulcan capsule" into the search bar. The animated Earth spun around and the Maps view followed a red line that lifted off of Earth and into space to where the capsule should be on its projected path. She rotated the view and zoomed in on the capsule. The Earth was still there in the background, a large blue ball. They wouldn't have gotten very far on their projected path. Through the portholes of the animated capsule was a rendering of herself and Brez, sitting in the pilot's seats. She took a screen shot and emailed the image to herself. She wished that was how the trip had really gone. She really wanted to believe in the official version of their take off and rendezvous with the planet.

As luck would have it, hers was the last shift before the big reunion with the Martians. She wouldn't be getting any sleep. She could see in the monitor that the men slept soundly and Brez's body was gone. She wouldn't wake the men but decided to take advantage of the rare wifi connection to catch up on Facebook, celebrity gossip, and world events. Then she'd stream a movie from Netflix, something romantic and melancholy that would make her cry. She'd tell the men about the visitors when they woke up.

6

The astronauts and the Trafalmadorans were seated at the two sides of the long levitating table, covered platters between them, with the air membrane splitting the table down the middle. The linguist explained that they would eat, and then the exchange of technology would occur.

The covers were lifted off the platters and in amongst the sauces, the spaghettis, the pizzas, and the casseroles, were recognizable body parts. The men had psyched themselves up for this. They knew it was the true test of their mettle and the last act they would have to perform before they returned to Earth heroes and celebrities. Major Tom was too eager as he plucked a finger from a serving dish and ate it like a chicken wing. Peg stared ahead, her plate empty. The linguist sat up stiffly like he might give a speech, but no one made eye contact with him, so he looked around and nervously waited for the right time to blurt out something about peace between peoples. Dr. Leonard chewed slowly while tears welled up in his eyes. He tried to remain stoic, but he eventually lifted his napkin to dab at the corner of his mouth first, and then to wipe away the moisture from his eyes. Captain Nick ate, but only the fixings. Any recognizable chunks of meat he pushed to the rim of his plate, or he spat discretely into a napkin.

The Trafalmadorans ate with relish. There was no difference between their consumption of Maxim Brez and their ingestion of Agent White. Because they were encased in clear hard shell suits, there were visible and recognizable pieces of Brez suspended in their gelatinous bodies. Peg tried to look on the bright side. Brez had wanted to be a space traveler and this way he was far-flung across the galaxy.

Another dish was carried over by a Trafalmadoran server and placed in the middle of the table. The cover was lifted to reveal Brez's brain, intact but floating in a curried sauce and pickled by something that had turned it pink. The dish was closest to Dr. Leonard who wept openly, his face buried in his napkin. The Trafalmadorans nodded toward their guests to indicate both the importance of the dish and that they wanted the astronauts to try it first. No one went for Brez's brain for an uncomfortable minute, then Peg got up with her clean plate, which pleased the Trafalmadorans who nodded toward her in appreciation of her refined tastes. She had apparently known Brez's brain was coming out and had waited for it. She was not only the one who spoke the language of pi, but the most intelligent and cultured of the astronauts, most obviously their leader.

Peg reached into Brez's pink pickled brain with her hand, she pulled off a large chunk of him, placed it on her plate, went back to sit down, and she ate with a knife and fork as if his brain were a slice of pie. She had no experience with pickled meats, which weren't really very California, but the texture of brain matter and the essences with which the tissues were infused made for a pleasant culinary experience. Peg had resigned not to eat her boss, but here she was presented with his brain, and she wasn't going to pass that up. The other astronauts shot her sideways glances, impressed by her composure, which none of them could match. Once she had finished, she set her silverware down and she wiped her mouth with her napkin. The Trafalmadorans continued to eat while all the astronauts had stopped. Soon enough Brez was eaten and the presentation of the gifts of technology could begin.

What none of the astronauts expected was that each new

device that was brought out, demonstrated, and placed in front of Peg, was for her to try and for her to keep. They saw her as the most worthy and they gave her the offerings. She knew these slight objects contained powers our scientists hadn't yet harnessed, that they were invaluable, and that Brez had hoped to use them for the betterment of humanity and the increased profitability of his company. As the only Findability representative aboard this vast UFO, Peg stepped up to the task. She nodded as the aliens demonstrated the functions of each new device, and she placed each, unceremoniously, into the zippered pockets of her jumpsuit.

She was given a voice translator that had telepathic responsiveness with the notable side effect that pointing the oval device at the linguist rendered him paralyzed, to be moved around as if by remote control with her thoughts, or to make him speak sentences in a flat voice that didn't originate from his own mind.

"I'm a jack ass!" she made him say.

This wasn't funny to anyone except Peg, though the astronauts pretended to laugh because they didn't want her to point it at them next.

There was a food processor, also with telepathic responsiveness, that would combine whatever raw edibles one had with whatever recipe one had in mind. While it wasn't clear what the Martians chucked into the thing for their demonstration, the astronauts understood that this funnel-shaped device, or one like it, was used to turn Brez and Agent White into dinner. Peg had great fun squeezing out a tube of pie in one end of the funnel and watching an actual slice of pie pour out. She had the feeling their interplanetary voyage was going to be greatly sped up with the help of the Martians, otherwise this cone-shaped object would make their long trek far more simpatico. She took the slice of pie and put it back through the food processor, so that it came out noodles. And she put the noodles in to get a peanut butter sandwich, which she put in while holding the empty plastic tube over the small end, and the original pie-goo came out and refilled the plastic tube where it had come from, how Peg preferred to eat these days anyway.

Yet another device with telepathic response was placed in the middle of the table in front of her, and it was obvious to Peg that this telepathy chip, or crystal, or whatever it was in these handhelds was what Brez had been after. What Findability might do with this technological leap, or how it might be integrated with silicon chip technology was unclear to Peg, but she was immediately leery of the ethical implications of handing over such devices to a company that relied on personalized ads for profit, and/or to NASA, which was too closely aligned with the military, despite their official civilian designation.

The last device was rectangular pane of glass that she held up and looked through, and as Peg recalled memories she saw them through the glass in front of her in the large room, like a film made from the progression of her thoughts: from the last looks that Erin's teacher shot at her, disappointed with Peg for taking Erin out of her class; to a naked Brian Clark who was embarrassed and excited to be alone in a hotel room with her after their fondue date; to her mother in a casket, unmistakably gone, but familiar, and Peg even to this day remembering the sound of her voice and never getting out from under her; to the face of the tired gray cop who arrived to escort her to the police station the time she was caught shoplifting, the cop leveling no judgment, even bored with her and the banality of her transgression as he asked her questions and wrote things down.

The device was better and worse than TV, and Peg was too ashamed to show anyone else what she saw. She wondered if they would be able to see what she saw, or if they would only see what their own minds remembered, and she also wondered why, if the Trafalmadorans had this kind of thing, they hadn't used it to better communicate? Could they have avoided eating each other? Were there simpler less destructive gestures that would have been accepted? This rectangular glass wouldn't fit in any of her pockets, but it would fit in one of the iPad cases, so she held on to it, and tried her best to clear her mind so as not to activate it.

There was no sharing of antigravity or artificial gravity devices, and Peg, who had found herself in charge during this negotiation, had no idea what to give them. What would Brez have given them? She realized then, because it was smaller and did fit in her suit pockets, that she had her Kindle with her, and that she could give them that. It was a poor example of the best of our technology, but the value was in what it contained.

She showed them how to turn it on, she demonstrated her password for them, and she pulled up the Merriam-Webster's file that came loaded on the device.

"Here is our language," she said.

They picked up the Kindle and crowded around. If they had been using the Internet, they could have easily found a dictionary there, but maybe they hadn't known about dictionaries. She felt cheap presenting an English-language dictionary as "our language," since she was a representative of the whole human race, but it was all she had, and the Kindle made them happy.

One typed clumsily at the Kindle with thin shell-cased appendages and after a few tries presented what looked like an algebra equation.

The linguist sat up straight, his eyes glossed over, and he said, his voice in a lower register so he was obviously channeling the thoughts of one of the Trafalmadorans: "*Our* language."

Dr. Leonard glanced over at the mathematical equation that was their bonus gift to humanity and said to the astronauts, "I'm not positive, but I think we already have that one."

"Maxim would have known," Major Tom said.

"I'm friends with a mathematician," Peg said. "I could ask."

"We can't exactly reach him," Captain Nick said.

"I've had luck getting through," Peg said.

They took a second look at the Kindle screen, to commit the equation to memory, and they backed away slowly down the long hall until they were out of sight, and they crawled through the tunnel that extended all the way back to their capsule and living quarters.

Once they were settled, Peg got out an iPad and she saw that the wifi was still connected. She pulled up Skype and Brian Clark was online and available. But she didn't call him right away. Instead she looked into the rectangular glass the Martians had given her and she watched scene after scene in the progression of her relationship with Brian Clark: when she was new at Findability and he had befriended her, obviously smitten and physically affected by her near proximity during any interaction with her; she watched as they settled into a friendship routine, with his hopefulness so obvious; then on into his self-fulfilling disappointment as he continued to pine for a Peg who would never feel the same way about him. She decided she couldn't call him, that it would be awkward and confusing for them both. They'd left things at "friends" and he was also sleeping with someone else. She had too often disregarded his feelings, she had taken him for granted, and sometimes she even resented him.

She pulled up Findability and searched for the equation, which didn't appear at first, until she recognized it on one of the worksheets on the website of a high school trigonometry teacher. What the Trafalmadorans had given Peg was the Pythagorean theorem, only written in a less-recognizable and non-standardized form. So it wasn't a gift but a signal of mutual intelligence. Just as she had made reference to pi in her dealings with them, they alluded to an equally important mathematical keystone. Whatever the future of Trafalmadoran-human relations, Peg was optimistic that both races acknowledged and valued intelligence, and if there had been miscommunication during first contact, she took stock in the final gesture of the gift of the Pythagorean theorem. She didn't tell the crew what she'd found, because she was sure that just as she was uplifted by the equation, they'd be disappointed.

7

Outside her house she half-expected to be apprehended, but there was no one there, so she went up to the door and knocked. Cecilia answered, delighted and confused to see her, and she was welcomed back into her own home.

"Mom! Mom! Mom!" Erin said, and they embraced in a long bear hug where neither would let go.

Ronny came into the room, also smiling, but skeptical and suspicious that Peg had made them the subjects of some elaborate reality-TV prank. But no, Peg had been to Mars and back, and she would tell them her story, though they would have to take the truth with them to their graves under the threat of death. She didn't know that was the case. No one had ever told her this directly. But there were things that had happened in the past few weeks she would not be allowed to reveal, and having revealed them, she had now put this onus onto her family.

In the morning, she hadn't planned on it, but with nothing else to do, and with Erin off at the public school all day, Peg put on a navy blue suit with sensible flats, got in her Corolla, and drove to work. She went to Building Eleven, where there were no longer any food courts, and the moving walkways were empty. The Findability Channel didn't play on the flat screens but CNN Financial was omnipresent. There were very few cubicles left on her floor, many of them empty. The changes had already been implemented.

She walked over to Kevin's cubicle and hardly recognized him. He was there in a suit, with a few personal items on his shelves but no Star Wars dioramas, no action figures, no graphic novels. His Bowflex was gone. He kept his back to Peg and he was busy typing.

"I did it," she said.

He paused and turned slowly in his chair. He couldn't believe she was there. He looked around to see if anyone else noticed her, but there was hardly anyone on the floor now, with Peg's old cube one of the ones that had been cleared out.

"I'm a science fiction hero," she said.

"How are you even here?" he whispered.

"You'll have to become an expert on me."

"I don't get to do that anymore," Kevin said, and Peg felt bad. He looked up at her from where he sat, uncomfortable in his suit, bald spots on the top of his head. There was no longer the atmosphere where he felt he could wear a t-shirt to work.

"I walked on Mars," Peg said. "I met aliens. We hitched a ride inside a purple spaceship and now I'm back."

"That was fast," Kevin said. "You didn't really have time to read."

"I do now," she said. She didn't have her Kindle, because she'd given it to the Trafalmadorans during the technology exchange. "I'm going to have to download the books again."

"You *left* them?" Kevin said.

"I *gave* the books to them."

"To the aliens?"

"Oh shit," Peg said.

"Do they even know what a novel is?" Kevin said. "What are

the ramifications? What will they do with the sum of human technological fantasy and fear?"

"I hadn't thought of it that way," Peg said. "We *did* misunderstand each other a lot. Brez is dead."

"You told me," Kevin said and he shook his head. "We were all hoping things would return to normal when he got back."

"It seems corporate around here."

"You were lucky to get out."

"I'm not out," Peg said. "I came to work."

"Pick a cube," Kevin said. "But if you're surfing the Internet when Alicia comes around, you'll have to explain. She's a terrible boss."

"Her name's Alicia?"

"You'll find out."

Peg went over to the nearest empty cubicle, sat down, and tried her old login, which worked. She had a lot of catching up to do, and she saw herself on website after website. She was a meme now: she was Wonder Woman in a spacesuit, the Bionic Woman on Mars, or her photo was reduced to look small and she rode a Mars rover like it was a bucking bronco, or she was made enormous and gazing down on the Findability campus from the sky. When the space girl memes ran dry, she went back to her old stand-bys: Fail-Fail Double-Fail, Cakewrecks, Funny or Die.

With hardly anyone else on the floor, with Kevin a few cubes away and typing furiously, and with the threat of a supervisor, Peg felt like she was wasting her time, and she hated to think it, but she was afraid that the Internet itself might be a big waste of time. She could look at the Internet at home and not blow her cover. Whatever they would have her doing when she came back, she most certainly wouldn't be paid to surf websites any longer. Even as she recognized this glaring truth, she hated that Kevin would no longer be paid to do what he loved, whether their work was a waste of time or not.

She had brought her Martian glass in its iPad case to show Kevin. She stood on her chair to see above all the cubicles and to gaze through the glass at her floor as she remembered it. Through the glass she saw a paper airplane with a propeller circling around, she saw more cubicles, and she saw Brian Clark smiling back at her. She had it made then. She hadn't known this, but she did now.

"Come here," she said to Kevin.

He reluctantly saved his document, got up, and trudged over to where Peg stood on her chair.

"You've got to try this," Peg said.

He rolled a chair next to hers and stood with her as they both looked out over the office and remembered what it had been like to work at Findability when Brez was alive and the company flourished.

"Back to work, Kev," someone had said from one of the cubicles. It wasn't Alicia, but someone who wanted to remind Kevin of her.

"I will," he said. "Just let me have one more minute."

<u>Acknowledgements</u>

Thank you to friends and family, most especially my parents and my teachers. Thank you to all the editors who saw something in me and through their good work made my work better, especially Dan Cafaro at Atticus Books, Christopher Monks and John Warner at McSweeney's Internet Tendency, Madison Scott-Clary at Hybrid.Ink, Christopher James at Jellyfish Review, and Ellen Parker at FRiGG. Biggest thanks of all to daily source of joy, Giacomo and Katrina.

<u>About the Author</u>

John Minichillo is the author of the novels *The Snow Whale*, *EOB: Earth Out of Balance*, and *The Last Workshop*. He teaches in Tennessee and lives in Nashville.

About the Publishing Team

Nate Ragolia was labeled as "weird" early in elementary school, and it stuck. He's a lifelong lover of science fiction, and a nerd/geek. In 2015 his first book, There You Feel Free, was published by 1888's Black Hill Press. He's also the author of The Retroactivist, published by Spaceboy Books. He founded and edits BONED, an online literary magazine, has created webcomics, and writes whenever he's not playing video games or petting dogs.

Shaunn Grulkowski has been compared to Warren Ellis and Phillip K. Dick and was once described as what a baby conceived by Kurt Vonnegut and Margaret Atwood would turn out to be. He's at least the fifth best Slavic-Latino-American sci-fi writer in the Baltimore metro area. He's the author of Retcontinuum, and the editor of A Stalled Ox and The Goldfish, all for 1888/Black Hill Press.